Malcolm Storer was born in Manchester in 1957.
He is currently living in Bowdon, Cheshire
and is terrified of going bald.

Acknowledgements
Cover design - Gig Pincham
Back cover photography - Richard Grasby
Illustrations - Samantha Campbell-Allester
Map illustration - Aidan Connolly
Typesetting - Lynne Watson
Publicity - Colin Taylor, Helen Guthrie
Editorial - Nick Roberts, Sue Acott, Jackie Morgan
Production - Karen Sixsmith

Malcolm Storer

The Wilmslow Comet

A **billy**_pickles_ publication

Published by Billy Pickles Limited

16 Anscome House, Great Heathmead, Haywards Heath,
West Sussex. RH16 1FB. England

http://www.billypickles.com

Billy Pickles Limited, Registered Office: Great Heathmead, Haywards Heath,
West Sussex. England

First Published in Great Britain by Billy Pickles Limited 1998

Copyright Billy Pickles Limited, 1998
All rights reserved

ISBN-0-9533755-0-1

Printed in Great Britain by : Em-En-Ess Printers Ltd

To my mother and father

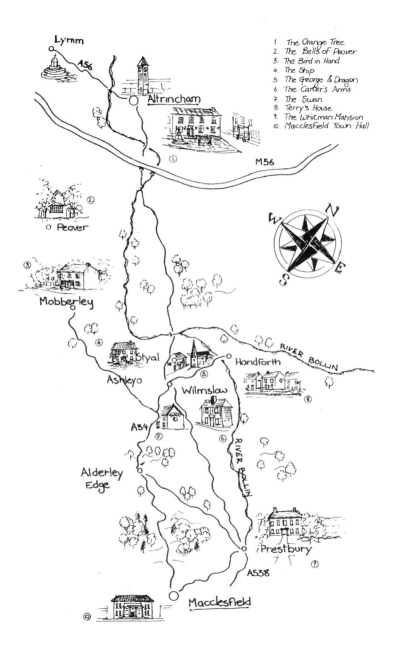

1. The Orange Tree
2. The Bells of Peover
3. The Bird in Hand
4. The Ship
5. The George & Dragon
6. The Carter's Arms
7. The Swan
8. Terry's House
9. The Whitman Mansion
10. Macclesfield Town Hall

Lymm

A56

Altrincham

M56

② o Peover

③

Mobberley

④ Styal

Ashley o

⑤ Wilmslow

Handforth

RIVER BOLLIN

⑧

A34

⑦

⑥

RIVER BOLLIN

Alderley
Edge

Prestbury

A538

⑨

⑧ Macclesfield

Chapter One

Terry Howarth always found the regular weekly meeting with his editor a complete waste of time. What was there to discuss? What earth-shattering event could possibly transform this affluent suburb of South Manchester into the world's hottest news spot? Bored, he scanned the pink venetian blind whose many tilting blades threw shafts of morning sunlight across the office. He shifted in his chair. His three colleagues did likewise. All four were sitting in various degrees of interest around the editor's large, cluttered desk. Suppressing a longed for yawn, he scratched his nose then looked down to read the front page of that week's edition of the *Wilmslow Comet*........................

CHIP PAN INFERNO, screamed the banner headline, **Late night supper led to tragic death of disabled mum**.

Not bad that, thought Terry, smugly satisfied one of his articles had made the front page. He always got a kick out of seeing his work in print, knowing that every household in an area encompassing Wilmslow, Handforth, Styal, Alderley Edge and Mobberley would be treated to *his* words, *his* descriptions of local events -- they had no other choice, the *Comet* was a free newspaper. But this feeling of self-flattery didn't last long. Underneath, Terry Howarth was a frustrated journalist who dreamt of working for one of the national dailies --*The Guardian*, *The Daily Telegraph*, who knows even *The Times*: proper newspapers you had to hand over money in order to read. His frustration was made even more unbearable by the fact that the man sat opposite him, his editor Frank Piper, once worked as a reporter on *The Times*.

Terry despised sitting in Frank's office; it was like a museum to his vanity. Adorning the walls were treasured mementoes of over twenty happy years spent working in Fleet Street: frame after cheap frame displaying some of the more important articles he'd written; photos of himself with other well known reporters, even, (and Terry really hated this) an award shared with two other journalists for unmasking a certain corrupt Liberal MP. On leaving *The Times* in 1986 -- a victim of Murdoch's hatchet men -- he decamped up North and worked as a senior reporter on the *Manchester Evening News*. After a two year stint he decided enough was enough and took on the job as editor of the sleepy *Wilmslow Comet*. He'd been there ever since, enjoying what was for him eight years of semi-retirement, free from the tight schedule of a daily edition. Frank was a tall man, well over six foot with a muscular build that defied his fifty eight years of age. And who wouldn't look healthy, being a member of Wilmslow's golf, tennis, and rugby clubs -- oh yes, Frank pampered himself. His long nose, like ex-President Nixon's, occupied a face that was tanned and well travelled -- he'd spent part of the late seventies as foreign correspondent in Athens, though everyone knew he had a sun bed tucked away at home. And what a home! A detached house on Broad Walk no less, where doctors, dentists and a scattering of Manchester United footballers resided. Not bad for the editor of a trashy local paper who earned a mere thirty grand a year. Frank had done well out of life's snakes and ladders by marrying his second wife, Jean, the daughter of a wealthy accountant. His first wife had divorced him and returned to live in their native Kent after he was caught having an affair. Frank was left on his own for two years feeling totally rejected -- his three grown up children married and living in various parts of the country -- until he met Jean one desperate evening at Wilmslow Tennis Club. From that moment on his life changed. Jean, twenty years his junior, set about such a restoration job on Frank that were his first wife to bump into him now, she'd swear an image consultant had been consulted. Out of the window went his unfashionable clothes and hairstyle, and in came a check-shirted, loafer wearing Calvin Klein with teased short hair greying at the temples. No doubt about it, Frank was a lucky sod. Some might say blessed.

"Can I just point out to everyone that most of next week's edition will be used to cover the public inquiry at Macclesfield Town Hall, concerning the proposed Mottram Hill out-of-town shopping development that has caused so much fuss."

Terry was snapped out of his dream world by the effeminate voice of the sub-editor, Nigel Harrison. Terry couldn't stand him. Not that he had anything against chubby, middle-aged homosexuals. It was just the little things that got under his skin; like the man's snooty demeanour; the way his green cords and brightly coloured Thomas the Tank Engine sweater supported a blob of a head with its thinning crust of mousy hair, button nose and gold rimmed spectacles; the way his minuscule eyes always begged to differ; the way he'd prance around the office while bellowing in his posh Prestbury accent comic extracts from the latest Gilbert and Sullivan operetta his pitiful choral society were forever putting on.

"I'd like to cover that if it's all right with you, Frank," said Vanessa enthusiastically, sensing the beginnings of an important environmental issue; her eyes widening behind a pair of enormous glasses that Terry thought didn't quite suit her, whereas in Frank's opinion they gave her a sultry, almost bossy look.

"I'm sorry, Vanessa," said Frank in his lazy Kentish drawl, leaning back in his chair thinking about lunch, "but this story's got to be handled properly. It's a very delicate matter."

Vanessa folded her arms in annoyance. "Look, all I want to do is tell our readers the truth!"

"Vanessa! Vanessa!" Frank loved saying her name, it almost sounded Greek. "Please don't take this the wrong way, but we all know the kind of extreme views you hold on the environment. The last thing the owner of the *Comet* wants is his newspaper turning into a kind of Green mouthpiece. We're a free local paper, and that means reporting both sides of the issue. If anything we should be standing up for things like local jobs which benefit the whole area."

"What about the countryside? Who benefit's from that when it's all been torn up?"

Frank completely ignored her. "I've decided to let Terry cover the story. "

Terry looked at Vanessa with a half smile, flattered at being given the opportunity to report something worthwhile for a change. He shrugged his rounded shoulders and opened his palms as if carrying a tray. "The boss wants someone who can assess the facts and write a piece that's not sensationalist," he pronounced in his nasally Manchester accent that was cocked and full of itself.

"What!" shouted Vanessa angrily. "You, not a sensational-ist.......?'Chip Pan Inferno!' Come off it, Terry."

Coming off it was the last thing on Terry's mind. "At least I give our readers a bit of entertainment. At least I don't shove my extreme political views down their throats at every opportunity. Jesus, it's like a one-woman crusade with you, lady. You've got conspiracy theories coming out of your ears."

Vanessa hated being referred to as *lady*, it was so demeaning, so council estate. She hit back, "And you've got a bad case of wax coming out of yours."

It was true; Terry's pride in his appearance had receded years ago along with his wispy blonde hair. He was a balding dishevelled bundled into a dark suit that shone of wear. His harsh angled face -- so resembling a cheap cabaret magician, the type usually seen at children's parties whose fixed grins haunt the toddler's nightmares for weeks -- was gaunt and sallow and speckled after a particularly bad hailstorm of acne in his teens. A pathetic attempt at a moustache hovered fuzzy yellow over thin red lips which, when angry, produced a jumbled row of even yellower teeth echoing to black. His frayed collar and cuffs spoke of a lifetime of making do. Terry Howarth was a thirty nine year old emaciated wreck.

"That's enough," said Frank, Vanessa's cruel jibe interrupting his mentally played six iron from dropping pin-high onto Wilmslow Golf Course's lush thirteenth green. "I've said Terry's going to cover the story and that's that."

Leaning back nonchalantly in his chair at the right hand corner of Frank's desk, the outline of his handsome young face not quite eclipsing a blue plastic bubble of water dispenser, was the final member of the *Comet's* editorial staff, the sports reporter Steve Barlow. Steve was everything Terry wasn't: 22 years old, single, good looking, middle class, with a thick mop of curly blonde hair. He was dressed in a collarless white shirt and dark green Yamamoto trousers, and his eyes were fixed upon the glorious swell of Vanessa's large breasts which, because of Terry's triumph, were betraying their existence and heaving angrily beneath their usual camouflage of baggy black sweatshirt. Vanessa was painfully shy of her breasts, hiding them at all costs under the most outrageously oversized jumpers and T-shirts. She wasn't fooling anyone, though. Steve took in the wonderful swelling mass of dark cotton ocean. Frank was quick to notice his young reporter's maritime interest, "Steve," he butted in. "That article you've just finished on Wilmslow Rugby Club for next week's edition. You know, the profile of the captain, what's his name, Eric Peters?"

Steve sat bolt upright in his chair realising he'd lost his ten pound bet.

He glanced over at Terry who had a look of triumph written on his face. Their weekly bet consisted of trying to see who could get as many words as possible in one sentence, beginning with the same letter and running consecutively, passed Frank without him noticing. A different letter was chosen each week. That week's letter was P.

"I mean," said Frank, shaking his head. "What the hell's going on? The article has real promise until, **Peters princely performance punctures opposition packs pride**." (almost a flawless score of seven) "It won't do, Steve, you'll just have to re-write it."

Terry was delighted, safe in the knowledge that his long standing record -- **Teenage thug terrorises topless temptress then takes thirty tranquillisers** -- would stand for all time, or at least until Frank next went on holiday.

Nigel Harrison stood up and adjusted his brightly coloured sweater so that plumes of steam emanating from Thomas the Tank Engine's funnel disappeared over his left shoulder. "If that's everything covered, I wouldn't mind going for an early lunch," he minced, rolling his eyes in a delicious manner while noticing the sun had thrown liquid reflections across the office, like the inside of an aquarium, as it struck the bubbling water dispenser. (A real aesthete was Nigel.)

"Not quite everything," said Frank annoyed at Nigel's haste. "Due to the number of letters I've received over the past few weeks, I've decided to bring back Pet's Corner. Terry, you can deal with this." He moved quickly in an attempt to quell Terry's protest. "Don't worry, it'll only be for about a month, until that young student starts her work experience with us in July. She can take over when you've shown her the ropes."

Now it was Steve's turn to look pleased.

"But Frank, you know I don't like animals," objected Terry, the investigative journalist within him seeing red. "Why don't you give it to Vanessa, she's obsessed with them? Anyway, I'll be far too busy working on the out-of-town shopping development story to bother about problem pets."

Vanessa was quick to extract her revenge. "Surely answering a few children's letters won't use up *that* much of your precious time." She then puffed out both cheeks like Shirley Temple and said in a high pitched, childish voice, "Dear Uncle Terry, my *liccle* kitten keeps doing naughty poo poos on the kitchen floor. Can you help?"

This innocent girlie cameo turned Frank on. He imagined himself rubbing baby oil all over her naked body as she cooed for more, stretched out alluringly on silken cushions, calling him Daddy, begging him to.... *Jesus*, he thought, *women really know how to push all the right buttons, and without even trying!*

The Friday morning meeting drew to its usual raucous close. Terry, Vanessa, Nigel and Steve were about to go for lunch when a phone call came through to Frank's office.

"Dear, dear," he commiserated into the receiver. "What a dreadful thing to have happened. I'm very sorry to hear about that. Yes, Mrs. Grasby, I'll send someone round in about an hour. Yes, don't worry, it will be dealt with in the strictest confidence. Thanks again for calling the *Comet*."

As Terry's shabby suit was about to evaporate behind frosted glass, Frank summoned him back into his office. And in weighty tones that promised a once in a lifetime scoop, he leant forward with his hands clasped together prayer-like and said, "After lunch I want you to go into Handforth and interview this old dear. Her name's Joan Grasby."

"Not another mugging!" laughed Terry.

"No. Those idiots at the Town Hall have been at it again. They've sent her late husband a council tax demand, along with a court summons for non payment."

"Naughty."

"So I want you and Keith to go along and,"...Frank's distinguished features suddenly wrinkled, mirroring his beige corduroy shirt. "By the way, where is Keith?"

"Er.... He's been at the dentist all morning."

"Dentist!   It's Alcoholics Anonymous that lazy swine needs."

Terry was quick to jump to his friend's defence. "Come on, Frank, Keith's been bad with his teeth all week, you know he has."

"And just when is his Lordship going to grace us with his presence?"

"I've arranged to meet him in the Swan for lunch. I can pass on any orders you've got when I see him then."

"The Swan, that's typical."

"But we always go there on a Friday."

Frank was in no mood to have his train of thought derailed. "Do you know I saw him last night drunk as a lord stumbling along Hawthorn

14

Street. Jean and I were driving past the Carter's Arms when she turned to me and said, 'There's that photographer chapie from your newspaper over there.' I couldn't believe it, he could hardly stand up." Terry searched the rag-and-bone cellar of his imagination and dredged up, "What's the betting he was a bit apprehensive about his dental appointment today, and had a few jars to calm his nerves."

"A few jars! Jesus Christ, I could have yanked half of his teeth out with a pair of pliers and he wouldn't have cared. The state of him. He was holding on to a lamppost, Terry, with his penis hanging out, urinating in the street. You should have seen Jean's face! Thank God it was late and there was no one about. Can you imagine what would have happened if the Police had spotted him!"

Terry instantly saw the headline -- **POLICE POUNCE ON PAVE-MENT PERVERT**-- as Frank continued, "What makes him act like that? For God's sake, the man's forty five, not a young kid any more."

"Keith's been going through a rough patch since Rita left him."

Frank rose agitated from his desk and walked over to the window before shouting, "That was over a year ago! How long does it take? You know as well as I do Keith's always been a heavy drinker. His wife leaving him has just been an excuse to carry on regardless!" He then hissed through clenched teeth, "When you see Keith, tell him I want the photographs of Mrs. Grasby developed and on my desk by five o'clock...... And I *don't* want any of her smiling!"

"Course not," said Terry, heading for the door. "Keith knows the score on that front. See you later, boss."

As the door to his office closed, Frank thought, *Useless pair of idiots! Those two wouldn't have lasted five minutes in Fleet Street.*

Chapter Two

The *Comet's* two-storey office was set in a row of smart shops, banks and building societies along the newly pedestrianised Grove Street in the centre of Wilmslow. Terry left the building and joined a line of lunchtime shoppers who were walking along an invisible pavement -- almost frightened to explore the centre of this once traffic jammed street in case it might still produce the odd rouge vehicle -- to an intersection at the corner of Bank Square. The June sun felt eager to fry the speckled white of Terry's bald head as he crossed the busy road and wandered past a splash of town garden where office workers relaxed on park benches surrounded on all sides by soft blooms of roses and boarders of fiery chrysanthemums. The welcoming sight of the Swan lay directly behind this municipal oasis, and he quickly exchanged dazzling sunlight, the smell of flowers and traffic, for the instant dim sweetness of alcohol and tobacco. Though the pub was crowded, it didn't take Terry long to spot the unique figure of Keith hunched over a fruit machine -- his purple shell-suit a bud of colour amidst the sombre petals of businessmen.

"Bastard!" shouted Keith, the promise of a third melon slipping just out of reach. His voice was deep and guttural, sort of muffled, as though he spoke with a pillow pressed against his face. "Fuckin machine's fixed!"

Terry gathered behind him like a storm cloud, his trebly tones a lightening bolt cutting through the jumble of pub conversation. "You're up shit creek, mate."

Keith ignored him at first, hitting instead the flashing start button that spun the individual fruits into a purée.

"Is Frank in a bad mood then?" he asked eventually, completely unruffled, feeding the machine pound coins with one hand while pushing crisps into his mouth with the other.

"Just a bit. He told me to tell you...."

"I'm not interested in what that southern idiot's got to say. Now get the drinks in. It's your round."

While Terry queued at the bar Keith carried on gambling, the fruit machine's lights dancing in his bloodshot eyes, swirling jumbled patterns like brief tattoos across his booze ridden face. His hair was shoulder length and greasy, framing a tatty grey beard that gave him the look of a down-at-heel Rasputin. After slurping down pint number four, two buck teeth materialised as if by magic under a line of beer froth slowly evaporating over his grizzled top lip. If Terry Howarth was a wreck, Keith Miles was an entire scrapyard.

"Here we are," said Terry, plonking down a pint and a half of Boddingtons.

Keith looked at the offending half with disgust. "What's this? Why aren't you on pints?"

" I'm driving. Frank's lined up a job this afternoon."

"Can't you get out of it?"

"Not just me. He want's you along as well."

"Me? But I've just got back from the dentist! The bastard almost killed me! "

Terry laughed as they both eased themselves round an empty table. "That won't wash with Frank. He went absolutely ballistic about you this morning."

"Go on then," said Keith, reluctantly, about to swill down yet more ale. "Give me the gory details."

Terry didn't spare the horses, he gave it to him straight, word for word, even throwing in the odd insult of his own, just for effect. The part that really got to Keith was Frank's insensitive comment about his ex-wife Rita -- how a year was more than enough time to get over the separation. This had Keith fuming, "The sanctimonious bastard! He's got no room to talk. Do you remember what *he* was like when his ex left and ran off back to Kent? A right miserable sod for two years until Jean came along. I remember driving into Altrincham with him one morning at least eighteen months after she'd walked out. He just sat there staring out of the window feeling sorry for himself. So I put the radio on thinking a bit of music might cheer him up. Well, talk about bad timing. On came that song, you know, the slushy one by what's her name......Witney Houston."

"I will always love you," shouted Terry, surprising the next table.

"That's the one. Anyway, Frank starts to get all depressed, starts to get all choked up, and in front of me. He turns the radio off and says," -- Keith then mimicked Frank's Kent accent, exaggerating it Worzzel-like -- "This was my babes' favourite song. I don't know what I'm going to do without her."

The pair collapsed in merriment, with Keith continuing to muck-spread, "He cried like a baby. It was pathetic. Then, when he'd final-ly got hold of himself, he begs me not to say anything, begs me not to embarrass him in the office. Well, I've been true to my word until now, and this is how he pays me back! The ungrateful.........."

Terry shattered any thoughts of revenge by mentioning that Frank and Jean had spotted him urinating in the street the previous night.

"Christ Almighty!" exclaimed Keith, open mouthed, the blood draining colander-like from his pitted red nose as a retrospective of drunken images blurred through his brain. "They didn't did they?"

Both men wandered aimlessly out of the pub, crossed the busy main road and walked the sort distance to where Terry's battered Fiat Uno stood not so much parked as abandoned. Keith had a blue nylon holdall slung over his shoulder. It contained amongst other things his Minolta camera and flash. Dressed as usual in his purple shell-suit, he looked for all the world as though he was about to begin a sponsored walk.

The spluttering Uno turned left and headed out of Wilmslow in the direction of Handforth. Though the journey was less than two miles, a startling decrease in house size and tree population told the visitor an inferior neighbour awaited. Handforth, home to both Terry and Keith, was a buffer zone between the riches of Wilmslow and the crime riddled council estates of Wythenshawe: a no-man's-land of endless cul-de-sacs, old people's homes and litter-strewn shopping precincts. It was outside one of these self-same retirement homes, 'The Gables', a yellow bricked three story establishment with cell-like windows and hanging baskets, that Terry's car came to a halt.

"What's the script on this old dear then?" asked Keith, reaching over the back seat to grab his blue nylon holdall.

"Someone's cocked up at the Town Hall and sent her dead husband a council tax bill," answered Terry, totally disinterested, shaking his head and tutting at the mundaneness of it all, knowing that out there in the real world stories of great significance were just waiting to be covered. Take Bosnia, for instance. He'd be on the next available flight if the opportunity arose to do a bit of war corresponding out there. In Terry's opinion scrambling about in a flack jacket interviewing the odd Croat wasn't dangerous -- it was money for old rope. If Kate Adie could get away with the same routine on TV every night, then so could he. Granted Martin Bell got shot, but that was through his own stupidity, far too near the front line. Terry wouldn't have made that mistake. Let's face it, getting yourself too close to a load of foreigners who were going at each other's throats was asking for trouble. Sandy Gaul had the right idea; pretending to be slap bang in the middle of a skirmish when in reality he had his feet up in some posh hotel miles away from the front line bawling into a microphone while his sound man played back library tapes of screeching jets and artillery barrages. That was the way to cover a war. Christ, though, Kate Adie! Talk about overkill! If there was the slightest hint of trouble anywhere in the world you could guarantee she'd be there; pan faced, oozing sugary sentiments about the plight of defenceless civilians caught up in some minor Third World conflict no-one else was the least bit interested in. And disasters -- you just couldn't keep her away -- she seemed to revel in them. If Terry was to hear that tired old cliché roll out of her sour mouth one more time about how the body of a dead child lying in the street resembled a 'broken doll', he'd kick the fucking television screen in! But what got on his nerves most of all was her appearance; a straggly-haired bag-lady faking hardship when the chances were she had a luxury cara-van tucked away just out of camera shot.

Keith buzzed the intercom and an elderly warder dressed in a smart blue uniform opened the door. "What can I do for you?" he asked, stifling a yawn.

"We're from the *Wilmslow Comet*, and we've come to inter-view a Mrs. Joan Grasby," answered Terry, noticing straight away that smell.

They were led by the white haired warder into the Gables' reception hall and asked to take a seat. Cemented into the wall between a bur-geoning rubber plant and a portrait of the Queen was a brass panel dotted with black buttons. The old man pressed one and spoke softly into an invisible microphone. "Joan, it's Arthur. There's two gentle-men from the press here to see you."

"Send them up," came the distorted reply.

Jesus, thought Keith, *Who's up there, Greta Garbo?*

"Go along that corridor there and you'll come to the lift," said the warder, pointing vaguely down a fuzzy tunnel. "First floor, room sixty three. If I know Joan she'll be putting the kettle on as we speak."

Opposite the lift was a large sunlit room where twenty or so O.A.Ps could be seen slumped zombie-like in high winged chairs glued to an ancient black and white film broadcast on a flickering television set. As the lift doors closed behind them on the first floor, Keith whis-pered, "It reminds me of a joke I heard in the Carter's Arms last night: What's twenty foot long and stinks of piss? -- The conga in an old people's home."

"You noticed the smell too, did you," laughed Terry, knock-ing on the door of room sixty three.

"Just a minute!" said a high pitched, worried voice.

After a delay of sliding chains the door eventually opened. Before them stood a frail sparrow of a lady with a hooked nose and rounded shoulders wearing a pink nylon dressing gown. Her thinning hair had a yellowish tint and was lacquered to a nodding head that craned from the folds of pink nylon like some prehistoric tortoise. Terry thought, *Why is it old folk's dressing gowns never fit?*

20

"Come in and sit down. I've just put the kettle on."

The tiny flat seemed all gas fire, knick-knacks and budgerigar cage. Terry coughed and pronounced in a loud, deliberate voice, "Please to meet you, Mrs. Grasby," nodding his head in mimicry. "We represent the *Wilmslow Comet*. This gentleman here's Keith. He'll be taking a few photographs of you. You don't mind, do you?"

"What the bloody hell are you talking to me like that for?" said the feisty old girl. "I'm not like that senile lot down there in the Sunshine Room. There's a good few years left in me yet…... And I'm not deaf either!"

The thing about Terry and Keith was they never took an assignment seriously. Their sick sense of humour always got the better of them, and turned any situation, no matter how sad or depressing, into one big joke.

" Of course you're not, luv," said Keith, taking out his camera while noticing the old woman's feathery pride and joy. "Tell me, Joan, what's your budgie called?"

"Joey. He's called Joey," answered Mrs. Grasby proudly, gazing up milky eyed toward her fluffy blue bird balancing fast asleep on its perch. "Aren't you, J..o..e..y."

After demolishing his cup of tea and half a packet of chocolate digestives, Terry began, "Those heartless buggers from the council been at it again, have they? Swines they are, Mrs. Grasby, absolute swines. Now, have you got the offensive letter they sent you handy?"

"It's on the mantelpiece," said Joan, attempting to raise herself from the flowery patterned armchair.

"I'll get it, luv. You sit there."

Terry gave the letter a quick scan through and realised straight away it was a computer error. But there was no way he was going to let those awkward bastards from the Town Hall get off lightly, especially after he'd received a court summons from them the previous week threatening to send in the bailiffs. And what a domestic bust-up that caused. He had to make up all sorts of excuses while his wife stood there humiliating him in the bathroom, going on and on about how he was a failure and how they could lose their house if he didn't pull his finger out. He was going to make them pay for that.

"Disgusting," ventured Terry, putting down the letter, eyeing up yet another chocolate digestive. "I can't believe it, in this day and age they're hassling old age pensioners."

"I know," agreed Mrs. Grasby, a lump appearing in her throat. "And my Bert fought in the war for people like that."

War hero. Couldn't be better.

"You don't happen to have a picture of your late husband in uniform, do you Joan?" asked Keith, reading Terry's mind.

"I have luv, somewhere."

Joan rose purposely from her armchair and inched slowly sideways passed the coffee table like a Hermit Crab resplendent in its pink shell, before disappearing into her bedroom. There was the sound of rummaging in boxes, then, after a good deal of muttering, the return of the fantastic crustacean holding in its claw not only a dusty old photograph of her husband, white faced and looking barely sixteen in his World War One uniform, but a polished row of jingling medals.

"Will these do?" she asked.

Terry could hardly contain himself. "Perfect, luvy."

Keith then took over. He sat her down and began to arrange the props.

"Joan," he said, looking through the lens. "Can you just nestle the photo of Bert in the crook of your left arm. That's it, close to your heart." Keith felt a quick pat of congratulation on his back. "And with your right hand can you hold the summons from the Town Hall out towards the camera."

"What about the medals?" whispered Terry in a panic. "You can't see the medals! It'll ruin the effect if the readers can't.......... I know, I'll pin them on her."

"Don't be ridiculous!" snarled Keith. "They look alright where they are resting in her lap. Just let me get on with it will you." Keith was all set to snap the shutter when he noticed the expression on Joan's face. A mask of serenity had descended as she gazed lovingly at her husband's photo. Whatever fond memories were now flicking through her mind, they seemed to be knocking twenty years off her age. It certainly wasn't the effect Keith wanted.

"Er.... Joan," he began, barging into her dreams. "I don't wish to appear rude, but is it possible you can look a little less happy."

The old woman was transported back from her wedding night. "Sorry. What was that?"

Keith felt the crunch off eggshells. "I was just saying, the idea of the photograph is to show our readers that an injustice has been done. *And to* show those heartless sods from the Town Hall that their letter has deeply upset you. Well, Joan, if you don't mind me saying so, the

22

expression on your face… it looks as if you've just won the lottery."

Joan laughed, "I'm sorry, luv, but looking at Bert's picture has made me feel all warm inside. It's taken me back. And you two gentlemen have been so nice to me this afternoon – you see, I don't get many visitors, my son only pops in now and again – that I'm beginning to think I've caused a lot of trouble over nothing. I mean to say, that letter from the Town Hall, it's obviously a mistake. Thinking about it now, I've no wish to cause any more trouble. So shall we just leave it be?"

Terry could see the prestige of another front page slipping away. "No, I'm afraid we can't! A complaint's been made so we've got to follow it through."

Joan didn't like the tone of his voice one bit. "Surely that's up to me. You're not the police or anything."

Through his camera lens Keith noticed the old girl's expression steadily decaying. He knew Terry's expertise would soon bear fruit.

"Your husband, Bert. Suffered at the end did he?"

Terry's quip caused Joan's face to become all agitated. *Confusion*, thought Keith, *well, it's better than nothing.*

As he took the picture, the explosion of flash suddenly woke the budgie from its peaceful slumber and induced a violent fit of flapping. Sand and blue and white feathers cascaded down from the metal cage like confetti. One moment the bird was a fluttering blur, the next it clung to the bars all thin and bulgy eyed, then it was off again, thrashing about in a bell ringing, mirror spinning rage of blind terror.

"JOEY!" squawked the old woman in such a high pitched voice it could easily have been that of a giant parrot's. "YOU'RE FRIGHTENING MY JOEY!"

In her shock Joan clasped the court summons to her mouth and began to weep. Terry stood there nodding his head as Keith let off a volley of shots in an orgy of stroboscopic celebration.

Chapter Three

After filing his copy onto the computer under the headline: **NO ARMISTICE FOR WEEPING WAR WIDOW – Council bureaucrat's cruel blunder reduces pensioner to tears**, Terry left the office and drove home in an up-beat mood. It was Friday evening, the weekend lay ahead, and Frank's last minute instructions, 'Make sure you arrive at Macclesfield Town Hall before nine o'clock Monday morning. I don't want the Comet to miss a single detail of the public inquiry pertaining to the Mottram Hill Shopping Development,' repeated themselves in his head. *Pertaining*, thought Terry, *Frank's such a pretentious idiot sometimes.* The low opinion of his boss was suddenly masked by a debt of gratitude for having been chosen to cover such an important story. *He's not that bad, a bit*

pompous, but he obviously knows a good reporter when he sees one.

A warm feeling of vanity caused Terry to drum his fingers lightly on the steering wheel in time with the car radio as his rusted Fiat Uno sped along Manchester Road towards Handforth. Driving along in the evening sunshine, he glanced enviously down the shaded drive of each passing mock Tudor mansion and imagined a different life. A life where he would cruise into one such gravel drive in his convertible BMW after a hard day's editing of say the *Telegraph*, and be met by his stunning blonde wife: Natasha? Cloe? Jemma? – he couldn't care less so long as she had huge tits – who would lead him by the hand into the conservatory where a gin and tonic awaited. Then, after an evening spent discussing literature in a cosy French restaurant in Alderley Edge, he would arrive back at his tree lined mansion and make love to his achingly voluptuous……..."Facking shite!" Turning into Windermere Drive, Terry's iridescent fantasy of elegant living suddenly dissolved when he saw his mother-in-law's car parked outside his three up two down ex-council house. "What does that nosy cow want!"

Climbing from the rubbish-strewn interior of his car he noticed the privet hedge still hadn't been cut. What did his wife do all day? A child's bike and red plastic paddling pool next met his eye, littering the small patch of unkempt lawn at the front of the house. Terry rammed his key into the paint bubbled door and fumed, "Cheryl! Blake!"

Two small voices answered in unison from upstairs, "What?"

"How many times have I told you not to leave your toys out on the front lawn. Now go and put them away…..And don't 'What' me."

"But Dad…."

"Now, you little swines!"

As he prepared to open the lounge door, Terry heard the unmistakable throaty rasp of his wife Dawn, "Someone's had a bad day," and after ten years of marriage it wasn't difficult for him to visualise the sight that would next meet his eye. The room would almost certainly be a bomb site of magazines strewn across the floor, half finished cups of tea dotted about like chess pieces, pyramids of cigarette ends overflowing a variety of scooped marble ash trays, and in the middle of all this domestic detritus would be the fat Buddha herself, glued to the television set encased in wispy blue clouds of Benson and

25

Hedges, wearing her usual bad taste summer attire of pink shorts – rolls of milky flesh oozing off her saggy thighs – and an oversized T-shirt baring the legend: '**Boddingtons -- The Cream of Manchester**'. Terry wasn't to be disappointed; or rather he was. For there on the sofa was the equally hideous sight of his obese mother-in-law Kath, kitted out in tight black leggings – *Christ, the woman's almost sixty five!* – and a flowing deep purple blouse of tent-like construction mushrooming over her huge arse. (Kath had once read an article in *My Weekly* that proved dark colours can help make a woman look thin. What Kath failed to appreciate, or more likely get into her thick skull, was the fact that accompanying the said article was a photograph of supermodel Kate Moss).

Terry grunted his hellos and edged his way nervously through to the kitchen, desperate for a soothing beer: he was drinking more and more the more his marriage slid further down the pan into the septic tank of despair. If the front room was an aperitif, then surely here was the main course. To his left, mounds of damp washing dripped from the breakfast bar onto a floor that hadn't seen a mop for weeks. To his right, dirty dishes piled high in the sink rubbed shoulders with fag ends, crisp packets and several dead tea bags resembling bloated carcasses floating down an African river. *People live better than this in Rwanda*, thought Terry. A nauseating smell of low-cost cornedbeef greeted his nose as he opened the fridge door; *One can left out of a six pack, so that's what the lazy bitch has been up to all day*. Terry didn't blink. He was used to it. With his usual round shouldered stoop he walked out into the glow of early evening sunlight bathing his scruffy back garden, sat on a white plastic garden chair and fizzed open the can of bitter. A tart desert awaited. Littering the lawn were the jolly remnants of his wife's busy afternoon: a scrunched up red towel used for sunbathing had for its satellites two erotic paperbacks, scatterings of chocolate wrappers, five empty beer cans – crushed of course – a large plastic bottle of cheap suntan lotion, various magazines, a Sony Walkman, two Cliff Richard cassettes (Terry despised him), and three plates that had seen lunch but were now a venue for flies doing the Cha-Cha. It wasn't a large back garden but it was secluded – enclosed on three sides by high hedges of tendrilous, overgrown privets – a place where a man could grieve without the bother of nosy neighbours. Talking of neighbours (the theme tune was now blasting out from the front room) Terry found

26

brief solace in recalling the moment when the young couple who'd recently moved in next door had stopped him in the street to introduce themselves. Keeping a straight face he'd rushed back inside to tell Dawn the hilarious news: that their new neighbours were called Campbell, and the man's first name was Donald. His wife failed to see the joke. Terry had to explain a second time, "Don't you get it, stupid. He's called Donald Campbell! And he's come to live on Windermere Drive!"

Not a hint of a smile appeared on her bloated, piggy face. Instead she snorted, "For God's sake Terry, grow up!......And by the way, it was Coniston, not Windermere."

He took another swig of beer and stared into the abyss. It hadn't always been this way. He remembered how in the old days Dawn used to laugh at his jokes. She was pretty then. Chubby, yes, but he liked girls who were generous in proportion, with big hips, big lips and big tits. Gradually over the course of their marriage these assets had been cruelly highjacked by violent explosions of flesh, leaving her body nothing but a rotund caricature of its former self, an obscene tribute to the gluttonous one Kath.

They had met twelve years ago at North Cheshire College where, as a mature student, Terry was doing a creative writing course. Dawn worked in the canteen at the time serving food, and they'd fallen for each other across deep orange vats of baked beans and acres of fried sausages – she a giver of sustenance, all rosy-red-perspiring in her starch white uniform beneath plumes of steam, wisps of short dark hair sticking to her cherubic face, desperate at the age of twenty five to marry and settle down -- he an undiscovered writer, so cool in the dog-tooth of his herring-bone jacket and the polka dot of his tatty cravat. A twenty seven year old misunderstood genius with a receding hairline that spoke of endless nights poured over classic novels. A man who always sat by himself in the canteen due to the obvious envy of fellow students. A man who was all set to take the world of journalism by storm.

"Terry, we're off out now. I've left you some tea in the oven. The baby-sitter's due round in about half an hour. If you're not going out telephone and cancel. No use wasting ten pounds. Bye, luv."

"Where are you going?"

"What do you mean, where are we going? It's Friday night...... Bingo night!"

"Aren't you going to tidy up first?"

"Can't *you* sort the house out for a change? Me and me Mum are in a hurry."

In his rage Terry saw the headline: **BINGO TWINS BATTERED TO DEATH BY BELEAGUERED HUSBAND; 'I just couldn't take it any more,' sobbed the distraught slaughterer.**

 Terry jumped up and stormed back inside the house determined to give his wife a piece of his mind, only to hear the front door slam followed seconds later by cheery clip-clopping high heels and the unmistakable sound of Kath's flemmy laughter. He looked through the window but as if by magic both women had vanished, so he returned to the kitchen. Terry did not dare look upon the 'Tea' that lay hidden in the oven like some dreadful secret. He knew all about the intricacies of mash, beans and burnt sausages to last him a lifetime, thank you very much. There was only one thing for it, he'd have to telephone Keith and go out for a few pints. More than a few!

Inside Keith's tip of a one-bedroom council flat overlooking a disused railway line, the phone's harsh ring skidded across an icy layer of loneliness.

(Could it be Rita?Please God let it be Rita) "Hello!"

(He sounds desperate) "Keith, it's me."

(No!!!!!!) "Oh, hello Terry."

"Fancy a pint?" *(Does the Pope shit in the woods?)*

"I thought you weren't bothering tonight." *(He's always changing his mind)*

"I've changed my mind."

"Is it Dawn?" *(Who else!)*

"In one."

"See you in the Ship in half an hour."

"Cheers mate."

After changing into jeans and T-shirt then giving a lecture to the kids about behaving themselves, Terry waited for the baby-sitter to arrive before calling a cab. He adored the kid Vicki who always sat for them, loved her almost. She was a sixteen year old hairdresser's assistant whose young body caused many a curtain to flutter as she fluttered up Windermere Drive. Her hair was dyed blonde with emerging black roots (an imperfection that hinted the slut and gave Terry licence to pull at himself) and her two front teeth were slightly bucked causing her top lip to pout in a maddeningly sexy fashion.

Add to that perfect breasts that had no need of a bra, a waist dizzying in its slimness, and a soft girlie innocence just begging to be defiled, well, that was Vicki Carson. Terry fantasised about her constantly. It was always the same scenario; Dawn would be staying overnight with her mother or strapped to a life support machine at Wythenshawe Hospital following a near fatal road accident, and he'd arrive home unexpectedly to find Vicki upstairs wearing one of his shirts and little else. He'd take her there and then, with the lights on, gazing deep into her mascara ringed eyes while she…..There was a sudden knock at the front door but Terry had already prepared himself. He'd scattered about the room various classic novels and put on an Oasis CD, Vicki's favourite. Armed with a man-of-the-world smile he'd practised in the mirror earlier, Terry opened the front door. To his dismay, Vicki had her delicate arms folded around a scruffy looking youth with thick wavy hair wearing a black leather jacket in the style of Marlon Brando in the *Wild Bunch.*

"Hi, Terry. This is Troy, my new boyfriend. You don't mind if he baby-sits with me tonight, do you?" she asked, all innocent.
Terry felt deflated. Betrayed even. For a moment his smile resembled a sneer. "Course not, come in."

The Ship public house was situated on Altrincham Road, a quiet country byway in the leafy borough of Styal. Though it was only a stones throw from Handforth, it may as well have been the other side of Mars, such was the difference in landscape. With creeping vines spread across its whitewashed exterior like a giant sea fan, and half a dozen parasoled tables dotted about its cobbled entrance, the Ship was a perfect Friday night rural retreat. The interior spoke of the nineties; horse brasses for the middle classes and fruit machines for the under eighteens. It was just after seven o'clock when the taxi dropped Terry off. He wandered inside to find the pub half empty and Keith sat all by himself in the corner of the snug, beneath a stuffed fox. He still had on his purple shell suit. Terry thought, *Scruffy sod.* Keith on the other hand took one look at Terry's miserable face and thought, *What's he got to moan about. At least he's got someone to moan about.* Both men hid their indifference behind friendly smiles, companions in the same rudderless boat. Keith was quick to gulp down the dregs of his third pint and order two fresh foaming ones, accompanied, as it was Friday night, by a pair of triumphant triple malt Scotches.

"Here, guzzle these," he said greedily. Funny how alcoholics love to entice the unwary into their crumbling world.

Terry sank down on a red velvet chair close to the bar while sinking in one the fiery Caledonian classic whose tint resembled tea and seemed not at all threatening.

"Nice one!" said Keith in admiration, realising a session was on. "That bad is it?"

"Worse than bad, fuckin terrible," sighed Terry, the scotch triggering an avalanche of self-pity. He put his hand across his mouth and mumbled, as if buried under snow, "I'm sick to death of her. She's the laziest bitch in the world. All I want to do is come home and find the house tidy for a change. I mean, it's not as if I'm Howard Hughes or anything; you know, obsessed. But it would be nice if now and again she at least tried. Christ, we're living like rats! Correction, rats eat better. Honestly, Keith, the kind of slop she serves up is fuckin rancid! It's a wonder the kids haven't left home. And another thing, her bleedin mother's always got her arse parked in the chair. I know she doesn't like me, the interfering cow never has. The pair of them went off to bingo happy as Larry, leaving me to see to the kids. That Kath does it on purpose. I'm sure she's trying to split us up."

Keith saw an opportunity to mischief-make. "Do you think she's see-ing someone else behind your back?" he asked, keeping a straight face while staring deep into Terry's eyes searching for any sign of weakness. What he got back didn't please him one bit.

"I hope not. I don't want to end up like you."

"What's that suppose to mean?"

Terry realised he'd gone a little too far and tried to paper over the cracks. "You know, living on your own in that flat, and….."

"And what?"

In order to escape the embarrassing cul-de-sac Terry found himself in, a battering ram of home truths was required. He scratched his chin and released the inevitable, "Let's face it, you're a wreck. Everyone knows you've let yourself go since Rita left."

Whether it was hurt or astonishment spreading across Keith's craggy face, Terry knew not. Whatever it was forced him onto the defensive. But he just made matters worse.

"I'm not blaming you," he said nervously. "I know Rita walking out like that must have hurt. I mean, if my wife had left me for another woman I'd be devastated…......"

"Hang on a minute. Who said anything about a woman?"
Terry froze as he remembered the amazing conversation he'd had
with Dawn in bed one night. Though it was well over a year ago, he
could still hear her words, "For God's sake don't tell Keith, but Rita's
shacked up with someone from Altrincham. And you'll never guess
what, it's a bleedin woman!"

"Woman!" blurted Terry, his face a twitching beetroot distorted in the reflection of a copper kettle. "Did I say woman. I meant
to say man!"
Keith was having none of it. "But you said woman, Terry, I heard
you."

"But I meant to say *man*!"
"But *you* said woman!"
"But I *meant* to say *man*!"
"What's the matter, don't you know the difference?"
Their ping-pong conversation had attracted spectators. A young couple sitting in the far corner of the snug next to a Grandfather clock
were all ears, so was the barmaid. She had dipped below the counter
like a marauding crocodile eager for tit-bits, pretending to replenish
the stock of fruit juice. Keith's stomach was spinning like the many
machines in a laundrette. He could barely contain himself. The only
thing that held him together at that moment was his quest for the
truth; a truth that had alluded him for more than a year. Noticing
Terry all of a fidget, he calmly asked, "What man's this then?"

"What man?"

"Yeah, Terry, what man? You see, *I've* always said Rita took
off because of my drinking. I've never *ever* mentioned anything about
another bloke being involved. So I'm asking you again, what man?"
There was menace in his voice. Terry could feel it. The whole pub
seemed to hold its breath, just waiting for an answer. Each tick of the
Grandfather clock grew louder and louder as Keith's boozy face grew
redder and redder. The clock chimed seven thirty. It was time for the
truth. Terry swallowed hard. "When I say man…......I, I mean woman."
Thousands of miles away in Antarctica, a huge iceberg broke away
from the main ice-flow causing a thunderous crash as it fell into the
ocean. Keith felt the vibrations. Other things now fell into place; like
his wife's long standing membership of the local hockey club; her
keen participation in women's cricket; her two year abstinence from

31

sex, her extended weekend trips away with 'The Girlies' on hockey tour followed by the incessant playing of K.D Lang. Jesus, what an idiot he'd been.

"So Rita's a dyke, is that what you're telling me?"

Terry didn't know what to say. "I don't know what to say. Dawn told me out of the blue one night that Rita was living in Altrincham with some woman. I couldn't bring myself to tell you. You were in a right state at the time. I thought news like that might have, you know, pushed you over the edge."

Simultaneously kicked in the teeth and balls Keith slumped back into his chair as if the life force had been drained from him. His body resembled a dried sack, a punctured blow-up doll. He was now on automatic pilot, a pathetic zombie struggling for the right words. "She…. She…. Have you any idea who this woman is, the one she's shacked up with?"

Terry fired a quick sideways glance at his friend's rigid face; it was ashen and appeared to have aged centuries. "I haven't, mate. I'm sorry but I can't help you there," he replied, drenched in embarrassment. He then sought to be constructive. "Do you want another drink?"

Keith's mouth began to move of its own accord, loose hinged like some macabre ventriloquist's dummy, his bloodshot eyes rolling inside their papier maché encasement, "Drink?......Cheers, Terry……. I'll have a Carlsberg Special."

The following morning, as Terry gazed at Dawn's enormous backside bent over the freezer cabinet in Sainsbury's, his thoughts returned to the previous night. He recalled the drunken taxi ride back to Handforth; how Keith had begged him never to take Dawn for granted, and how he wished Rita had been a lazy fat slob instead of a marauding lesbian; his inane ramblings about loneliness and the meaning of life; his self confessed decline into the mire of hard-core pornography; his unsavoury interest in dog fighting; his dark suicidal thoughts. All were digested in stony silence with the occasional nod of the head. Then watching from the back seat of the cab as he stumbled towards his flat, cursing Rita's gay philanderings at the top of his voice before spewing up on the pavement. Then, after stumping up Keith's share of the taxi, rushing back home to tell Dawn the juicy scandal, only to find her jumping around the front room with news of her own; that she'd won five hundred pounds at bingo. What a night!

And finally in the bedroom because she was so worked up – "Oh Terry, luv, come here, we've not had a good bonk for weeks," – grappling with the same massive arse that now eased its fatty bulk further and further into the freezer compartment hunting for the bumper pack of fish fingers.

"Caught you, you *liccle* bleeders," chuckled Dawn, surfacing whale-like from the icy depths, drunk with joy at last night's bingo jackpot. Money! Boy what a feeling! She nonchalantly tossed the frosted packet in Terry's direction. As if tied by an invisible thread he began following her towards the continental cheese section, keeping the trolley at a respectful distance. Up and down the aisles they strolled, passing saucy comments on the myriad of strange looking vegetables now available from far off lands. It was such a pleasure shopping in Wilmslow. Dawn felt like a million dollars. Mixing with the Cheshire Set instead of the usual lot down at Kwick Save in Wythenshawe certainly took the biscuit. This was shopping at its most refined; piped Vivaldi amidst the low murmur of posh families whose accents would have graced Harrods. And the staff were a lot nicer too, better looking in fact. What a strange place Wilmslow was; an island of South Kensington floating in a choppy northern sea. Imagine being wealthy enough to shop here every Saturday! Imagine living here! Oh for a lottery win.............

Chapter Four

Alas there was no lottery win for the Howarth household that week-end. Instead, the clock radio switched itself on as usual at 7.45 am. Monday morning had arrived to the strains of Michael Jackson whimpering about how much he loves the children of the world. Terry lay in bed thinking that if he had his kind of money it wouldn't be the children of the world he'd be loving. The gaseous bulk that was Dawn shifted and spluttered beneath the duvet, "You'll have to make your own breakfast this morning. The kids are off school till Thursday, so I'm having a lie in," before returning to her rhythmical, throaty wheeze.

Terry crept along the toy strewn landing toward the bathroom. He noticed in the dull curtained light that his son Blake had stuck a life-size poster of Eric Cantona to his bedroom door. "Morning Eric," he whispered.

Terry was in good mood, despite having spent Sunday at Dawn's mum's listening repeatedly to the victorious bingo story; about how they'd waited for what seemed like an eternity for the number twelve to come up, and when it did Dawn could hardly speak so Kath had to scream at the top of her voice the all important "HOUSE!" Christ, if the encore was anything to go by it was a wonder they didn't hear the loud-mouthed bitch in Inner Mongolia, never mind Outer.

The reason for Terry's vibrant mood was simple. At 9am he would be sitting comfortably in Macclesfield Town Hall covering the public inquiry into the proposed Mottram Hill out-of-town shopping development. This was the chance he'd been waiting for, to prove to everyone at the *Comet* what a fabulous writer he was, and he intended to ram a dazzling piece of journalism down their throats. Who knows where an opportunity like this could lead? One of the quality papers might pick up the story and offer him a job down south. Scoop! You never know in this game. While Terry stood carefully shaving his pitted face in the mirror, a ravaged lunar landscape, he imagined the kind of impact his in-depth article might have on local people's lives. Obviously a story of such importance would be spread over a number of weeks, and if that were the case his own opinions would naturally come to the fore. He had no intention of writing a series of long winded articles stating nothing but dry facts, the readers would soon get bored and turn to the sports pages. No, the more he thought about it the more it made sense: they would have to be led through this complicated political maze by someone with high moral standards and a nose for rooting out corruption; someone who wouldn't be ruffled by rich bully-boy entrepreneurs or fanatical Greens. He would set himself up as judge and jury; the people's journalist who calls a spade a spade, and let the Devil take the hindmost.

After egg on toast and a quick scan through the *Daily Mail*, Terry decided to wear his best suit. It was a silvery grey affair, the type common to South American businessmen, though Dawn had purchased it from her mother's catalogue. She'd chosen it because one of the male models took her fancy; a dark brooding chunky character with mountainous hair, a square jaw and the promise of a rippling chest. Dawn was so disappointed when the thing finally arrived and Terry tried it on. Honestly, advertising! It's all a load of bollocks.

Decked out in his glossy grey sheath, a jiggling skeleton inside baggy cloth, Terry took his place in the world. He opened the front door to be greeted by another bright blue June morning. A carpet of dew covered the bumpy lawn like Silver Shred marmalade spread across toast. Walking down the path he noticed his neighbour Donald Campbell drive off at terrific speed, obviously late for work. *Bluebird!* thought Terry, climbing into his own rusting hulk before starting the engine that always raced. Driving along the A34, elbow out of the window, radio on nice and full, he felt relieved not to be calling in at the Comet's office. Seeing Keith after Friday night's embarrassing fiasco was the last thing he wanted, and anyway Frank had told him to go straight to the Town Hall. *Mustn't upset the boss, I might need a good reference!*

He sped through Wilmslow, passing on his way the old Rex Cinema, Hooper's department store, and on past Sainsbury's along a road festooned with pink and red cherry trees exploding their blossom like miniature atom bombs. He followed the narrow road through Alderley Edge where large Victorian mansions curtained in discreet anonymity hugged the famous hillside; shrouded in wood-land, their rooftops and towers emerging only as faint clues. True wealth. On and upwards, over the Edge, until the vast panorama enclosing this affluent part of North East Cheshire came into view. The Derbyshire peaks. In the morning sunlight their colours combined emerald green and purple heather, distant waves of tinted stone. It made his heart leap to see Nature's glory thus revealed. Perhaps Vanessa did have a point after all.

His attention was diverted from spiritual to carnal as he approached the slate-grey outskirts of Macclesfield – a group of micro-skirted schoolgirls were gathered round a bus stop awaiting their transport to education. Terry slowed down to scan ice-cream legs and firm young bosoms, gifts from the gods, and imagined himself as their PE teacher leading them naked into the showers. Oh what fun they'd have. All that nubile flesh pressed up against him as he individually washed and caressed, scooped and sucked the hardening raspberry nipples of each of his vanilla-skinned charges. Terry's sex fantasy was rudely interrupted by the fast approaching back-end of a stationary bus. Just in time he rammed his foot on the brakes and came to a screeching halt. With inches to spare he'd manage to avoid disaster. That was a close one! Several shocked faces peered from the rear window of the bus as it slowly pulled away. They weren't the only ones staring at him accusingly. The gaggle of schoolgirls he was so fixated with were also unimpressed. One of their number shouted, as Terry drove off, "That'll teach you to keep your eyes on the road, you dirty old pervert!"

Macclesfield Town Hall stood in the centre of a town built on numerous hills, like Rome, though here past glories were derelict silk mills and Victorian pubs. Terry parked his car opposite the municipal hub and gained access via a grand Corinthian portico, its Doric columns shading the entrance doors. It reminded him of one of those buildings featured in American TV court dramas such as *LA Law*, where the accused is hassled by the press.

(What about the missing millions, Terry, and the dead blonde found in your swimming pool?

No comment! Speak to my attorney!

That's not good enough, Howarth, you'll get the chair for this....)

"Can I help you, sir?" asked a uniformed presence trapped

inside a glass fronted booth just inside the main door; a world within a world. Terry reached into his top pocket for his press pass and handed it through a slit in the glass. "I'm from the *Wilmslow Comet*. Could you tell me which room's holding the public inquiry?"

The old man, dressed in a black uniform not dissimilar to a traffic warden's, his hat far too big for his head, studied the photo for a good thirty seconds before handing it back. He leant forward menacingly, pushing his bespectacled face right up to the glass as if studying a rare species of insect.

"Which public inquiry? There's three running this week," he said, his voice a sarcastic muffle inside an echoing dome of hurried footsteps, slammed doors and bellowing council chit-chat.

"The Mottram Hill Shopping Development."

"Well, you should have said so in the first place. I'm not a mind reader."

Terry didn't like his attitude one bit. He noticed the black fingers of an enormous clock hung on a marble pillar above his head showed 8.55. Only five minutes to go and the public inquiry would be under way. He eyeballed the cynical veteran. "Listen, Granddad, I'm not wasting my time arguing with a no-mark like you. So just tell me which room the meeting's in, or I'll report you to your superiors!"

The old man, who'd fought for his country, blurted out in military fashion, "First floor! Turn left! Committee Room Three! Ignorant sod!"

Terry rushed up a sweeping staircase flanked by stone dragons, then along a hallway displaying vertical portraits of past civic dignitaries resplendent in their robes of office – some had jaunty expressions, other's looked as if they were about to face a firing squad. He stopped halfway down a deserted corridor and read the inscription on a gleaming brass plaque above two carved walnut doors -- **Committee Room 3**. He composed himself and entered. The meeting had yet to start. What luck.

The council chamber was packed with over a hundred people, its gothic stained-glass bathing all assembled in multiple rainbows of shifting colours. At the far end of the oak panelled room, under an arched central window depicting St George slaying the dragon, an eight strong committee of councillors sat bolt upright on high-backed red leather chairs behind a raised banqueting table, stern looks written across their faces suggesting the Nuremberg War Trials had come to town. Below them, on either side, two smaller tables cluttered with files held the representatives of the pro and anti shopping development lobbies. The rest of the chamber was filled with grey plastic chairs, each one containing a bobbing head eager for the meeting to get underway.

" *Oi*, Terry! Over here, lad."

A crazy waving hand flapping like an injured dove caught his eye. It belonged to Fat Charlie Peters, Terry's rival from the *Wilmslow Gazette*, and it beckoned him toward the press table situated halfway up the right hand side of the room. *I thought he'd be here*, thought Terry, swapping hellos with other local reporters before squeezing into his seat. Unfortunately for him it was right next to Charlie's.

"I've saved you a place," said Charlie, already the working space in front of him a clutter of chocolate wrappers, pens, that day's *Daily Star* turned to the crossword puzzle, and a thick Jumbo notepad with five pages torn out scrunched up into tight little balls. "What kept you?"

"I had a run in with that white haired old bleeder on reception. You know him, the one that got thrown out of the SS for cruelty. Pillock! I'll tell you what, if this had been a public inquiry into euthanasia he wouldn't have talked to me like that."

Charlie laughed to himself thinking, *Same old Howarth, the lad never changes*. He was fifteen years older than Terry and had been active on the local news front for more than twenty. He knew his place in the world, and also what the other reporters thought of him, *There goes Fat Charlie Peters, a right sloppy bastard, been in the same job for years, never make editor, doesn't take his work seriously enough*, -- and hopefully – *But he's a good laugh is Fat Charlie, got a wicked sense of humour, never do you down, always first to the bar, shame about Maureen, though.*

Charlie had recently lost his wife after a long illness, so the other reporters, including Terry, put up with his Fatty Arbuckle style of journalism.

"Hey," offered Charlie, digging Terry in the ribs. "That 'Chip Pan Inferno' headline. Brilliant! Absolutely bloody brilliant! I don't know how you think of 'em. Frank's definitely not paying you enough!"

There was a loud rat-tat-tat-tat as the pointy faced chairman called the meeting to order. He peered down upon the noisy throng in a distasteful manner through horn-rimmed spectacles, both lenses flashing aluminium as they caught the sunlight.

"Here we go," whispered Charlie, settling into his chair like an immense blob of dough hopelessly poured into a tiny mould, his flabby face and podgy nose glistening sweat. "Wake me up when it's all over."

That same morning Keith rode precariously to work on his *MZ 250* motorcycle – the two wheeled *Trabant* – in sombre mood through a light that felt sharp and terrifying as only it can after a weekend lost to drink. As he droned along the A34, golden sun knifes piercing the trees above slashed into a thin membrane of alcohol protecting him from his worldly woes; a chain-saw brain-abrasion similar to the tinny hornet buzzing between his legs. So Rita had run off with a woman, had she? The whore! Of all the low-down stinking tricks! Why him? What had he done to deserve such a humiliating kick in the balls? He'd tried to be a good husband. Alright he drank, and gave her a back-hander now and again. But so what? Millions of men do the same and their wives don't turn into lesbians. He'd always believed you had to dominate women; give them too much freedom and they'll walk round like bitches on heat. His father had ruled his mother with an iron fist and it never did her any harm. She loved him for it.

Keith padlocked his excuse for a motorbike in the Swan's car park. He hurried along Grove Street towards the *Comet's* office, hoping above all else that Terry hadn't spread their sordid secret. Imagine if it got out! At least if Rita had scarpered with another man he could expect a bowl-full of people's sympathy. But this! This would make him a laughing stock. Life really was a meaningless nightmare of suffering.

With his usual couldn't-care-less attitude he strolled into the office thinking, *Mustn't show any sign of falling apart, these jerks can sense it a mile off.* The first person to greet him was the sub editor, Nigel Harrison. He wore a pair of grey Oxford Bags, a lime green corduroy jacket, and a blue shirt coupled with a blood-red dickey-bow. *Another queer. I'm surrounded by them. How many more are there in the world?*

"Morning, Keith. I believe Frank wants to see you," he said, in his ever so posh Prestbury accent. Noticing the bleach-like pallor of his skin, Nigel atoned, as if centre stage in one of his cheap operettas, "Worry not, dear boy. I see no trouble on the horizon."

"That makes a change," laughed Vanessa, wearing yet another ultra baggy sweatshirt adorned with the Greenpeace logo. Her long dark hair this morning was set free, spilling over her shoulders like an inky waterfall. Keith put down his crash helmet and asked her, casually, "Where's Terry?" knowing full well where he was, just so she'd have to answer.

Vanessa attempted nonchalance."Err, I think he's gone to...."

"Oh yeah," he interrupted sarcastically, about to knock on Frank's door, "I remember. He told me Friday night. He's gone to Macc Town Hall. It's that Mottram Hill shopping doo-dar this morning, isn't it? You know, Vanessa, that environmental crap you're so uptight about." He then tapped lightly upon frosted glass. "I'll tell you this, lady, I hope they rip up every last tree in Cheshire........and gas all the wildlife in the process."

On receiving a pompous, "Enter", Keith turned and jibed before slipping through the door, "I bet Terry's signing up to drive the bulldozers as we speak."

"Morning, Keith," said Frank, relaxing in his chair, both hands cupping the back of his head so he resembled a giant wing-nut. "Come in and sit down. Did you have a nice weekend?"

Keith panicked and thought, *Hang on? What's he being so friendly for.....? He knows! He fuckin knows! That bastard Terry must have told him!*

"Err......OK, boss. And yourself?"

"Great, Keith, great. Couldn't have been better."

Frank's good mood was down to a hole in one at Wilmslow golf club the previous afternoon. Par three thirteenth, seven iron, 180 yards, wind coming from the right rustling the tree tops, perfect swing, head still, knees slightly bent, hardly felt the ball caress the club, one bounce and it was in. Oh the joy!

Sitting in a casual manner opposite Frank as if time was a beautiful thing to waste, was the *Comet's* young sports reporter, Steve Barlow. He acknowledged Keith's presence with a cheeky grin, his pale blue eyes lighting up mischievously under his curly blonde fringe.

He knows as well. The whole fuckin office knows!

"Now," said Frank, the miraculous golf shot pinging once

more through his brain, "This morning I want the pair of you to pop along to Knutsford Leisure Centre. At ten o'clock the Lord and Lady Mayoress are due to open three new astro-turf pitches financed by lottery cash. To commemorate the event, two teams from Knutsford High School are going to play an inaugural hockey match, teachers v pupils, that sort of thing."

Hockey! The place'll be full of dykes! thought Keith.

"Anyway," continued Frank. "Keith, I want you to get some pictures of the Lord and Lady Mayoress as they arrive. Get a few close-ups of whichever one of them cuts the ribbon, and then afterwards various action shots of the teams taking part. Steve, I want you to interview the woman responsible for getting the lottery grant. I've got her name here somewhere. Here it is, it's a Miss. Jenny Radford, the director of the Leisure Centre. I've already spoken to her this morning, so she's expecting you. Get a photo of her as well, will you Keith. And another thing, Steve, try to get a few words with the Lord Mayor. It shouldn't be too difficult, we all know he loves publicity." Frank's joyous mood knew no bounds. As the intrepid duo were about to leave his office, he sought to boost the flagging ego of a certain alcoholic photographer. "Before you go on your way, Keith, I just want to say that the photos you did of Mrs. Grasby last Friday were perfect. She must have really opened her heart to you and Terry. Well done, and keep it up."

Inside Keith's silent lair -- his cramped darkroom just along the corridor from the main office, where a trio of plastic trays half full of wondrous chemicals produce images as if by magic under an eerie reddish light similar to the light in *Hammer Horror* films when Count Dracula is about to be put to the stake but the sun unfortunately sinks bathing the vault in a fiendish glow allowing him to grapple with Professor Van Helsing (why this extermination routine isn't carried out at midday, God only knows) – he grabbed his Minolta and several cartridges of film. He then checked in one of the wooden drawers that served as a plinth for the enlarger to see where his light meter had got to. He eventually found it. Rooting in the drawer his hand touched something familiar, glass and comforting; half a bottle of vodka. Gulping down the liquid pain suppresser, a loud bang echoed inside the darkroom. "Hurry up, Keith! What are you playing at, man? We're going to be late," causing a nostril back- flush of Vladivar.

"Christ, Steve!" he coughed angrily, his eyes blurred with

tears. "I'll see you downstairs in five minutes."

They set off for Knutsford in Steve's brand-new pillar-box red Ford Probe; the name of which delighted the young owner. "I've got a two litre Probe," he would boast to any attractive girl that took his fancy. And there were many. Although he had a steady girlfriend, he still made a play for the opposite sex, with spectacular results. Steve Barlow was the kind of honeypot most upwardly mobile Cheshire girls buzzed around. Whereas Terry and Keith appeared to these same girls as meaningless shapes, like wisps of something nasty emanating from within a compost heap, Steve on the other hand stood out bold as a granite statue. He was good looking in an *Old Spice* aftershave type way: fair skinned, chunky build, curly blonde hair grown just over the collar to suggest the rebel, and a face healthy in its cut of high cheekbones and flashing pearl-white teeth. Terry often thought that if reincarnation was a state that might actually exist, he wouldn't mind coming back as Steve. To add insult to injury – as if Nature's generosity knew no bounds, or She was playing a silly joke – he came from a wealthy family who'd purchased as a twenty first birthday present his very own duplex apartment in the affluent Curzon Mews, close to Wilmslow town centre. But most attractive of all he had the easy-going confident manner of someone who didn't really need to work. Life to Steve was an enjoyable event where one acquired as many ego-trips as possible, each one collected and savoured with pride as he travelled down the endless river of his own vanity. He'd come up the usual middle class route: Manchester Grammar School, then on to university before deciding on a career in journalism. Because his English degree was an embarrassing third, the only newspaper prepared to take him on was the *Wilmslow Comet*, and then as a lowly sports reporter, and then because his farther played golf with the proprietor. Steve didn't give a damn. At the age of twenty-two he'd long since realised that ambition was for lesser men like Terry, men who weren't fortunate enough to have a trust fund set up by two doting parents.

Cruising through the traffic lights past the old Rex Cinema, Steve suddenly remembered he'd left his Filofax at home. This was the ideal opportunity to show off his new property, a real sickner for someone living in rented council accommodation.

"You don't mind if I just pop to my apartment for a second, do you?" he asked with a smirk, "I've forgotten something."

It was the first time Keith had visited Steve's new home, or 'apartment' as he insisted on calling it, and a spark of envy ignited his thoughts. *'Apartment'. What a tosser. Apartments are what they have abroad. What if I went round telling people I lived in an 'apartment'? Probably get my head kicked in.*
You should have seen the look on Keith's face as the car turned off the Kings Head roundabout and entered the heady precincts of Curzon Mews; a modern development of two storey Cheshire-brick town houses surrounded by a high wall.

"I won't be a tick," said Steve, parking next to a neighbour's brand new Mercedes convertible, purposely not inviting his scruffy confederate in, realising a glimpse of the exterior would have his mind racing as to the sumptuousness of the interior.

"Well hurry up then," barked Keith, envy pumping through his veins. "I thought we were running late."
Steve vanished behind a black panelled door similar to 10 Downing Street's. Keith swore out loud, "The privileged bastard!" Both he and Terry had become infected with the miasma of jealousy from the very first day he'd joined the *Comet*. For twelve months their hatred had mushroomed. It was obvious why, he was from another world. Frank got on well with him, so did Nigel - *probably fancied his tight little arse*. The way Nigel gazed lovingly into his eyes first thing in the morning whilst mincing, "Coffee, Steve?" made Keith feel sick. And Vanessa didn't fool anyone with her socialist views and sarcastic comments about the rich, she obviously fancied him too. And why not, the whole world fancied Steve Barlow. Keith would often bumped into him at lunchtime in the nearby delicatessen on Grove Street, only to witness a sickening carnival. Each pretty young girl working behind the counter would stand gazing at him all doe-eyed, like he was some kind of pop star, then fight for the thrill of serving him, whilst he, Keith, didn't get so much as a second glance. On other occasions he'd be sat by himself in some pub or other enjoying a quite drink when suddenly Steve would appear, laughing and joking in the company of a stunning girl, throwing his money around as if a comet was about to slam into the Earth. It wasn't fair. How is it God deals such a lucky hand to one man, yet leaves nothing but a fistful of jokers to another?

Steve climbed the stairs and gently tiptoed into his bedroom. He carefully made a grab for his bulging leather-clad Filofax lying on the dressing table, only to knock over a bottle of Hugo Boss after-shave. A sweetly curved leg, tanned and smooth as a pebble, appeared from under the single white bed sheet, followed moments later by an arm, then a mass of auburn hair. It was his girlfriend, Natasha. He half thought about jumping in beside her, but remembered Keith was waiting outside.

"What time is it?" came the girlie groan.

He knelt at the side of the bed and delicately stroked her long wavy hair. "Look, Tash," (her cute nickname.) "Sorry to wake you up, but can you do me a favour?"

"What? What do you want?" she asked, expecting a sexual demand. Steve just couldn't get enough.

"Put your see-through nightie on and come downstairs. It won't take a minute. I want to give someone a surprise. The guy's a real loser. It'll make his day."

"WHAT!"

"Come on, Tash. Just for me."

Outside there was a loud impatient blasting car horn -- *BEEEEEEP!!!* Steve looked through a chink in the bedroom curtains to see Keith's grizzled face pressed up against the windscreen. It reminded him of one of those hideous reptiles exhibited in a zoo's Hot-House; all head shaking and tongue flicking inside a mouth miming obscenities. Keith's gnarled hand beckoned like a claw scooping hot sand against glass, followed by more *Beep! Beeep! Beeeeps!* Steve laughed to himself while the gorgeously naked nineteen year old Natasha slipped on the flimsy silky nightie he'd bought for her only two days ago from Hooper's department store. *BEEEEEEEEEEEP!!!!!!* One behind the other they descended the bronze spiral staircase linking bedroom to lounge; a charming curl of iron like one of Natasha's ringlets. Downstairs in a spacious living room boasting fine Italian reproduction furniture – though tasselled red drapes still drawn against the morning sun revealed little but the scrolled back of a curved sofa and the dim distant outline of six high-backed dinning chairs – Steve made ready his fabulous creation. Just enough shoulder, more than enough cleavage. By now Keith was fuming, "What's that spoilt twat playing at!"

The Prime-Ministerial front door opened and out bounced Steve without the slightest look of remorse. Keith was all set to go nuclear. He turned sideways to confront his middle class tormentor as he climbed into the sleeky Probe. "Where the *fuck* have you been?" There was a shimmering presence beyond the curly blonde of Steve's head, a presence that seemed to float just outside the driver's window. A Vee of silk announced two fabulous breasts, then a sweeping neck-line, then a face of startling beauty framed by a halo of auburn hair. "Sorry to have kept you waiting, Keith," sang the vision.

He thought, *She actually knows my name!*

"Take good care of my *Stevey* today, won't you."

Steve fired up the engine and casually flicked on a Bon Jovi CD. Just before turning up the volume he turned and asked proudly, "Well, what do you think of Natasha? Not bad is she."

To the thumping beat of 'Living on a Prayer', they headed towards Knutsford along country lanes fresh with summer's burgeoning fra-grance; a time to wind down the window, lean out an elbow, and take in the blurring hedgerows as they roller-coaster by. Keith tried to get the gorgeous Natasha out of his mind, and the stomach churning thought that Rita might have fancied her, by mentally re-running a dog fight video he'd seen at the weekend.

Keith loved dog fighting. He couldn't get enough of it. The sight of two crazed Pit Bulls going at it hammer and tongs sent shiv-ers down his spine. What a spectacle! The way the dogs flew at one another other for no particular reason, the shear power of each animal as it snarled, ripped, bit, tore, growled and shook its opponent throughout the vicious bout made Keith an instant disciple. There was no pussy-footing around as in boxing. Quite the opposite. In dog fighting they couldn't wait to get at each other's throats. With their shadowy owners bawling messages of encouragement from the side of the pit like, "*GowwwwOnnn!*" or "*GuuuuwwwwOnn Boy!*" you knew a savage death awaited one or other of the plucky contestants. Simply breathtaking. And all the dogs seemed to have glorious names like Caesar, Spartacus or Tyson, and one particular champion who'd reigned undefeated for twelve consecutive fights was crowned, fittingly, Emperor. What Keith would have given to see him let loose at Crufts! He was introduced to the sport completely by accident in a pub one night. What started out as an innocent exchange of hard-core pornographic videos between himself and a friend, ended up, because they were both so drunk, with Keith being handed the wrong tape. It was like a door into another world. Instead of tits, cocks and arses, he was royally entertained by three smashing fights produced on a home-made video. Granted the quality wasn't all that it should have been, but so what, here was something far more exciting than any skin-flick, and from that moment he was well and truly hooked. Keith could never understand why such a marvellous sport was banned and forced underground. As far as he was concerned you may as well try to ban people from going to the lavatory, or making love – why interfere with the natural cycle of things? One video in particular seemed to prove his *avant-garde* theory correct. Entitled 'Pit Bull Mania,' the cameraman must have had itchy fingers because instead of showing the usual badly lit room and empty pit ready for the coming battle, the action mysteriously began outside a derelict barn. Two battered Escort vans then appeared carrying their snarling cargo. What happened next proved beyond doubt Keith's rationale. No sooner had the vans stopped and their back doors flung open, than both dogs ignored their owners and immediately started a ferocious set-to right in the middle of the yard, without any prompting whatsoever. Proof, if proof be needed, that these proud beasts would savage one another whether or not there were any humans present to enjoy the frenzied encounter. Keith thought it a real shame that in a free and democratic society the government should deny its citizens access to this kind of scintillating entertainment.

"What did you do at the weekend?" asked Steve as they approached the gates to Knutsford Leisure Centre, totally disinterested really but knowing the journey's long drawn-out silence was due to him cruelly exhibiting Natasha.

Keith shuffled in his shell-suit and scratched at his tatty grey beard. "Nothing much. Watched a few Vids."

Steve thought, *I bet you did, you dirty bastard.*

A crowd of school children, teachers, members of the public, various leisure centre staff conspicuous in their brightly coloured track suits, and a sprinkling of council officials were gathered under a banner proclaiming **WELCOME, LORD AND LADY MAYORESS**. They all stood around waiting patiently for their special guests at the rear of the leisure centre, in the shadow of its massive breeze block sports hall. Behind them, enclosed by a ten metre high wire-mesh fence, were three brand-new emerald green astro-turf pitches, smooth and silent like stagnant swimming pools overgrown with watercress. Steve parked his Probe next to a mini bus that had 'Knutsford High School for Girls' written on its side. He noticed a bunch of lily-white faces peering from within. Keith began to load his camera with film while Steve took a sly glance at himself in the rear-view mirror. Well, you never know. All of a sudden there was a commotion. Jolted from the inner workings of his camera, Keith looked up to see a police motorcycle pass through the entrance gates followed moments later by a black Daimler limousine, an heraldic flag elegantly flapping atop its shiny radiator. Keith snapped shut the back of his Minolta. "Christ, they're here!"

"Who?"

"Who? Who do you bleedin think? Hitler and Eva Braun?" Both he and Steve leaped from the Probe in unison and ran across a shimmering car park that smelt of treacle toffee baking under the hot June sun. Steve's hurrying was nothing more than show, to show those baby faces in the minibus that, yeah, that's right, I'm a journalist.

"This is your fault," snarled Keith, resembling Emperor. "Wasting time showing off your fuckin '*A-part-ment*', and your fuckin girlfriend! It's alright for you, you can write your bullshit copy back at the office! If I don't get a picture of their Worships getting out of the car, I'll be up shit creek with Frank!"

Running alongside Keith through the dense morning heat, already noticing he was out of breath, Steve found it hilarious that he should use their official title in such circumstances; he couldn't have cared if it was the President of the United States waiting to be photographed.

"Don't blame me," said Steve, gliding effortlessly across the tarmac. "You took your time pissing around in that darkroom. And don't think I didn't smell the booze."

"BOLLOCKS!"

Keith's vulgar yell caused a gap to appear in the crowd crowding round the inky black Daimler, funereal in its appearance save for the colourful twitching pendant. It certainly wasn't the kind of welcome the Lord and Lady Mayoress were expecting. Climbing out of their stately limousine the regal couple stood for a moment in shock, looking round for the foul mouthed offender, allowing a panting Keith the chance to stop, take aim, and fire off several shots from his Minolta. That was a close one.

"There, I told you we'd make it," laughed Steve.

Terry and Fat Charlie Peters, along with several other local

47

reporters, had adjourned for lunch in the Hog's Head, a legendary watering hole behind Macclesfield Town Hall. The smoky Victorian pub was as usual crowded with people eager to sample the lunchtime delicacies advertised with such poetic gusto on its chalkboard; an unholy alliance of cheap frozen food made to sound as if the nectar of the gods was available to anyone willing to sacrifice a mere £6. 50. **Fresh Loch Salmon, Chips, Mushy Peas. Saddle of New Zealand Lamb with Mint Sauce, Potato Scallops and Beans. Grilled Pork – cooked to your liking – Roast Potatoes and Sprouts.** Terry wondered if anyone had ever ordered it not cooked to their liking. And the piece de resistance, **Giant Yorkshire Pudding filled with Spicy Sausage floating in an ocean of Onion Gravy.** A veritable Mount Olympus of succulent flavours. Fat Charlie swore by the place. Terry gazed at what was on offer, then pronounced in his broad nasally accent that sounded like he was talking through an empty cardboard toilet roll, "I'll have a cheese sandwich."

Fat Charlie ordered the food and was about to join his fellow reporters in the Pool Room when he noticed Terry's miserable face. "Fancy a quick game?" he asked. "It might cheer you up."

"No thanks. You go ahead. Don't let me stop you."

Terry found an empty table in a quiet corner and sat down. On the chair next to him was an abandoned copy of the *Guardian*. He picked it up and read the headline; **Scandal In The Beef Industry**. Now here was a real story. A wave of envy coupled with nausea swept over him as he took a sip of bitter and reflected on his own useless existence. The public inquiry that morning had been a tedious bore in which nothing of any significance had occurred; just the opening salvos from both sides and a few inane technicalities concerning the why's-and-wherefore's of the Ancient Woodlands Act. It was worse than listening to Dawn's mum going on about her haemorrhoids. No wonder Fat Charlie had fallen asleep. Terry's dream of a journalistic coup was disappearing faster than his pint of Robinson's. *I'm just kidding myself*, he thought, submerging into yet another deep depression. *There's no way I'll ever get to work for a decent newspaper. Nothing's worth writing about in this one horse town. It could do with a savage murder to brighten the place up.* His macabre fantasy quickly dissolved. *No such luck. I don't know why I bothered coming here this morning. I should have let Vanessa cover the story, at least she'd have stirred things up.* It was as if a match had been struck in a dark cavern. He recalled the public's mood at the meeting; almost all seemed to favour the pro shopping development lobby. Ever since childhood Terry had never been one for the majority. It stuck in his throat to agree with anyone, let alone a bunch of get-rich-quick Cheshire businessmen bent on a juicy profit. And for what? A sodding great eyesore of a building spread across ten acres stuffed with posh boutiques selling over priced crap the ordinary person could ill afford. It would rip the heart out of town centres like Wilmslow and Handforth! Not only that, Dawn would almost certainly make a fuss about shopping there every Saturday, dragging him along in the process, forcing him to traipse around for hours on end under a magnificent centre piece dome of chrome and tinted glass – a 'Cathedral of Shopping' according to the developers – with its piped muzac, Amazonian fountains and Perspex elevators, humiliating him every time he argued that such high prices were far beyond their tight budget. Terry felt a crusade coming on. There was no way he was going to end up like Thomas A'Becket. He remembered what Frank had said about writing a balanced piece, reporting both sides of the issue in an even handed way. Balls to Frank! The time had come to take a more controversial stance. At least it would be more interesting than writing about dead pensioners. And just think of all the letters that would flood in!

As he was formulating his grand stratagem, he gazed through the pub's stain-glass window across the hazy expanse of Town Hall car park. What he saw puzzled him. A group of well dressed businessmen, one of whom he recognised as being the spokesman for the pro-shopping development lobby, were gathered in a prayer-like circle beside a Seychelles blue Rolls Royce. The luxury auto bore the personalised number plate, **AW 2**. *Arthur Whitman?* Thought Terry, climbing onto a chair to get a better view. *No, it can't be. He drives a red Merc, and his number plate's AW 1.*

"What are you doing, lad? Eyeing up the town's skirt? And you a married man."

Terry spun round almost falling off the chair to be confronted by Fat Charlie, his jacket speckled with tomato ketchup and his shirt buttons set to pop after an enormous lunch. He was holding out two pints as though they were trophies.

"Here, have a drink…..My treat…..I won at pool…..Can you credit it."

49

Terry looked again through the window but the Rolls Royce and raven-like assembly of dark suited businessmen were nothing more than a memory. "Cheers, mate," he said, stepping down from the chair. "We'll sink these then get back to the meeting."

"I'm in no hurry, lad," scoffed Charlie.

Chapter Five

6 / . ' [5 " " 0 - g k g £ ^ 7 k £ k m j y 7 5 n $ i k - ; x f . . P a m e l a - Anderson,,;;kv/@8*7>63op^h5rg80kj kl9l o. The next morning Terry was sitting at his computer, doodling. Agitated, he was unable to make up his mind whether or not to complete the article condemning the Mottram Hill Shopping Development, or write something a little less controversial. Although the public inquiry had been adjourned the day before, it still had a further three days to run. In their wisdom the committee decided that each session should be held on the following three Mondays. The reason given for this unnecessary delay was that a cooling off period was to be enforced so that people might have the chance to assess the facts and not jump to the wrong conclusions. But Terry knew that if his article was published, containing as it did such a strong, negative tone, it would be very difficult, if not highly embarrassing, for the *Comet* to suddenly do a *vault-farce* and change its stance. Terry also knew the instant Frank read it he would hit the roof while doing his own *vault-farce* and make him write a more balanced piece. But fate had taken a hand, the same mysterious hand that silently plots the destiny of planets with scant regard for anything other than its own Divine strategy (obsessed by his hole-in-one, Frank had decided to take advantage of the glorious June weather and award himself the rest of the week off to enjoy a short golfing holiday with a friend). To avoid being interrupted by one of Nigel's futile phone calls, Frank stated his destination pompously as, "Somewhere along the timeless Scottish coast."

The thought of Frank striding regally across the Caledonian countryside dressed in tweedy plus-fours, whacking a ball about and guzzling delicious malt whiskey from his initialled hip flask – a present, no doubt, from a grateful editor – finally made up Terry's mind….......... *Sod him! The arrogant swine shouldn't have gone walkabout.*

To get around Nigel spoiling his journalistic time bomb, Terry decided on a brilliant piece of subterfuge that had worked well in the past. He would put off asking him to check through the article until late Wednesday afternoon (Nigel always left around 4pm every Wednesday, *"Three'ish"*, if Frank wasn't there, thus giving himself plenty of time to spread his wings and do a bit of shopping before sprucing himself up prior to rehearsals at the operatic society). Terry's plan seemed fool-proof. This particular rehearsal was even more important than usual because Nigel had been chosen – *"Nay beseeched!"* – to direct the Prestbury Local Opera Group in their forthcoming production of 'The Pirates of Penzance'. There wasn't a chance in hell he'd risk turning up late for his first evening *'At the helm"* just to read through a piece of Terry's unimaginative garbage. So caught up was he in his directorial debut that had the Martians landed in Wilmslow town centre, Nigel's reaction would almost certainly have been a defiant, *"The show must go on!"*

The office seemed almost too peaceful that Tuesday morning: Frank away on holiday smashing golf balls around a mysterious part of Scotland; Nigel absent doing the thing he liked best, reporting crimes and misdemeanours from the press box at Wilmslow Magistrates Court (the sight of a beefy young thug being sentenced to six months imprisonment, no doubt having to share a cramped sweaty cell with another beefy young thug, never failed to excite his artistic imagination), Steve out interviewing the new manager of Macclesfield Town football club, and Keith locked away in his dark-room. The only other person in the office at the time was Vanessa, typing away furiously, a crest of dark hair bobbing above her computer screen. Terry's creamy-white desk faced Vanessa's desk head on, like their relationship, across a ravine of green nylon carpet. The desk immediately to his right belonged to Steve Barlow, which stood opposite Nigel's – the way he intended it would from the very first day the blonde bombshell walked through the door. It was a small open plan office, no more than eighty square meters, with an inner quartet of work stations each forming the corners of a disconnected square. A line of dreary grey filing cabinets faced Terry and Steve, while Vanessa and Nigel enjoyed a bank of tinted blue windows. Frank's office stood at one end, and at the other a pair of teak coloured doors. The first opened onto a modest reception hall leading to the stairs. The second announced a long corridor accommodating the toilets and a rest room furnished with six easy chairs and a coffee machine. At the far end of this corridor, as if banished from civilisation, was Keith's sordid sanctuary.

For the third time that morning Vanessa felt terribly uncomfortable, as if her privacy was being invaded. Once again she looked up and this time the problem was solved. Rising like a new moon above the horizon of his computer screen, the smooth arc of Terry's bald head revealed two staring eyes. Without giving him the chance to blink, Vanessa barked in her contrived working class accent that still contained a hint of her prep-school past, "What's the matter, Terry?"

"Matter, Vanessa? Nothing. Nothing's the matter."

"Well why do you keep staring at me?"

"Staring? I wasn't staring, I was just thinking."

Terry *had* been staring, though, *and* thinking, both at the same time, a trick he'd managed to perfect as a child. All morning he'd been urging himself to go ahead with the explosive article; sort of publish and be damned, but somewhere along the line his courage had deserted him. Only in the last hour had he realised that an ally was essential; someone who could back him up and take most of the flack. But who could it be? Nigel was out of the question; far too close to Frank *(he wished)*. Steve couldn't be relied upon in the slightest; he spent half his time on Planet Narcissism. Then it struck him. Of course, the answer had been there all the time in the gorgeous shape of Vanessa Garland. But there was one small problem to overcome -- Vanessa hated his guts.

Daughter of the late Dr. Angus Garland from Alderley Edge, Vanessa had been brought up within the strict confines of an upper middle class family. Her mother Grace was a terrifying 63 year old blue rinse battle-axe who was used to getting her own way, especially within the confines of the Wilmslow WRVS where she had reigned as unopposed president for the past six years. Many's the time her steely will and gothic appearance struck fear into the hearts of those who sought to deflect the path of Tory self-righteousness. After her husband's death, even though Vanessa and her older brother Sam objected, she continued to live on in the family home, a large Victorian house close to Nether Alderley. Vanessa had inherited many things from her mother – stubbornness, an iron will, unshakeable self believe, but unfortunately for Grace being a Conservative wasn't one of them. Since Durham University, where she graduated with an honours degree in English, Vanessa, much to Grace's consternation, had become a hard-line Socialist with links to the Animal Liberation Front. She lived in a quaint terraced house near the centre of Wilmslow with her boyfriend Ian, a thirty two year old unemployed joiner by trade and budding musician by design. Grace hadn't spoken to her for almost a year since she shacked up with Ian, who she described as a wastrel. Vanessa didn't give a damn. Everything in life seemed to be going her way. She was an attractive, articulate twenty five year old who owned her own house – purchased from the proceeds of her father's estate – co-habiting with a man of working class stock who definitely knew the meaning of the word imagination when it came to sex. Not for her the cheap Cheshire charms of immature lads like Steve Barlow, with their pathetic Boy's Toys and wide-eyed wine bar mentality; Vanessa needed and got the love of an angry man. She did, though, have one burning ambition; the hope of one day becoming a freelance journalist, able to utilise her investigative zeal for rooting out corruption in order to shake the very foundations of the state.

Vanessa continued typing, **a police spokesman said they were completely baffled as to who set fire to the shed, and went on to warn tenants of the Morley Green allotment to be on their guard in case the arsonist returned.**

"Thinking!" laughed Vanessa, sarcastically, putting the finishing touches to her in-depth article on local crime. "Thinking about what? Your next drink?"

Terry hated being tarred with the same brush as Keith. Nevertheless, he swallowed his pride and began to lure her expertly into his swim. "Honestly, Vanessa, the things you say." He then dangled the bait with all the expertise of an assured angler. "If you must know, I was thinking about asking you for some advice on the Mottram Hill shopping development story. But if you're not interested…........"

Hook line and sinker.

Vanessa had been dying to ask Terry all about what had gone on at the public inquiry the day before, but didn't want to give him the satisfaction. This was the chance she'd been waiting for. Gathering together her charms, she paddled her swivel chair around the side of her desk and set sail across the great green divide towards Terry territory, accompanied by a soft breeze of air-conditioning. Dropping anchor, she immediately noticed the faint mangrove swamp of under-arm perspiration. Absolutely sickening. The things she did for the environment. Terry couldn't help noticing her bounteous cargo, huge and exhilarating under a loose fitting T-shirt that bore the distinct logo, 'No Second Runway'.

"Well, what do you want to know?" she asked, wary of land mines.

Terry swallowed hard. He then pressed the shift key on his computer with such drama as to suggest the launch of a nuclear missile, exploding the screen saver.

"Please read this, I'd be grateful for your opinion."…...He hadn't spoken to a woman in such cultivated tones since going through a period in his early twenties of mimicking Sebastian Flyte when *Brideshead Revisited* was all the rage.

Terry decided to give Vanessa the chance to read through the article in her own time, without his bony knees causing a distraction. So he rose from his desk and headed for the coffee room. When he got there he found Keith slumped in a chair reading Photographers Monthly. They hadn't seen each other since Friday night, and once more the fateful evening rolled through their minds like an embarrassing home movie. Keith was the first to speak. He came straight to the point while Terry fumbled at the coffee machine. "I'm glad you told me about Rita. It's made things a lot clearer. Christ," – his voice climbing from deep guttural morose into a pathetic attempt at humour – "I must have been a complete idiot not to have guessed. Talk about naïve. Every time I made a grab for her in bed she suddenly came over with a thumping headache. Anyway, I just want to say I'm sorry if I made a dickhead of myself, and I hope you won't mention it to anyone, especially anyone who works here."

Terry took a sip of blistering hot coffee and turned to see a broken man in pieces slouched in the chair.

"I won't breath a word, mate. You can rely on me."

Keith had the pained expression of a dog who receives a gentle pat from its owner following a good kicking. Terry threw another kind scrap as he leant against the door of the coffee room, his mind elsewhere. "Fancy a pint in the Swan at lunchtime? Do us both good."

"Brilliant," said Keith, rising from the chair, about to wander back to the unknown pleasures of his darkroom. "See you at one o'clock."

55

Vanessa re-read the final paragraph of Terry's article. She couldn't believe it. The whole thing was a complete revelation from start to finish. She thought it impossible that he could have written such a devastating, such a dynamic piece of journalism. She couldn't have put it better herself: from the greed of the developers right down to the horrendous damage lying in wait for the countryside. It was all there, and more! This certainly wasn't the Terry she knew, the Terry that had sat opposite her for the past three years chortling over every house fire, bizarre gardening accident, cruelly mown-down cyclist and viciously mugged pensioner; the same man who once wrote an article about a terminally ill child's visit to Disneyland (courtesy of Wilmslow Rotary Club) under the banner headline: **LEUKAEMIA LAD LETS HIS HAIR DOWN**.

Two thoughts now criss-crossed her mind. The first was that she had misjudged him, and that his apparent change of heart could have been due to some mystical experience within the council chamber. The second, and most likely, was that the whole thing was a wind-up, concocted by himself and Keith. But why? Why would he go to the trouble of writing such a long and complex piece for the sake of a joke? Things didn't add up. One thing she felt certain about, though, was that if the article managed to get into print, it would deal the pro-shopping development lobby a severe blow. With this in mind, she intended to play him at his own game.

Terry walked back into the office and found Vanessa still sitting at his desk, eyes fixed to the computer screen.

"Well Vanessa, what do you think?"

She cocked her head to one side and looked up, her dark eyes peering intently through her enormous glasses as she attempted to look the gift horse in the mouth for any sign of tooth decay.

"I'm impressed, Terry. But there's a couple of things I don't understand."

"Like what?"

"Like for instance why you've written it."

Terry was about to explain when all of a sudden Nigel Harrison pushed open the door and sauntered in, fresh from his morning in court. Vanessa noticed Terry go all coy at the fairy's entrance, so she waited until Nigel had walked into Frank's office (he always used it when Frank was away) before speaking. Nigel overheard Vanessa's low murmuring invitation as he closed the frosted door, "How about

56

lunch in the Carter's Arms? We can discuss it there if you like."
Nigel rolled his eyes and thought, *The Carter's Arms! With Terry!*

In the reddish developing light, like a Caribbean sunset, or the inside of a Turkish brothel, Keith could be seen hunched over his desk carefully examining a spreadsheet of photographs through his viewing lens. He was trying to decide which of the twenty or so black and white prints taken of the Lord and Lady Mayoress best captured the occasion. He eventually chose one, and marked the corner of it with a black felt tip pen. As per Frank's instructions, he'd also taken various action shots of the schoolgirls playing hockey. Peering through the viewer at frozen billowing skirts, dazzling white legs and the occasional slash of navy blue knicker, he tried to imagine how many of these Cheshire *belles* might turn out to be lesbians. Was it in them from birth for instance, already fully developed inside the womb, primed and ready like a poisonous seed to reek havoc amongst men, or did it just sort of happen years later because they got bored with their husbands? He had no idea. Women were a complete mystery to him.

"Shit!" he said out loud, noticing the fingers of his watch pointing to quarter past one. "I'm missing valuable boozing time."
He grabbed his purple acrylic jacket, locked the darkroom and hurried along the corridor towards the main office. When he entered he found the place deserted. Frank's office door opened and out strolled Nigel in the manner of editor in waiting.

"What's happened to Terry? We're supposed to be going to the Swan together. You've not sent him out on a job, have you?" asked Keith, annoyed.

"As a matter of fact," said Nigel, "You'll *never* guess where he's gone, and with whom, *never* in a million years."

"What are you talking about?"
Nigel began nodding his head like a crazed fun-fair dummy. "He's gone out to lunch with Vanessa. Yes, that's right, and you'll never guess what else, *she* asked *him*! "
Keith's jaw dropped open for a second. "Bollocks!"

"Please don't swear. I'm only letting you know. They left together about fifteen minutes ago. It's true!"

"Gone out where? Where have they gone?"

"To the Carter's Arms if you please. Went off like two lovebirds they did. And by the look on your face it's obvious Terry didn't want *you* to know. Oh, I am sorry. I seem to have put my foot in it.......again."

Keith slammed the office door and went trundling downstairs, thinking, *What the hell's Terry playing at?*

The Carter's Arms was Vanessa's local. A spruced up Victorian affair resplendent with hanging baskets, it was situated on the corner of Hawthorn Street and Chapel Lane, a quiet intersection close to the town centre. She lived just across the road from the pub in a charming three bedroomed red brick terrace modestly referred to as Railwayman's Cottage, though it was hard to imagine your average railwayman of today being able to afford such exorbitant house prices. Nor was it likely the railwayman of yesteryear ever envisaging his quiet street being taken over by luxury automobiles such as Saabs, BMW's and Jaguars. Approaching the pub, Vanessa glanced across at her house and noticed the bedroom curtains were still drawn – her darling Ian was having a lie-in. Bless him.

She insisted on buying the first round of drinks, and they both stood at the bar perusing the lunchtime menu. Terry felt strange being out with such an attractive woman, giddy almost, as if he were inhaling electricity. Vanessa must have sensed this, for she immediately said to the young barman, "By the way, Colin, this is Terry. A colleague from work."

Terry didn't like that one bit.

They ordered lunch and found a deserted table at the back of the pub. Vanessa went straight onto the attack. "Are you really serious about wanting to publish that article?"

"Deadly."

"But you'll never get it past Frank."

Terry smiled, unfolding the first part of his plan, "But Frank's not here, and no one knows where he is or how to contact him."

"What about Nigel? There's no way he'll let an article as controversial as that go to press. It'll be more than his job's worth."

Terry took a sip of bitter and relaxed further into his chair. He gazed at the mini jukebox, smiled a second time and asked a question of his own, "What day is it tomorrow?"

Colin the barman brought over two plates of scampi, chips and salad. Vanessa picked up her fork and said, "Wednesday. Press day. Why? What about it?"

"And what does Nigel do every Wednesday afternoon, especially if Frank's not here?"

Vanessa understood the implication, and a look of astonishment swept over her face.

"Jesus, Terry! Do you mean to tell me you're going to send it to bed completely unauthorised? You'll….You'll get the sack!"

"No I won't."

"Of course you will. Frank'll go ape-shit."

Terry swallowed a mouthful of scampi, put down his fork and said calmly, "Let's start with Frank then, shall we. He's supposed to be the editor of this newspaper, the man in charge, yet he's disappeared off to God knows where." Terry then pretended to be the sarcastic innocent. "Honestly, I tried my best to contact Frank so he could check the article, but he left without telling anyone in the office where he'd gone."

Vanessa couldn't help but admire the plan, and she completed it with gusto, her voice in similar mocking mode, "And Nigel wasn't available to check it either, he'd gone and finished early the very afternoon I needed his guidance most. So what was I to do? I had to publish something."

The pair of them fell about laughing at the simple ingenuity of it all, realising more important heads would roll before Terry's. It took a few moments for them to calm down, then Terry got to the crux of the matter.

"I want to ask you something," he said, his voice gathering seriousness. "Would you consider putting your name to the article alongside mine? I mean, you'd be free to add anything you like. I just think it would look better done in tandem. Give the piece more gravity."

Vanessa didn't see anything wrong with his suggestion, and much to Terry's relief she said, "I'd love to. I'd be more than happy to do my bit to stop that shopping mall ruining the countryside. Those greedy bastards have got it coming as far as I'm concerned."

Terry was thinking how attractive she was in the midst of her anger, when she suddenly asked, "One thing I don't understand, Terry, is why the sudden conversion to Green issues? I thought you didn't give a shit about anything like that."

This threw him. He felt a crimson tide wash over his face. He tried to regain his composure but nothing of any significance came out. Instead he began to ramble, "I've been doing a lot of thinking, you know, recently. I mean, a lot of what you've said in the past is true, you know, about the environment and all that. Yeah, true, true, it's true."

What was he blathering on about? Even *he* was confused. He realised that anymore bullshit would seriously damage his proposal. His mind raced, desperate to find a convincing theory, but more of the same rubbish poured forth. "When I was driving to Macclesfield on Monday morning, Vanessa, I noticed all those green fields: Nature in the raw so to speak. And I thought, what a pity it would be if we lost any more of it – you know, the *Nature*. Not to put too finer point on it, it would be a bloody calamity…......"

Vanessa was touched. It seemed to her that Terry's inability to express himself was down to an almost childlike sincerity, the pure emotion of someone only recently converted to the cause. Someone who had yet to learn how to put their true feelings into the kind of words that come out in the right order.

"You're right, Terry, it would be a calamity," she said with conviction.

Sitting there in the pub, watching Terry hunched over his plate trying to locate the last piece of scampi from under a mound of soggy chips, she began to think that perhaps she had misjudged him, and that his outlandish behaviour in the past was probably down to Keith's satanic influence. She also thought of the old adage: 'My enemy's enemy is my friend', as she continued, now in full battle cry, "Anyway, it's up to us to do all we can to stop the shopping development from going ahead. One good article should put a spanner in the works for the time being."

Excited at Vanessa's complicity, Terry fell into the silence of his own hidden agenda. He then thought about visiting the loo. He glanced at his watch; 1.45. *Damn!* They would have to make a move in the next five minutes. He hated rushing things when it came to the intricacies of his inner plumbing. You see, Terry was what you'd call a long bog man. He liked nothing better than to while away the odd hour sitting alone on the toilet, reading, or doing the crossword. He enjoyed the feeling, especially in the comfort of his own home, of brewing up a mighty load that would cause his bowels to elasticate until they could take no more. Then, with the determination of a B-52 about to take off with its explosive payload, he would grab the nearest newspaper or magazine and slip upstairs on his own personal bombing run. Once secured in his seat over enemy territory, he would read a while just let his bowels know who was boss, then wait for that luxurious painful feeling of surrender deep down in the lower gut before finally letting rip with a jettison of stinking cargo. Lovely jubbly. But sometimes, in his attempt to reach the zenith of pleasure, he would forget to check if there was any toilet paper left on the roll. When this happened he would be forced to close the bomb doors, abort the mission, and set off in search of *Kleenex*. This dreaded scenario occurred only last weekend, just as he was about to unburden a freight-load of chicken Korma carefully stored from the night before and primed for detonation by means of a large cooked breakfast. He had eased himself upstairs, slyly, and after a good twenty minutes read was ready for countdown. T-minus 7…6…5…. countdown suspended. To his dismay he looked sideways and noticed an empty cardboard toilet roll dangling helplessly off the metal chain. He suddenly remembered seeing a full one perched on the dressing-table in his bedroom (Dawn used sheet after sheet to remove her thickly applied Bingo make-up), so he edged out of the bathroom with his trousers around his ankles, grabbed the precious roll off the dressing-table and scrambled in a crab-like motion back to his cockpit. Disaster struck. As he lurched inside the bathroom, he overbalanced slightly and thumped down a little too hard on the lavatory seat causing one hell of a premature discharge, culminating in the 'All Clear' staccato siren of farting. That was it, the shite was ruined.

"Shouldn't we be getting back?" asked Vanessa, her voice dissolving Terry's toilet tale like a splash of bleach. "You know what Nigel's like when he's in charge."

"A right pain in the arse if you ask me," said Terry, oblivious to the analogy.

Inside the Swan, Keith continued feeding the fruit machine pound coins until he had no more. He gulped down the remaining dregs of best bitter, sighed, and headed out into the sunshine to begin the short walk back to the office. Yuppie couples cavorted on emerald green park benches as he skirted round the town garden. Love was in the air. Terry's lunchtime date with Vanessa played on his mind like an old 45;   first his wife had deserted him and now his best friend. *What the hell was he up to?* thought Keith. Suddenly, halfway up Grove Street, he spotted them shimmering towards him through the suburban heat haze. They were walking close together and laughing.

Laughing at what? The fact that Rita was a lesbian? Keith left behind the sunny pavement and ran upstairs to his darkroom, fuming.

Steve Barlow was sitting alone at his desk when Terry and Vanessa walked back into the office. He looked the typical sports reporter in black jeans (*501s*), a pale blue denim shirt (Lacoste), and Nike trainers. Nigel had already told him about their '*never in a million years clandestine rendezvous*," and a pang of jealousy drilled his stomach. Steve had been desperate from day one to get his hands on Vanessa's large breasts, to have them jiggle in his eye sockets. He'd always assumed attractive women like her were put on the earth for him and him alone, not balding jerks like Howarth. He swivelled round in his swivel chair, cupped the back of his head *a la* Frank, and asked cheekily, "Was the Carter's Arms full then?"

They had been rumbled.

Terry froze like a scarecrow. Vanessa came to the rescue in her usual self-confident manner, "As a matter of fact it was half empty. Why?"

"Just wondered. Just wondered what the special occasion was, that's all."

"No special occasion, Steve. Just fancied a change."

Steve raised his eyebrows and looked at Terry. "A change is as good as a rest, eh Vanessa? I hope Ian doesn't find out."

"Shut it, Barlow!"

Terry remained silent, thinking that by now Keith would know about the escapade. He decided without further ado to face his nemesis, and made the excuse, "I'm going to get a coffee. Does anyone else want one?"

"No."

"Not for me, thanks," said Vanessa, her amiable reply infuriating Steve.

Terry walked down the corridor and tapped lightly on the darkroom door. "Are you in there, mate?"

The door opened half an inch to reveal a knife blade of Keith's face; a slice of tatty beard and one bloodshot eye. A smell similar to alcohol mixed with chemicals met his nostrils while a reddish light bled from within.

"Oh, it's you. What do you want?"

"Listen, I'm sorry about not meeting you at lunchtime, but I had something important on."

"On your arm walking up Grove Street, so I saw."

"Don't be stupid, it's nothing like that."

"What is *it* like then?"

"Let me in and I'll explain."

Upon entering Keith's enchanted cavern, Terry noticed, pegged to a kind of washing line above the deep marble sink, several black and white photographs of little old Joan Grasby in various states of despair. Each horrified expression more animated than the last, she clutched her dead husband's medals and council tax bill against her petrified breast.

"They're brilliant," laughed Terry. "Just look at her face."

Keith was in no mood to accept false praise. "Never mind about them, what have you been up to?"

In the main office, Steve had begun his article profiling the new manager of Macclesfield Town Football Club. Try as he might, he just couldn't come to terms with the fact that Vanessa had spent her entire lunchtime in the company of Terry Howarth. He himself had asked her out many times, and always received the same answer – a firm, unequivocal 'No'. So what did Terry have that he didn't? What was the attraction? Had she finally succumbed to the fantasy, spread around by those with less hair than a golf ball, about the virility of bald men? Steve brushed back his thick curly hair with his right hand, purposely showing a smooth forehead. He turned to Vanessa and asked, "What are you doing going out to lunch with that jerk?"

With this question she saw revealed the soft underbelly of Steve: a man whose outer shell of apparent self confidence could be shattered as easily as a crystal vase, a man whose shameless vanity prevented him from believing that women could find other men apart from himself attractive. She gladly took revenge for all those months of sexist remarks, all those months of endless *double entendres*. Though it was extremely hard for her to say, like swallowing hot gravel, she grabbed the opportunity to wound the office Adonis with a well timed, "Actually, Steve, I find Terry rather handsome, in a mature kind of way," producing the desired result. His ego splintered into a thousand pieces. Poor Natasha, she was in for a long night of sulks with mardy-pants Barlow.

"I had no choice," explained Terry, encompassed in a fuzzy red light. "I had to go out for lunch with her, she insisted. Look, I need her on my side. Once the article's been published I'll need all the friends I can get."

Keith shook his head. "You must be mad, going against Frank's orders like that. He'll hit the roof when he reads it!"

"Don't worry, I took out an insurance policy this morning by phoning his wife."

"Jean?"

"The very woman."

"What did she say? What did you say to her?"

"I rang up and said I had to get in touch with Frank. That I wanted his opinion on something I've written."

"And?"

"Well you know what Jean's like – the snotty cow. When she realised it was *Comet* business, she said, in that posh accent of hers – 'Oh no, I couldn't possibly tell you the exact whereabouts of my husband. I've haven't got a clue myself. He left on Tuesday morning with a friend and said he was going to play golf somewhere in Scotland. I'm afraid that's all I know. Now if you don't mind I'm rather busy.' – I could tell Frank had primed her."

Keith's mind raced ahead. "And Vanessa's agreed to help you?"

"Yeah! This type of thing's right up her street."

Envious of Terry's lunchtime tête-à-tête, wanting to experience for himself life's hidden dangers, Keith sought a piece of the action. "Listen, if there's anything I can do to help, you know, photos and things, just let me know."

"Cheers mate, I will."

So Terry wouldn't be under any illusions as to whose idea it was in the first place, Keith added, as a cowardly after thought, "Bloody hell, I hope you know what you're doing!"

Chapter Six

Nigel Harrison was having a barbecue!.....Yes, it was true! Not only that, he'd gone and invited everyone from the *Comet*, including Keith. Utterly incredible. The man whose private life could only be guessed at, was flinging open the doors to his house this coming Saturday for all the world to see. Everyone at the *Comet* knew he was gay. Nigel had never tried to hide the fact. Well, he couldn't really, it screamed from his every gesture. But to be invited to his home, to glimpse his inner circle of friends, that was another matter.

The shock for one and all came the following morning -- Wednesday -- press day. Terry, Steve, Vanessa and Keith were summoned to Frank's office, where Nigel had set up temporary camp, to be told the good news. He was dressed for the day in a white shirt, marmalade coloured tie and dark blue slacks, and when the four of them entered he stood up and leant forward with both palms resting on Frank's desk. Peering through gold rimmed spectacles he had the look of a chubby overgrown schoolboy, an up-to-date Billy Bunter, his thin cupid lips pursed in anticipation.

"I have decided to invite you all," he said, with immense dignity, "to my home for a barbecue this Saturday evening, where I will be celebrating, along with my friends and fellow members of the Prestbury Local Opera Group, my directorial debut. As you all know I have been chosen to direct our forthcoming production of The Pirates of Penzance."

There was a gothic silence. Nigel looked at everyone expecting a round of applause. None came so he carried on with his performance undaunted. "Please bring your better halves with you" – he shied a glance at Terry – "if you so wish. Keith, just bring a friend. I do hope you can all make it. I'm sure it will be a lovely evening, weather permitting."

He then handed out stylish invitation cards depicting individual characters from various Shakespearean dramas. Steve got Romeo gazing up at an empty balcony. Vanessa got Lady Macbeth rubbing her hands together in a kind of frenzied glee. Terry got a sneering, stooping Richard III, looking as if he were about to carry out some dastardly deed, and Keith got the old drunk Falstaff, sat on his fat arse swigging ale out of a pewter tankard.

"Does this mean it's fancy dress?" asked Keith, staring at the invitation with some concern. "If it is, there's no way *I* can afford to get kitted out like that."

"Course not!" said Nigel, acidly, looking up flabbergasted toward a Heaven of blue polystyrene tiles, annoyed that his stab at good taste had failed to hit the mark, had fallen into the realms of pretentious absurdity.

"That's a shame," laughed Vanessa. "He's already got a head start with the beard."

"And the beer-belly," added Steve.

"What about Frank?" asked Terry. "What character's on his card?"

"Othello," sparked up Keith. "He'll come back looking like Tiger Woods after all that fresh air and sunshine."

Trying his best to ignore the waggish remarks emanating from the cheap seats, already regretting giving Keith the invite, Nigel explained, "I'm not sure if Frank will be back in time, but I've sent Jean an invitation just in case." He then added, with great decorum, "Please take note as to what it says on the card; smart dress, eight o'clock sharp."

Nigel's *Grande Gesture* to his lowly colleagues had come about for two reasons. First, not only did he want to finish early that day, about lunchtime, but he wanted to take the whole of the next day off, *and* Friday; no use spoiling the opportunity for a long weekend - - he hadn't enjoyed one of those in ages. And tonight being rehearsal night, his first *at the helm*, certain members of the cast had planned to throw a party in his honour; partly out of friendship, but more likely because most of the main roles had yet to be decided. This meant he would be drinking champagne until all hours, and he always woke up with a *stinking* headache after champagne. The second and most important reason was due to a telephone call he'd received the previous evening. Nigel had been listening to Verdi's Requiem at the time, a piece that always reduced him to tears, when out of the blue the phone rang. His heart almost stopped beating. On the other end of the line, *nervy* as *hell*, was the most potent man in the cast, Roger Harvey; a closet homosexual just waiting to be unhinged. He was a forty eight year old dentist who had recently left his wife for artistic reasons, but had yet to dabble in the love that dare not speak its name. All the gay men in the Prestbury Local Opera group were after him; they could smell fresh meat a mile off and boy were they ravenous. He was *sensational*; tall, good looking, athletic, but most important of all he was the nearest thing to a *straight* a gay man would ever get. And now look what the cat had dragged in! He was presenting himself on a plate solely for Nigel. "The obvious choice for director as far as I'm concerned," Roger had said, along with, "Do you think there might be an outside chance of me playing the lead?" and, "I would be ever so grateful," and, "Could we possibly discuss it over lunch in the Bells of Peover, say Thursday?"

The Bells of Peover, thought Nigel, *with* Roger Harvey. *I can't believeeeeeeeve it!* You could have knocked him down with one of his old feather boas.

"So what this means," continued Nigel, "is that I'll be finishing early today, and taking tomorrow and Friday off in order to sort out the arrangements for Saturday. There's *lots* to do, honestly." Fearing mutiny in the ranks, he quickly changed the subject and got down to the business of the day. "Now, about this week's edition." –

Terry swallowed hard – "As you've all finished your respective articles, apart from Terry, I've managed to finalise the general layout on my computer. Obviously the Mottram Hill shopping development story goes on the front page. Local news as usual on pages two, three and four. Vanessa's in-depth article on crime takes up page five. Page six deals with the court reports and gardening tips. And finally the back pages are of course Steve's domain. Can you *please* make sure it's e-mailed to the printers well before the six o'clock deadline. Now, are there any questions?........ Come on, don't be shy."

Nigel took the stony silence as a negative, then made the same corny joke he always made, "And by the way, if there's any problems, don't you *dare* call me at home. "

Terry and Vanessa stared wide-eyed at each other across the golden arc of Steve's curly mop. It seemed their plan was being sanctioned by the gods. Steve couldn't help but notice this furtive lover's glance, and thought perhaps Dawn might be interested to find out her husband was about to play away from home.

At around twelve fifteen Nigel left the office with a breezy, "See you Saturday everyone. Don't be late."

The relief was tangible. It wasn't long before Steve took advantage and disappeared for an early lunch, followed moments later by Keith. Once the coast was clear Vanessa pushed her swivel chair alongside Terry's desk and together they went through the finer points of the article. Vanessa wanted to make a few changes, to give the piece real bite, so Terry sat back and let her get on with it. As far as he was concerned, the more she put in the more she would share in the blame. Typing away furiously, her long slender fingers a dextrous blur, Vanessa said, "Oh, I forgot to tell you. I've been in contact with the anti-shopping development committee, to let them know what we're doing. They're all for it. Said the article would really help the cause."

Terry nodded his head. "Good, I'm really glad about that."

"Isn't it great to be writing something worthwhile for a change, instead of the usual crap?"

He couldn't have agreed more. To him this was journalism at the cutting edge. Even though he didn't give a damn about the countryside, they could tarmac the whole lot for all he cared, at least he was fulfilling his prophecy as a reporter by being controversial. He recalled an old Marx Brothers film he'd watched several times as a child. During the map-cap movie Groucho sang a song that greatly influenced the young Terry; it might have been specially written for him. The lyrics went something like this:

> **It doesn't matter what they say**
> **It makes no difference anyway**
> **Whatever it is, I'm against it.**
> **And even when they try to re-arrange it,**
> **I'm against it.**

Before transferring the article to Nigel's computer, where the entire layout of the paper could be viewed in electronic miniature before it was sent to the printers, Terry carefully read through Vanessa's contribution. Was she angry! Talk about revolution! He hadn't expected such vitriol. He thought for a moment, then tried in vain to get her to moderate the article by saying, "Er, do you think you might have gone a bit too far, Vanessa, here in the second paragraph where you suggest to the readers that they chain themselves to the bulldozers?"

"No, not at all. That's what I'll be doing if they……....Hold on a minute, Terry, you're not getting cold feet are you?"
He felt as though he was ascending a rickety staircase, with no banisters. Carefully choosing his words, he hid his anxiety behind comic bravado normally associated with the reluctant sky-diver. "Cold feet!!!!! Me? No chance. I'm in this all the way, *Jose*. It's *asta la vista* to those developers!"

"Good, just checking."

Time didn't half fly for Terry that day. No sooner had Steve and Keith come back from lunch than it was five o'clock and they were on their way home. During the afternoon he'd thought up several good reasons why the article shouldn't go to press. But each time he plucked up the courage to face Vanessa, to explain to her that the whole thing might be a terrible mistake, that they should at least moderate the tone, he took one look at her beautiful determined face and lost his nerve. By the time five thirty had come round, the time to contact the printers, he'd accepted the inevitable with the stoicism of a firing squad appointee.

"I think this calls for a celebration, Terry," said Vanessa jubilantly, after pressing the enter key on Nigel's computer, sending yet another edition of the *Comet* down the information superhighway to Ackroyd Printing Works in Stockport. The paper was now well and truly tucked up in bed.

What the hell, he thought. *At least a condemned man is entitled to his last drink.* "Sure. Where do you want to go?"

"Bank Square Café Bar would be nice. It's not too busy around this time."

"OK, I'll just give Dawn a quick ring to let her know I'll be a bit late. Are you going to phone Ian?"

"What for?" asked Vanessa, incredulously.

Her remark seemed to sum up the situation. There was to be no secret border crossing, now or in the foreseeable future. Terry dialled nervously, and after a few rings heard the theme tune to *Neighbours* blast in his ear followed by Dawn's screeching voice, "WHO IS IT? WHAT DO YOU WANT?"

"For God's sake, Dawn, turn the television down. It's me!" Terry then whispered to Vanessa, his hand placed over the mouthpiece, "She always has the tele on too loud."

"Oh, hello Terry," said Dawn, glad to be talking to an adult after being with the kids all afternoon, even if it was only her husband. "What time are you coming home?"

"That's what I'm ringing about. I'm going to be a bit late."

"Why, what are you doing? I've just this minute put the tea on!"

Vanessa stared at Terry and watched him flush crimson, from scooped throat to bald pinnacle in less than a second. He pressed the phone hard against his ear. Time seemed suspended. How was he to answer his wife? He couldn't tell her the truth and say he was going for a drink with Vanessa; on the odd occasion Dawn had met her there was an instant dislike, followed by the raging jealousy of someone who'd married young and was living to regret it. He didn't want to appear a wimp in front of Vanessa, either, by lying to Dawn about working late. Suddenly, bravely, Terry closed his eyes and trusted in fate, "I'm going for a drink….."

"Oh, I see," said Dawn. "That's very nice. You're off out gallivanting with that piss-head Keith I suppose?"

"Yeah, that's right," said Terry, looking directly at Vanessa in a way that suggested the masterful husband, "I'm going out for a drink. You don't mind, do you?"

The phone had to be clamped even tighter against the ear so Dawn couldn't be heard letting rip, "YES, I DO FUCKIN MIND. AND TERRY, DON'T EXPECT ANY TEA WHEN YOU GET HOME, CAUSE I'M GIVING IT TO NEXT DOOR'S DOG!"

He calmly replaced the receiver, his right ear throbbing like a bass drum, and thought, *But next door don't have a dog.*

Vanessa grabbed her faded denim jacket from the back of the chair. "Shall we go?"

They walked the short distance to Bank Square Café Bar, an old branch of Barclays recently converted to charge glasses instead of interest. It was the first time Terry had been in since the metamorphosis, and he was surprised to see how much of the original interior had changed. The morbidly dark wooden counter with its glass partitions had been replaced by a light, art nouveau style bar; separate folds of pine nestling between castle-like turrets. And instead of smartly dressed tellers white- aproned waiters vied for currency, serving drinks against the backdrop of a huge mirror that featured a scrolled metal sculpture hovering above optical illusions. The eggshell blue walls and lofty gold-leaf cornices that so impressed the saver of yesteryear were now almost entirely covered in trendy minimalist painting: vivid canvases of shocking pink and Amazon green. The only original feature to remain was the wooden floor – now stripped and polished – a sprinkling of honey coloured tables and chairs populating its waxed surface. They had tried to capture, the interior designers, the atmosphere of a Modern Art gallery. The prices too, of course, were ahead of their time.

Pushing open the electric-purple door, a kind of piped easy jazz hummed in the background as they took their seats and scanned the wine list. Terry hated this kind of nondescript muzac. It reminded him of when he was a child watching early episodes of the Saint in which Roger Moore use to invite different girls back to his flat for a drink. During these little escapades the *Saint* would always put on the same type of record – usually slow jazz punctuated by a lazy wooden glockenspiel – so banal it was hard to establish what, or if, any tune was being attempted. Terry used to imagine the *Saint* popping into his local record shop and purchasing the *cool* album, probably on the recommendation of *Danger Man*, then rushing back home excitedly to sit and listen to it by himself, before getting up halfway through the first track feeling utterly cheated and turning the crap off.

Vanessa chose a bottle of *Jacob's Creek*, a deep blackcurrant red all the way from Australia, and they tipped their glasses toward one another in salutation. It seemed befitting she should choose such a wine, from such a country, as henceforth their world would no doubt be turned upside-down. "Cheers!" Terry settled back into a relaxed atmosphere, the alcohol slowly infusing his brain with an audacious confidence. He glanced around the wine bar and began to feel a touch decadent, strangely at home amongst the ever growing number of sharp-suited businessmen with their bleached-blonde accessories. This was altogether more enjoyable than sitting opposite Keith in the Swan listening to him drone on about Rita's sexual blasphemies. But as he began to speak, to tell Vanessa his dreams for the future in which their burgeoning partnership might flourish, in walked Steve Barlow and his girlfriend Natasha. *Shit!* They made their way to the bar and as usual Steve gave the place the once over, just to check if any female might be secretly adoring him. What he saw swiftly replaced vanity with envy. There, in the corner, with her back to him, under a monochrome photo of Paris in the twenties, was Vanessa, her long black hair spilling over her pale blue denim jacket. And sat opposite her, cosy as you like, his shocked expression a testament to guilt, was the bald one Howarth.

"What's the matter, Terry?" asked Vanessa, noticing a sudden reddening of the gills; his face seemed brittle, almost a jagged, pitted shell.

"You'll never guess who's just walked in? Steve – Mr. I love me who do you love – Barlow. And he's coming over!"

"Well let him. It's a free country."

Terry had to admire the woman's couldn't-care-less-ness.

"Mind if we join you?" asked a flashy presence, carrying four fluted glasses and a bottle of champagne – bought on the spur of the moment in order to embarrass what he thought was Terry's cheap plonk. "Care for some *shampers?*"

Vanessa cringed and thought about her poor unemployed Ian, who's meagre bi-weekly dole check barely covered this expensive bubbly, waiting patiently at home for his daily dose of undying love and affection. She glanced at her watch. "Sorry, Steve, I've arranged to meet Ian for a drink in the Carter's, and I'm late already."

"Terry, how about you?" asked Steve, determined to split the lovers up.

"Oh, no thanks. I'd better be getting home. Dawn'll be doing her nut."

With that they rose from their chairs in unison and headed for the door, leaving behind as a silent confession a half-finished bottle of *Jacob's Creek.* It was obvious to Steve what was going on, and his jealous thoughts turned to the Moat House; a nearby hotel where on many a summer evening he had enjoyed covert sex. The reality was far different. Terry and Vanessa parted amicably outside Bank Square Café Bar, wishing each other well for tomorrow.

She crossed the busy road and made her way up Grove Street, the early evening sun glinting on *Dixons* shop window. Terry felt an immense foreboding take rise in his chest. He glanced at his watch: 6-15pm, Tea would have almost certainly been deposited in the peddle-bin by now, and the wrath of Dawn a festering consequence. His throat felt brick-dust dry and yearned for cold larger. But which boozer would best accommodate his thoughtful mood? He stared at the Swan's whitewashed façade and decided on a change. So he turned right and headed towards the George & Dragon public house, which lay at the end of Church Street. Barely two hundred meters long, the right hand side of the street was dominated by a glass fronted Safeways – scene of shame for a local TV personality – and on the left a spacious Café Rouge outlet. He crossed the dipping street and walked passed this French frippery, stopping for a second to take in its Parisian interior. Fifty meters further was his goal. The

George & Dragon stood uncomfortably close to St. Bartholomew's church, and looked out over a war memorial and quaint public park whose grounds rose to meet the traffic clogged A34. Terry marvelled at the kind of Divine inspiration that allowed churches and pubs to be built next to one another, and thought perhaps it might have something to do with spirits. Expecting to find the pub empty at this early hour, he found instead the rear bar haunted by Fat Charlie Peters. He was in the process of purchasing his third pint and fourth packet of Pork Scratchings when he noticed a familiar face. "Hello Terry, lad. Do you want a pint? I've just this second got them in."

There would be no escape. Since the death of his wife, the last thing Charlie Peters wanted to do was to go home and face an empty house crowded with her memory.

Terry obliged. "Go on then."

The session was on.

Chapter Seven

The flimsy bi-plane Terry was attempting to land headed inexorably toward the sheer cliff face of an enormous mountain. He tried with all his might to pull back on the joystick and gain height. To no avail. While the engine roared and the wind tore at his face he knew his only chance of survival was parachuting to safety. He struggled to free himself but found his uniform had been welded to the interior of the cockpit. Seconds later there was an almighty crash and he sat bolt upright on the sofa, sweating profusely.

Bulgy-eyed he stared about him, dim silhouettes of armchair, gas fire and television set bearing silent witness to his terrifying nightmare alone in the stratosphere. His mouth felt parched, feathery dry, as if he'd just swallowed Joey. Outside, beyond the drawn curtains, he could make out the paper boy's receding footsteps and realised the tremendous crash was the letterbox greedily smacking its lips after swallowing the morning paper. The morning paper! He threw off the musty continental quilt Dawn had thrown at him the night before – "If you think you're sleeping with me tonight you've got another thing comin, comin in at this hour," – and lurched into the hall where the Comet lay unfolded on the copper coloured doormat. Perspiring still more, he read the front-page headline as if for the first time.

NO TO SHOPPING DEVELOPMENT
By TERRY HOWARTH AND VANESSA GARLAND

After attending the first in a series of four on-going public inquiries into the proposed Mottram Hill Shopping Development, we at the Comet believe it is our duty to speak out and condemn the plan. There are several reasons for coming to such a swift conclusion. 1: An area of outstanding natural beau-

**ty two miles north of Wilmslow would be completely ruined if the
go-ahead were given to…..** *"Daaaaaaaaaad!"* Terry's nine year old
son Blake, his brown eyes wide as saucers, peered through the banis-
ter rail at the top of the stairs unable to comprehend his father's
bleach-white nakedness. Fiddling with his pyjama bottoms, he asked
innocently, "What you doin? Why havm't you got anyfink on?"
Terry scrunched the newspaper firmly into his groin and jinked into
the front room, saying, "That's for me to know and you to find out.
Now get back to bed, you cheeky little bugger!"

"Hey!" shouted an invisible, groggy-throated Dawn. "Don't
take it out on the kid."

"I'm not taking anything out on the kid. He shouldn't have
been spying on me."

"What are you talking about, spying on you! He was only
going to the toilet."

"How do you know, can you see through walls?"

"Oh, do us all a favour and piss off to work. You spend more
time at that stupid *Comet* than you do with us."
Fuming, Terry began to get dressed, his clothes a sloppy pyramid on
the floor. He imagined his wife lay in bed, snug beneath the duvet, the
immense bulk of her, like a giant hamster, dispensing her critique
without even bothering to lift her fat head from the pillow. *Stupid
Comet, is it*, he thought, pulling on his creased jacket while heading
for the door.

"At least I don't lie in bed all soddin day!" was his final ver-
dict, accompanied by a judiciously slammed front door. *Christ! That
woman!*

Not even the sight of a subdued Donald Campbell strolling
to his car amused Terry that baking hot morning, nor the sight of him
fast disappearing down Windermere Drive into what seemed a
watery, heat-haze oblivion. No, the only thing on his mind as he
clambered inside his sticky oven of an Uno was the *Comet's* front-
page headline. *What's Frank going to think when he reads it? What
have I done!* Forced to set off for work earlier than usual he decided
to call at Keith's flat, partly for moral support, mainly for an achingly desired breakfast. Dawn had chucked last night's tea in the dust-
bin, so he'd gone to bed on an empty stomach. Keith didn't live far,
just a mile away in a row of two storey, orange brick council flats
backing on to a disused railway line. The street had its problems. You

could tell by the countless flats boarded up and the way raggedy-arse kids snook around with emaciated dogs trailing in their wake. He parked his car and walked up a weed infested path, carefully avoiding oozing mounds of dog shit, each a shade greener than the last. *What did those vicious swines eat?*

Keith lived on the ground floor. Terry was glad of that, because as he waited for his knock to be answered he noticed a disgusting smell of stale urine drifting down the concrete stairwell leading to the upstairs flat – an old woman nobody ever saw lived up there, Keith had once told him.

Keith opened the door bleary eyed wearing a tartan dressing gown and tan coloured moccasins. "Come in, I'll put a brew on," he said, not at all surprised to see Terry this early in the morning. His flat consisted of a short poky hallway leading from front door to lounge, along which a small bathroom and kitchen faced one another – very hygienic. The smell didn't help either: a musty, sweaty, fatty, damp outpouring that permeated the nostrils with invitations to heave. A few steps further, past the bathroom on the right, was a single dimly lit bedroom. Clothes, discarded beer cans, empty bottles of cheap scotch and porn mags lay scattered about, suggesting a frantic search for the winning lottery ticket. Although Keith had lived there for over a year, he'd done nothing to the place. The walls in the lounge were still covered in the original woodchip wallpaper painted a ghastly blue the previous tenants had thought modern. The furniture was even worse. Two black plastic armchairs (he obviously wasn't expecting many guests) faced each other across a spindly Formica coffee table like two Sumo wrestlers poised for battle. An Hawaiian drinks bar complete with fake grass awning stood in one corner of the room – Keith had to fight Rita tooth and nail to keep that – while in the other a battered TV and video partnered a small glass cabinet that was home to at least fifty video tapes. The carpet had seen better days: a threadbare, peach coloured oversized rug that defied any vacuum cleaner, so greasy was its surface. The view from the window wasn't much better -- an overgrown railway line slithered past a meat packing factory, hence the filthy net curtains. It was hardly Curzon Mews and Keith knew it. Still, he did try to make the place nice and homely with the addition of several framed Constable prints, bought as a job lot off Wythenshawe Market, decorating the walls. All in all, though, it was a shit-hole. Terry looked round and shuddered as he took a seat while his friend put the kettle on.

"I suppose you've seen the *Comet?* " shouted Keith, rattling about in the kitchen.

"Yep."

"Got any regrets?"

"Nope."

"That's the idea. Fuck 'em all, that's what I say," was his advice. He entered the room like a penniless Scottish laird, with two steaming brews balancing a plateful of burnt toast. "Get this lot inside you. Sorry the bread's a bit stale, I've not been shopping for a few days."

It wasn't quite the full English breakfast Terry had expected, but at least his friend had tried. He also tried livening up the morning with a bit of light entertainment.

"Fancy a laugh?" asked Keith, flicking on the TV and video.

"How do you mean?"

"I picked up this little gem from a bloke in the pub last night. You want to see it. Absolutely awesome."

Before Terry had the chance to take a second bite from his toast, on came the carnage. Inside what appeared to be a barn of some sort, populated by several balaclaved aficionados, two snarling Pit Bulls were tearing a helpless Badger to pieces .

"Just look at that. Listen to it squeal," said Keith proudly, turning up the volume.

A spine tingling screech in conjunction with hideous horrible snapping ripping growls filled the flat, while in the background coercive threats and triumphant praises could be heard emanating from the hooded handlers.

"Jesus Christ Almighty!" spluttered Terry. "Turn it off!"

Getting the wrong end of the stick, Keith said, his eyes transfixed to the flickering screen, "Don't worry about the noise. The old girl in the flat upstairs is as deaf as a post, and no one lives either side of me. So just relax and enjoy. Now watch this, there's a cracking bit coming up. Here it is. Here it is…...HERE IT IS!"

There was a lot more carnage to come that day.

Terry gave Keith a lift to work, and they drove in silence along Manchester Road past oak-shaded detached residences. The Uno slowed to a gear-crunching halt beside a smart newsagents that stood directly opposite Blue Bell garage, a BMW dealership. Waiting for the traffic lights to change at the junction of Staneylands Road, their eyes lingered awhile on sleek new miracles of German engineering whose prices seemed to be displayed in lira. Keith, insulted at such auto decadence, switched his attention to the street corner newsagent. There, beneath a rainbow coloured awning, was proof of Terry and Vanessa's chivalrous deed; a yellow advertising board proclaimed in jet-black letters: **COMET SENSATION STUNS TOWN.**

Keith nudged his friend who was engrossed in a bright blue BMW 7 series. "Look, mate, fame at last."

The shock almost gave Terry a heart attack, and he stalled the car. When the lights turned green and he failed to move, a cacophony of impatient car horns made their debut, each one ordering him to get his Italian heap of crap moving. *PRONTO!*

"Bastards!" shouted Terry, finally pulling away with a lurch and a shudder.

Keith turned round and noticed the main offender -- a snotty little blonde driving a black Mercedes convertible sounding the horn and gesticulating wildly. He quickly wound down the window and stuck out two fingers. The girl eased over and accelerated past with nonchalant ease, shouting in her refined Cheshire accent, "*Facking pair of losers!*"

Now that wasn't nice, that wasn't nice at all. Terry put his foot hard down on the accelerator, desperate to follow the bitch. He had a split-second fantasy about running her off the road and watching with immense pleasure as the Mercedes first crashed, then exploded, incinerating the mad cow in a tidal wave of screams. Instead his car came to a juddering halt beside the kerb. He'd run out of petrol.

The sweat-drenched pair arrived at the office twenty minutes late. Pushing the deceased vehicle into a side street overlooking the cemetery followed by an exhausting mile and a half's walk had taken it out of them. Terry staggered to the rest room and grabbed himself a cold *Tango*. Keith on the other hand made straight for his darkroom where something stronger was stashed.

"You're in for it now," said a voice dripping with pleasure. Terry spun round to see Steve Barlow leaning against the rest-room door, an idiotic smile playing about his twitching face: like Bob Monkhouse when he sets the ball rolling on *The National Lottery Live.*

"What are you talking about?" he asked in mock bravado, already his bowels clamped in a vice-like grip (except this time it wasn't their objective to allow him the pleasure of a long awaited dump).

Steve's grin became even wider, showing off his perfect teeth. "Arthur Whitman's here!"

"Whitman! Never! Are you having me on?"

Terry was shocked. In over a decade working for the *Comet*, the only occasion he could guarantee the proprietor ever visiting the Wilmslow office was at Christmas time, regular as clockwork once a year to hand out the odd bottle of scotch and wish his staff a festive 'All the best'. One of the reasons he enjoyed working at the *Comet* was the fact that Whitman was a 'hands-off' type, never once interfering in what was written, even when it bordered on bad taste. Unlike Robert Acott – the owner of *The Wilmslow Gazette*, their rival paper – who incessantly poked his nose into the editorial column, Whitman was the complete opposite. Many's the time Fat Charlie Peters would moan to him about how Acott got on everyone's nerves by asking for this or that to be changed.

"I'm not having you on," boasted Steve. "He's come in especially to see you. He's in Frank's office right now giving Vanessa a bollocking, and he told me to send you straight in when you got here. You've really fucked up this time." He arrogantly swept back his blonde hair in a way that always infuriated Terry, then thought for a moment before asking, "What made you and Vanessa do it? I mean, Jesus man, are you two in love or something?"

He finished off his *Tango*, pushed past Steve and headed down the corridor. Terry realised the younger man was right behind him, so he blurted out, knowing it would hit the target and cause severe damage, "Yeah, that's right Steve, we're lovers. We just can't get enough of each other."

Approaching the frosted-glass door to Frank's office, Terry heard Arthur Whitman bawl in his thick Yorkshire accent, "What the *ell* do you think you're playing at?"

He steadied himself and walked in unannounced. There was brave Vanessa, arms folded in defiance, sitting tight-lipped at the corner of Frank's desk, while the huge figure of Arthur Whitman stalked the office in an agitated primeval rage, demanding answers. The man was a frightening sight at the best of times. A cropped-haired ex-wrestler from Barnsley who always wore an expensive dark suit, Whitman looked more like an ageing bouncer than a suave newspaper proprietor. He was at least six foot tall, with a gangling gorilla-like gait that had startled many a spectator in the late sixties packed inside the sweaty wrestling halls of South Yorkshire. Shortly after hanging up his trunks he'd married a wealthy publisher's daughter from Leeds, and thus began the first in a series of multiple *Comets* to appear over Northern England. Even though he was fast approaching retirement age he still looked a formidable opponent, with his massive barrel chest, log-like arms and menacing face. Yes, it was his face that disturbed Terry. On the few Yuletide occasions he'd swapped handshakes with the man, he couldn't help but notice his fearsome features: cruel and mean with a jutting jaw and bulging brown eyes. There was something else about the face, too. He'd seen the like of it only this morning on Keith's flickering TV screen, brutally tearing to pieces an unfortunate badger.

"I believe you wanted to see me, Mr. Whitman," said Terry, closing the door.

When at last Arthur Whitman caught sight of the bald miscreant, strolling in late for work dressed in a suit of many creases, looking as if he'd just spent the night on the sofa, which he in fact had, his anger boiled over. "You useless bastard, Howarth!" he spat, the veins in his temple throbbing like tiny purple eels. He snatched up a copy of the *Comet* lying on Frank's desk, pointed to the front page and yelled, "Ow dare you print leftist shit like that in my newspaper…."

"If I could just explain, Mr. Whitman….."

"…...... *My* newspaper, mind, that I've built up over the past twenty years. Do you realise that kind of garbage could ruin me? Do you? *Do you?* You scruffy bastard!"

Terry sat down and hung his head. Vanessa couldn't take anymore. "Look, Mr. Whitman, we were only trying to get the readership interested in what's going on in the environment."

If there was one thing certain to get on Whitman's nerves, it was a spoilt Cheshire bitch acting the working class Eco-warrior. He stared at Vanessa slant-faced, with one eye open and the other half closed, like Emperor sizing up his latest rival. "And who the *ell* gave you permission to do that?"

"No-one, we just thought….."

"You just bloody thought did you? What you're telling me

is, the two of you took it upon yourselves to go behind Frank's back and knowingly publish an article that would damage the *Comet's* interests.... I mean principles."

Vanessa was quick to notice the slip. "What interests?"

Wildman Whitman, as he was known in the halcyon days of professional wrestling, with its quaint two falls and two submissions or one knock-out to decide the winner, was quick to counter her surprise half-nelson with a deft forearm smash of his own, "Don't split hairs with me, young lady. You know full well what I mean. Jobs are at stake. Local jobs, and we're part and parcel of all that."

Terry interjected, trying his best to chivvy the contestants back to their respective corners while at the same time distancing himself from the furious bout, "We were attempting to start a debate, Mr. Whitman, so that the readership might have a chance to consider both aspects of the on-going proposal."

"That's complete rubbish!" said Vanessa angrily, realising her partner-in-crime was shifting sides. "We're dead against it. We wrote that article for one purpose and one purpose only, to inform local people that the Mottram Hill Shopping Development would be a complete disaster for the countryside."

Realising the benefits of sticking with the devil you know, Terry agreed. "You're right, Vanessa. Of course that's what we did it for."

Arthur Whitman calmly removed his jacket and took a seat behind Frank's desk, readying himself for the final round. His white shirt bore three blood red slashes; a pencil thin tie flanked by supporting braces. He stared at the enemy tag-team across a teak landscape dotted with a leather bound ink blotter, telephone, and token family photo, before deciding upon the *coup de grasse.* First he would play with them like he use to in the old days, when the crowd demanded even more punishment ought to be dished out to some half dead opponent -- loveable grannies shrieking like crones surrounding the guillotine. Terry's eyes shifted about the office, darting this way and that in blind panic. Arthur Whitman rolled up his sleeves, and said, "You two make me laugh. You think yourselves proper little reporters, don't you? Well let me tell you something. You're nothin but a pair of glorified office juniors." – Terry felt a plug being pulled, his whole life about to be washed down the drain – "Nobody out there, your readership as you laughingly put it, is the least bit interested in what *you* write. Let me give you a few home truths while we're on the subject. The *Comet's* function is to sell advertising space, pure and simple. That's why I set it up, to make money, not to provide a political platform for idiots like you. And another thing, ordinary folk don't give a damn about the *e.n.v.i.r.o.n.m.e.n.t.* They're happy as long as there's decent shops within easy reach. Take those morons at Manchester Airport, tunnelling underground. What good's it done? Nothin! A big fat zero! Tax-payer's money gone to waste. That's all those lazy swines have achieved."

"I wondered why Frank was so negative about me covering that story," said Vanessa, her temper reaching boiling point. "It's obvious now he had orders from you."

"That's right, little *girlie*. The only time I'd let *my* newspaper give any sort of publicity to those scroungers, is when one of their pathetic tunnels caves in and a couple of them get buried alive. Now that's what I call news!"

Terry had to stop himself laughing at that little gem.

There was no going back for Vanessa. She stood up, shouting, "You Fascist bastard, Whitman! I hope you rot in hell for saying that."

Terry's fate was also sealed. The giant ex-wrestler rose to his feet and shouted, even louder, "I'm sackin the fuckin pair of you. Now get out!"

You should have seen Steve Barlow's face when Frank's office door flew open and out marched the defiant ones, heads held high. Vanessa was Joan of Arc to Terry's Mark Anthony; he hadn't felt this alive since taking amphetamines years ago at college. When they were near enough to the outer office door, Terry let fly his own personal salvo, "You can stick your poxy job up your arse, you fat twat!" And like two giggling children they ran joyously down the stairs into a blanket of warm sunshine radiating Grove Street.

"God knows what I'm going to tell Dawn, or how she'll react," moaned Terry, sitting in Vanessa's charming mock-Victorian kitchen cradling a mug of freshly brewed coffee. During the short stroll to Railwayman's Cottage his spectacular speed-like high of telling Arthur Whitman where to go had completely vanished, like the bubbles in his frothy coffee into which he now contemplated disaster.

"She's bound to understand," said Vanessa, calmly watering a hanging basket that cascaded orange and yellow blooms outside the open kitchen door.

"No way! You don't know what she's like."

"I'm sure you'll sort it out. Come on, once you've explained to her what's happened, the way that bastard Whitman spoke to you, I can't see a problem."

"I can."

"Nonsense, Terry," said Vanessa, returning the plastic watering can to its shadowy place beneath the sink. "She's your wife for God's sake. If she won't stand by you, nobody will."

He couldn't help noticing a distinct lack of concern in both Vanessa's voice and body language. She had just been sacked, made unemployed, a prospect that terrified him, yet she pottered about the kitchen as if on an extended lunch break.

"Don't look so glum," she offered, first bathing with milk the waxy leaves of a rubber plant that stood beside a china-laden Welsh Dresser. "We've both done the right thing, you'll see," then refilling a wicker basket with apple-smoked logs destined for the polished Arga.

Terry was about to say that it was all right for *her* to be so optimistic, that by the looks of things she wouldn't have to worry about paying the bills for a while, when a flushing toilet was followed by the creak of stairs.

"Ian's up," said Vanessa, lovingly, slotting two pieces of wholemeal bread into the toaster.

The pine kitchen door opened to reveal a yawning, unshaven, claret dressing gown wearing Ian, his bloodshot eyes crinkled against the light. He stole a sideways glance at Terry and completely ignored him. Instead he sat down, turned to Vanessa and said, "You're home early. The noise woke me up."

Ian was of medium build with shoulder length dark hair tied in a ponytail. A goatee beard fringed his delicate mouth, and two carefully sculptured sideburns came to a halt below a pair of jutting cheekbones. Terry had to admit it, the man was good looking in a rock star kind of way; a loose-limbed slouch the type women queue up to take care of.

"Sorry, Ian. The reason I'm back this early is Terry and I have just been sacked."

Whereas Vanessa put on a working class accent, Ian cloaked his own scratchy tones within a Wilmslow drawl. "No shit. Wow!" He thought for a moment, and fearing his tranquil, aristocratic lifestyle might be affected by this wanton display of anarchy, he instantly became a pro-establishment, counter-revolutionary pillar of wisdom. "Well you'll just have to find another job. No use the two of us being out of work. Look, it's really boring dossing around all day. I can cope, I've got other interests to keep me occupied. But you, you'd die of boredom." Terry couldn't help himself, "And what is it you actually do, mate?" Ian hated this bald stranger, and hated having to justify himself so early in the day. "If you must know, I'm an unemployed musician currently looking for the right band."

Vanessa could tell by Ian's tone of voice, by the way he sneered and looked everywhere other than in Terry's direction, that he felt humiliated. She had seen this expression countless times before, at parties or following his return from the Job Centre after a particularly nasty grilling -- she knew what the outcome would be if he was put through any more embarrassing scrutiny; an afternoon spent sulking in the Carter's Arms feeling sorry for himself. Skilfully changing the subject, Vanessa said, "Ian, I've promised to give Terry a lift to the garage. He ran out of petrol this morning and had to leave his car near the cemetery off Manchester Road."

"How long will you be?"

"Not long. When I get back we can drive out to Prestbury for a nice pub lunch if you like."

Ian grudgingly accepted with a hang-dog look that infuriated Terry.

After visiting the petrol station – a revamped *Shell* garage opposite Little Lindow Park, with its sleek space-age pumps and alien looking attendant – they set off in Vanessa's metallic blue Honda Accord in a quest to resurrect Terry's heap of scrap. Glugging the miracle fuel into the unworthy Uno, in the shadow of a metal cross welded atop the spiky cemetery gate, Terry said, "Thanks for the lift. I'll no doubt see you around sometime."

Sitting in her car, watching the sloshing, spilling antics of this pathetic matchstick man, Vanessa couldn't help feeling sorry for him. She wound down the window and said, pluckily, "I'll see you Saturday night. At Nigel's barbecue. You're still going aren't you?"

Shocked, he spilt the last few dregs of precious petrol onto the crotch of his trousers.   "You can't be serious!"

"Why not? An invite's an invite."

"But we've just been sacked for gross misconduct."

"Not by Nigel we haven't. Anyway, he won't even know what's happened. Don't forget, he lives in Ashley, and they don't get the *Comet* delivered out there."

"Course he'll know. Steve's bound to have phoned him the minute we left."

"What if he has! We've done nothing wrong! As far as I'm concerned we should go to the damned barbecue, eat, drink and be merry and sod the lot of them. Come on, it'll be a good laugh, if only to see Keith drink Nigel's wine cellar dry."

Terry was easily won over. "You're right. What's the point in moping around. Dawn's been looking forward to it all week, so at least a free night out might help the situation, domestically speaking."

"Good," said Vanessa, firing up her car engine. "Don't let the bastards get you down." With that she drove away at great speed, hurrying to be with her beloved Ian, totally unconcerned as to whether or not Terry's car might start.

Unaware of the earth's stately progress through time and space, Dawn lay fast asleep in her overgrown back garden dreaming of yet another bingo win. She'd had a strenuous morning. After dragging the kids off to school then doing a bit of impromptu shopping on the way home, she was completely knackered. Rather than tackle the mountain of ironing that stood before her in the washing basket, she decided instead to accept the sun's dazzling invitation.

Her blubbery body oozed its milky flesh from beneath the folds of a one-piece bathing costume as she lolled about on the towel, grunting and snoring. These subconscious ejaculations fused into a hideous hog-like cackle when a sudden shadow passed between her and the sun. Opening one eye, expecting to find a lone cloud masking the great fiery disk, she was shocked to see Terry standing over her.

"Bleedin hell!" she rasped, convinced she had slept away the entire afternoon, and in doing so had left Cheryl and Blake at the mercy of any old paedophile that happened to be cruising for strays outside Handforth Primary School's main gate. "What, what time is it....? Terry, the kids!"

"Calm down, it's only quarter to twelve."

Dawn sat up, her veiny breasts blancmanging ripples of aftershock. "Quarter to twelve! Why are you home so early?"

His bald head blocked the sun, so that from Dawn's perspective it looked like the culmination of a solar eclipse. Had God placed the earth exactly 93 million miles away for just such a grand illusion? Terry swallowed hard. Nervous, he shifted his position slightly, causing the 'Diamond Ring' effect. "Listen, luv, we've got to talk."

And talk they did, for at least half an hour. He sat her down and told her how his crusade to protect the environment had led to his being sacked. The reasons for such a crusade, he explained, were for his children's and, God willing, his grandchildren's sake. In his own small way he was trying to fight the evil developers who were about to rob them of their birthright. Dawn read the article for herself, and yes there were references to their children. Not by name, of course, but in such glowing terms as 'future generations' and 'our precious spouses'. She was so proud of him. At long last he had proved himself a man. A terrible feeling of guilt for having banished him to the sofa the previous night rose within her – how could she have acted in such a callous way when her husband was wrestling with his conscience? Tears began to fill her piggy lids. Terry could scarcely believe Dawn's reaction; on his way home he was convinced she'd hit the roof. But now here she was, condoning his explanations with a nod of the head here and a dab of the eye with a paper handkerchief there. Pride and compassion were not the only emotions felt. She was filled with rage when he recounted the vile insults thrown at him by Arthur Whitman, and how he'd parried them with stoicism and dignity. "The arrogant bastard!" she said. Give Dawn credit, she could dish out the most humiliating home truths when necessary, but let anyone else try it, well, that was another matter. Rage turned to suspicion when she saw Vanessa's name alongside his beneath the front-page headline. This was Terry's *tour de force*. He told his wife that Vanessa had been so moved by the article, so enamoured by its powerful prose, she had literally begged for her name to be allied with his. She was so desperate, he said, to be associated with such a great piece of journalism that she instantly nailed her colours to the mast, thus going down with the sinking ship. When Terry explained that this meant Vanessa had been dismissed also, her suspicion turned to exaltation. Her man, *her man* had charmed that know-it-all-little-bitch into getting herself sacked. Powerful forces were unleashed. Terry's brave words and heroic deeds played upon her libido like the symphonic notes of a concert pianist. This strange music had aphrodisiac

87

qualities. For the second time in a week Dawn led her bemused husband upstairs for a, "Do whatever you want to me," sexual extravaganza.

Chapter Eight

The following day, after registering at the Job Centre in Wilmslow as an unemployment statistic, Terry decided to attack the back garden. A bout of good honest manual labour was needed to take his mind off things. He had to admit, there was a lot to be done if his scraggy wilderness was ever to rival Donald Campbell's neat, manicured vista. Dressed for action in faded yellow shorts, red T-shirt and brown leather sandals, he approached with caution his dilapidated old shed at the bottom of the garden. He hadn't been in it since last summer, and there was a strong case for it collapsing as soon as he opened the door. Before gaining access, he peered through its single, musty, mildewed window to survey the scene. Unlike Howard Carter who saw 'Wonderful things,' Terry was horrified at his own personal discovery. By the look of it tomb robbers had been in. A heap of garden tools lay strewn across the floor, covering what appeared to be the body of his ancient lawn–mower. Worse still, a rouge tree branch had pierced the back of the shed, stretching toward him like a ghostly arm. He fiddled for a second with the rusty *chubb* lock and let himself in. Sunlight flooded the dank wooden structure and before his eyes huge spiders ran for cover. A nauseating smell of rotting wood mixed with turpentine hovered in the air as he penetrated the eerie silence. After dismantling the pyramid of garden tools he finally exhumed the mummified body of his lawn mower (throughout the winter it had been conscientiously wrapped in a shroud of cobwebs). Terry shuddered; he hated creepy-crawlies.

He began mowing the lawn -- a back-breaking task made worse because of the intense heat and the discarded ring-pulls continually jamming the mower blades. The job was made even harder as his mower was an outdated push-me-pull-you affair. How he wished he'd invested in a state-of-the-art, friendly *fly-mow* that operates at the mere touch of a button and accepts commands from the weakest of wrists. This savage beast had a mind of its own. Terry was sure it was trying to get its own back for all those long winter months left alone under a tangle of rusting tools, without so much as a drop of oil.

Up and down the garden he trawled, convinced the exercise was doing him good. After half an hour battling with Nature, his whole body drenched in sweat, Dawn called from the kitchen, "Terry. Do you want a nice cold glass of lemonade?"

"I'll say."

She had been watching his struggles with admiration while doing the washing up. It was great to have her man at home, toiling under a blistering sun. Unnoticed by the passengers and crew of a lone jet streaking comet-like across the heavenly blue, Dawn, still in her pink pleated dressing gown, presented Terry with a chinking ice-cold tumbler.

"Magic! Just the job."

They both sat down on two white plastic garden chairs set beside the shady privet hedge. Terry rolled the glass against his burning forehead and asked, "You know tomorrow night…. Nigel Harrison's barbecue. Well, do you think it's a good idea if we go? I was just thinking, with all the trouble that's been caused, the last thing I want is for you to feel embarrassed."

Dawn was taken aback by such sweet concerns. She leant forward and placed her hand on his bony knee that felt like a damp prickly pear. "Course we'll go. You've got nothing to be ashamed of. As far as I can see they're the ones who should be embarrassed, not us. What you've done, Terry, it's made me so proud. And listen, I know you're worried about the money situation, the mortgage and all that. Well don't, we'll get through, even if I have to get a job myself."

Was it the heat, the physical exertion, the nauseous aftershock of the shed? No, it was his wife's love and understanding that made him feel faint, there, beside the overgrown privet hedge. He gripped her hand and was about to say how much he loved her when the phone rang. *Vanessa?* he thought

"I'll get," offered Terry, jumping to his feet.

He slithered into the house and picked up the receiver. "Hello?"

"Terry, it's me, Keith."

Disappointed in the fact that it wasn't Vanessa, and annoyed that his friend hadn't been in touch sooner, he said coolly, "Hi, mate. I thought you might have phoned last night."

"Sorry about that. I meant to, but I went out straight from work and got pissed with Fat Charlie. You know what it's like; one becomes two, two becomes three, followed by complete oblivion."

"Very nice."

I'm going out with him tonight if you want to come?"

"No thanks. I think it's best in the present climate if I stay in. Dawn's not even going to bingo! First time in about five years."

"Please yourself. Anyway, I did try to phone you yesterday lunchtime, after it all went off, but the line was constantly engaged." Terry remembered Dawn taking the phone off the hook prior to sex, and he stuttered, "Oh yeah, one of the kids must have been messing about."

Keith's voice took on that half-serious, half joking tone he always used to impart bad news. It was rapier-like in its delivery, and had an underlying hint of, '*you stupid bastard*'. He cut to the quick. "Frank's back. He came in this morning. He went absolutely ape-shit. He said he's been betrayed. "

"What!"

"Betrayed. You and Vanessa had betrayed him. Stabbed him in the back. Yeah. He said that in all the years he'd worked as a journalist, he'd never known anything like it. Not even in Fleet Street. Disloyal he called you."

This got Terry's back up. "Did he now. Well I don't give a shit." He did feel, though, a hint of satisfaction, having done something never before known in Fleet Street.

Keith parried his defensive thrust. "I would if I were you, mate. He said you'll never work for another newspaper again. That as far as he was concerned, you're finished as a journalist. D'you know what else he said? He said, 'Just let Terry or Vanessa ask for a reference. I'll give them a reference.' "

Bravado kicked in. "So what. I was thinking of quitting in the near future anyway."

Keith thought, *Course you were*. Realising he'd inflicted enough pain for the present, he switched the angle of attack, "Arthur Whitman's been in all morning giving Frank a load of grief. Very messy. Steve told me he heard Whitman bollocking him for not keeping more of a tight rein on you and Vanessa."

"And?"

91

"Hang on, this is the funny bit. Steve said it all went quiet for a good minute – Frank was obviously trying to calm him down, when Whitman suddenly exploded, 'What about that fuckin *ponce* Harrison! Where was he while this was going on?' He actually called him a ponce!"

"What did Frank say?"

"According to Steve, he didn't even attempt to answer the question. He closed ranks with Nigel and said that you and Vanessa must have set the whole thing up, behind everyone's back. He came out with all the excuses under the sun, saying that on press day things always run smoothly whether they're there to supervise or not. Anyway Whitman must have believed him, because he calmed down and told him to hire two new journalists, then he made a big deal about making sure nothing like this ever happens again."

"When are they…......?"

"Give me a chance, I've not finished yet. Steve said they both walked out of the office and Whitman ordered Frank to personally re-write the article and put in a disclaimer for what had already been written, apologising to the readers. He told him in no uncertain terms that he wanted the Mottram Hill Shopping Development cast in a more favourable light."

"That wont make any difference, let me tell you. The damage has already been…."

"For Christ's sake, Terry, let me finish!"

"Sorry. Carry on."

"Finally, Whitman says to Frank, 'See you at Harrison's barbecue on Saturday night.' "

Terry's heart sank. "Whitman's going?"

"By the sound of it, yeah. Nigel must have invited him along with the rest of us last week. Funny he never mentioned it, eh."

"Shit!"

"Why are you so bothered? After all that's gone on, don't tell me you're still thinking of going?"

Terry felt the rise of indignation. "Yeah, why not?"

Keith's laughter echoed down the phone line. Using his talent for sarcasm, he explained, as if to a small child, "Why not! Frank and Arthur Whitman are going to be there! And I don't think Uncle Nigel will be too pleased to see you, do you? "

"An invite's an invite. Correct?"

Keith held back trying to dissuade Terry any further. He realised the forthcoming event had all the makings of a classic set-to. His love of dog fighting had taught him that the best fights, the most ferocious of encounters, are the ones where each contestant has first been goaded into action with a few sharp kicks.

"You're right," said Keith. "The way those bastards have treated you, and the *things* they've been saying behind your back, you deserve a good night out."

Chapter Nine

Nigel's Barbecue

With two days to go before the opening salvos of Wimbledon fortnight, Saturday, 22 June arrived in this part of Cheshire as a misty morning promising yet another day of unbroken sunshine. The early sky seemed netted with a fine mesh of cloud the climbing sun would soon disperse. Perfect *barby* weather.

Time to press the pause button and take a glimpse at our characters frozen in their own particular mid-morning routines. **10am**. Frank has just placed the ball on the elevated first tee at Wilmslow Golf Club and is about to smash it for all it's worth down the fairway; par four, dog leg left. His wife Jean has settled into her black leather swivel chair at Barard Hair Studio on Grove Street and is in the process of demanding from David, her personal stylist, "Something with a little more *panache*, dear". Keith lies dehydrated in a heap on the sofa surrounded by last night's beer cans and Chinese take-away cartons while the TV fuzzes through the video channel. Steve Barlow is standing in the courtyard of Curzon Mews washing his Probe as the lovely Natasha showers herself in his pearl-white bathroom. Terry sits enthroned on the toilet teasing his bowels toward a magnificent release while Dawn is busy shopping at Kwick Save in Wythenshawe Precinct, hunting for bargains now that money's tight. Vanessa and Ian? Well, here I think it's best if we press the slow-motion button and enjoy a slice of their intense love making – Upon the mussed bed sheet, in the curtained half light, Vanessa, astride Ian, her back arching rhythmically she attains climax, his hands reaching forever upward caress her spectacular breasts, her dark hair spilling over her face she silently relaxes, her whole body trembling she bends forward to kiss the giver of this sensation, mouths entwine, arguments forgiven. **STOP.**

PLAY.

Nigel Harrison carried forth from his neat, fussy kitchen a varnished wicker tray upon which two bone china teacups clinked against a Royal Albert bone china teapot. From the back door of his house he strolled majestically into the morning sunlight wearing a silk dressing gown the colour of Blue John. (Whitman was right, he was a fuckin ponce). Careful lest the jittery teacups give away his nervousness, he shuffled across the redbrick patio and stepped lightly down three stone steps that introduced his wide, box-hedged garden. The clipped dewy lawn felt cool under his podgy bare feet. Yes, in an attempt to appear the savage bohemian Nigel had abandoned his slippers to the wardrobe. Like an attendant at a Pharaoh's funeral he made his stately way down the garden towards the shade of a lone apple tree. Beneath its fruit laden boughs stood a rustic set of garden furniture – in other words, one crooked table and four wobbly chairs cobbled together by the inmates of a nearby mental hospital and made to look antiquated by haphazardous measuring and sawing and numerous coats of creosote; each piece designed from a configuration of flaking pine logs nailed in place by childish hands no doubt under the instructions of an exasperated overseer. The effect was Old World charm, though Nigel had purchased the set only two months ago for a mere thirty pounds. Sitting ramrod straight on one of these

95

harsh chairs, the sunlight dappling his flowery shirt and baggy canvas trousers, was the object of Nigel's devotion, the *sensational* Mr. Roger Harvey.

Nigel and Roger had been in each other's company since their lunch date at the Bells of Peover, two days ago. Nigel's nerves were all of a flutter that morning as he parked his green Saab in the 14th century pub's car park, walked across the cobbled entrance and settled himself inside the snug bar parlour. He was purposely fifteen minutes early – he needed time for a large G&T to blunt his edginess. He loved this pub, with it's ancient wisteria guarding the entrance door, it's low ceilings and old-fashioned oak panelled bar and fabulous restaurant, set opposite a Norman church surrounded by rolling Cheshire countryside; frequented not by those *nouveau* Wilmslow types but by people similar to himself. Old money. Nigel was descended from a wealthy family of Macclesfield silk merchants and had been brought up in ostentatious Prestbury. His place in the sun assured, he treated journalism as a hobby, a way of passing the time.

He looked up at the clock above the bar: 12.30pm – it was time for Roger Harvey. To the accompaniment of peeling church bells in walked broad shouldered Roger, summeryfied in white canvas trousers, cream coloured shirt and sporting a red ribboned Panama. Whether it was a trick of the light or Nigel's dodgy eyesight, Roger seemed to carry about him a saintly aura, a nimbus, as if the sun haloed his handsome presence. It was enough to set Nigel's heart a-flutter. After a light lunch of lobster *en croûte* dispatched by a golden Chardonnay, they took themselves off to Tatton Park. Here, amongst aristocratic acres where red deer roamed at will, they walked and talked. "I'm offering you the lead in *Pirates*. You're the only one capable of pulling it off," said Nigel, as they approached Tatton Hall, its Georgian grandeur of phallic pillars rising into the air.

"Do you really think so?" asked Roger. "I can't believe you've got that much faith in me."

"Nonsense. You're perfect for the part. Absolutely perfect."

"I mean, *Frederick's* only supposed to be eighteen. What will the audience think? An old duffer like me playing the part of a young rascal!"

"They'll simply lap it up, don't worry. The thing is, you've got a fabulous voice. And more important, if you don't mind me saying so, you look stunning in tights."

The word *tights* tingled in Nigel's mouth, filling him with a kind of charged electricity. Evelyn Waugh put it more succinctly – 'A bat squeak of sexuality' – in one of his many homo-erotic novels. (He was another ponce).

The wine and oozy flattery did the trick. Later that Thursday afternoon, after making Hellenic love, Nigel asked Roger if he cared to stay the weekend. Roger agreed. Nigel was ecstatic. So ecstatic, that even Frank's phone call the next day informing him of the crisis and the sackings had little effect upon his mood. So ecstatic, that even when Vanessa rang late Friday night to ask, "In the circumstances, is it still OK if Terry and I come to your barbecue?" Nigel replied that, "Of course it is," and in slight chastisement, "I think both you and Terry have behaved like naughty children, but, *c'est la vie*."

Setting down the wicker tray beneath the apple tree, Nigel poured Roger a cup of Earl Grey. "Just think," he intoned, surveying his back garden. "In less than twelve hours my quaint little plot will be full of party goers."

They sat next to one another in perfect silence; the buggerer and the buggeree, each accepting the laurels with quiet dignity.

The clock had ticked round to 5.30pm. Terry was sitting on the loo in splendid isolation reading the latest Jeffrey Archer; the one where Murdoch and Maxwell are given different names. He sat pondering the immense volume and thought, *What a writer! Where does he get his ideas from?* He had shut himself away in the bathroom to escape Dawn, who as the afternoon progressed began to get more and more excited at the prospect of her night out with the Cheshire elite. During the past hour she'd tried on at least eight dresses, seeking Terry's advice with each new formulation. Finally she decided to wear what appeared to be a polkadot marquee that reminded Terry of Mama Cass. *All the leaves are brown, and the sky is grey*, he whistled to himself. Sitting there on his white enamel throne he felt content. The kids had been packed off to Dawn's mum's for the weekend and the only sound at that moment was Donald Campbell mowing his lawn. About to start chapter twenty-nine, Dawn called out, "Terry, phone."

He pulled up his trousers and jinked into the bedroom. His wife was sitting at the dressing table wearing nothing but a gigantic brassier. Her face was plastered in a mud pack, and her hair sprouted a set of plastic yellow curlers. As she turned to acknowledge his presence, Terry thought she resembled an alien sunflower programmed to attack. Dawn casually flung the cordless phone onto the bed. Wide-eyed within her concrete shell, she stared accusingly at him and mumbled, "It's Vanessa."

"Hi, Vanessa. What can I do you for," sparkled Terry. This friendly play on words bugged the hell out of Dawn.

"Do you and Dawn fancy meeting up for a drink before we go to Nigel's?"

"Yeah, why not. Great idea. Where?"

"How about Bank Square Café Bar?"

Terry thought for a second; thought about all the beautiful people he'd encountered there, then imagined Dawn traipsing through the place, fag-in-hand.

"I'd rather not, if you don't mind. Tell you what, why don't we meet up in the Carter's Arms? It's right across the road from you, and it's miles cheaper."

"OK," agreed Vanessa. "Ian prefers the Carter's anyway. See you in there around seven. Bye."

"Bye….Vanessa….Bye."

During their brief telephone conversation, Dawn, her face caked in mud like an African shaman, peered at Terry in the reflection of the mirror, looking for sighs. What she saw deeply troubled her. His expression was that of a schoolboy arranging his very first date with the class temptress. He was all round-shouldered and goofy-featured, hanging on to her every word.

"We're meeting her for a drink, are we?" asked Dawn, noticing her husband's pallor tint crimson.

"Yeah….er…. I thought we might."

"You didn't think anything of the sort. It was her idea."

"I know, I know. She's just being friendly."

"Terry, how many times have I heard you say in the past that you can't *stand* the bitch?"

There was real venom in her voice now, and her face-mask began to crack a mini earthquake. He decided it was time to play his ace in the hand. "Look, Dawn, if it bothers you that much we won't go. I've already told you, I'm not bothered about the *barby*. It's entirely up to you. I mean, if you intend to start the evening off in a bad mood, what's the point."

Dawn envisaged all that delicious food going to waste, and realised her jealous fit was a mistake. "Course we'll go. I'm sorry, luv. I've had a lot on my plate today."

The phone rang a second time.

"Who the bleedin hell's this now!" she muttered, her colossal breasts swinging like great cathedral bells as she bent to grab the receiver off the bed. "Hello! Speak!"

"*Hiya*, Dawn. It's me. You sound funny. Is Terry there?"

She raised her eyes to the heavens, this time spitting, "It's Keith!" before marching into the bathroom.

Terry picked up the receiver. "Hi. What's happening?"

"Why do you think I'm ringing you? To check you've not changed your mind."

"About what?"

Keith laughed, "About what? Going to Nigel's Do."

"Course I haven't!"

"You've got some nerve."

Terry kept secret the fact that Vanessa had phoned the previous night with the all clear from Nigel. "Spot on. There's no way I'm going to be frightened off."

"Good," said Keith, sinisterly. "Anyway, how are we getting there?"

"I don't know. Probably by taxi. Me and Dawn have arranged to meet Vanessa and Ian in the Carter's at seven. You're welcome to join us if you want."

"Vanessa! She's not going as well!"

Terry thought, *This twat's worse than Dawn.* "Calm down for Christ's sake!" He then lied, "She said it might be cheaper if we all go together, you know, taxiwise."

"That's not a bad idea, I suppose. Would it be OK if I come to your place about half six? I thought we might have a few before we go, just to start the evening off on the right foot, you know, drinkwise."

"Yeah, alright. But there's no need to rush things in that department. I've had it on good authority that Nigel keeps a well-stocked cellar. So don't fret, there'll be truck loads of booze."

"Brilliant!" said Keith. "I can't wait."

Frank poured himself a vodka and tonic and began to peruse his vast

CD collection. He was relaxing in what was laughingly called his study; a spacious downstairs room overlooking the garden at the rear of his detached house. It contained the usual objects found in genuine studies -- a leather inlaid desk with art deco night light, a presidential sized arm chair, wall to wall shelves crammed with books, and a small silver drinks tray and Hi-Fi cabinet whose polished glass doors reflected a Manhattan skyline of stacked CDs. Frank chose Glen Miller's Greatest Hits; track four, Moonlight Serenade. He loved the big brassy sassy sound of the forties, especially after making love. He and Jean had composed their own sweet music only half an hour ago. Convinced her new hair style would be ruined if she lay flat on the pillow, Jean insisted on being taken from behind, on all fours. Frank didn't mind, 'doggy' was his positional favourite. He also enjoyed the fragrance her freshly lacquered hair gave up, a sharp scented challenge, hastening climax.

It was now 7pm. Jean lay soaking in the bath. Frank had already showered and changed. He wore a candy striped shirt (*Next*) and sky blue trousers (*Burton's*) and he paced his study to the strains of Chattanooga Choo Choo. Thoughts of tonight's barbecue simmered in his mind. What if Terry and Vanessa showed up? What would he say to them? What if Terry got drunk and started causing trouble? What if Vanessa told Jean about their stolen Christmas kiss in Keith's darkroom? How on earth did he miss that easy three footer on the eighteenth green this morning? Like Glen Miller, he was flying into thick fog.

He needed some air. Grabbing his vodka and tonic, he opened the French windows and stepped out into the garden. The evening sun tinted with fire the serrated edges of his tall conical ferns, threw their lengthening shadows back towards him across the lawn. He adored this house; its detachedness, its moneyed respectability, its within-easy-reachness, its let's-nip-to-the-*Trevi*-for-a-nice-bit-of-pasta; the fact that Jean had paid for it lock, stock, and biscuit barrel. Jean, Jean, sweet mercantile Jean, she who had transplanted him to this oasis, like the ferns. Though the house was only two hundred meters from Wilmslow town centre, one got the impression, travelling along Broad Walk, with its tree-lined curves and set-back residencies, of driving through a red brick mini New England.

"Almost ready, darling," said Jean, framed by the French windows holding a crystal G&T. She looked ravishing in a white ankle length cotton dress specked with tiny red flowers (*Laura Ashley*). Jean wasn't the tallest of women but she was slender; a fine boned fairy queen whose pale complexion and delicate features resembled a porcelain figurine. At Barard's her blonde hair had been cut shorter than usual. The style, though boyish in appearance – David had stressed the need for nineties minimalism – gave her the look of a saintly Mia Farrow. Frank and Mia! Around her neck she wore a string of pearls. Frank thought this gesture cute considering what was playing on the CD. You had to hand it to Jean, she had real class. *Panache*.

She walked gracefully down the garden. Frank was struck by his wife's demur, feminine beauty. Why? Why did he continue to have affairs with other women when standing before him was his ultimate everything? A gift from God.

"Take your time," said Frank, lazily. "There's no rush." He glanced at his masculine *Tag Heuer* sports watch, the type older men go in for when married to a younger woman. "It's only seven twenty. The taxi's not due till eight. We've plenty of time for at least a couple more drinks."

They strolled back inside the house arm in arm while "In The Mood" and a glint of orange sunlight bathed Frank's study.

The taxi containing Terry, Dawn and Keith pulled up outside the Carter's Arms. Having already consumed more than half a bottle of scotch, the tipsy trio clambered unceremoniously from the belly of the black cab and tottered into the pub, giggling. Terry wore his silvery grey suit. Dawn had on the tented polkadot number. Her short curly hair was dyed ink-black and plastered to her head like some nineteen twenties film starlet – both cheeks rouged a la Betty Boo. Keith on the other hand was the surprise package. He'd 'splashed out' on some new clothes. Replacing his worn out purple shell-suit was a brown corduroy jacket, green denim shirt, mauve coloured tie and loose fitting tan trousers. A pair of classic brown brogues added the finishing touch. Spurred on by his shopping spree he'd even gone as far as to have his hair cut. Now, instead of a tangled mess lying about his shoulders, his steel-grey hair fell about the collar in combed fluffy strands. Hey presto, a ravaged Grisly Adams turned groomed Kris Kristofferson. You should have seen Terry's expression when he saw his friend walk up the path. Sitting in the house before the taxi arrived, Keith kept giving himself the once over. He leant forward on the sofa, a karate chop palm to the side of his mouth, rolled his eyes as if revealing state secrets, winked at Dawn and said, "I decided to splash out."

Inside the pub Vanessa was nowhere to be seen. While Keith and Dawn stood at the bar ordering the drinks, a distraught Terry gave all four corners a quick shuffty, pretending to look for an empty table. When Dawn saw him investigating every nook and cranny, she bawled out, "I wish you wouldn't haunt the place like that. You're giving everyone the creeps. There's plenty of seats over here! Look!" She threw Keith a flabbergasted expression, "Honestly, the man's a bleedin idiot sometimes."

They sat at a table near the door. Terry could see Railwayman's Cottage directly opposite. If only he had the power of X-ray vision, he would have seen a lot more. Vanessa was upstairs screaming at Ian, "What's brought this on? Why have you suddenly changed your mind? I thought you *wanted* to go! For Christ's sake, Ian, don't do this to me!"

He lay on the bed puffing at a cigarette. Eyes fixed to the ceiling, he eventually sulked, "I was going, before you told me *those* wankers were coming along. Did you see the fucking state of them getting out of that taxi! Did you see what that fat bitch had on! She looked like a fucking circus freak! There's no way I'm mixing with types like that, Vanessa, no way. Scum they are!"

"Scum? That's rich coming from you!"

Ian blinked nervously, "And what's that supposed to mean?"

In her temper she had transgressed an unwritten law. Not daring to cross the Rubicon concerning his rough upbringing, his long-term unemployment, his several brushes with the law, his total financial dependence upon her, Vanessa said calmly, "Nothing. But you're not stopping me from going," and walked out.

Terry's heart skipped a beat when he saw the coal-black, Georgian style front door to Railwayman's Cottage burst open and produce Vanessa. *Alone.* Good, he thought, *I hope that prick's decided to do us all a favour and stay at home.*

Vanessa looked flustered as she walked in, dewy eyed. With a woman's instinct for trouble, Dawn folded her arms atop her gargantuan breasts and asked, "Where's your boyfriend, then? Is he not joining us?"

"Ian's not very well. Food poisoning. We waited until the last minute, but it was no good. He keep's trekking off to the loo. Poor thing. Still, he did ask me to send you his regards, and he hopes we all have a pleasant evening."

"That's very nice of him," said Dawn.

Keeping her emotions in check, Vanessa raised her eyes from the floor and offered, "Can I get anyone a drink?"

Drink. The magic word.

"The round's three pints of Tennant's Extra, and whatever you're having," answered Keith, waggling his glass like a blind beggar.

"Hang on a *mo*," said Dawn. "I fancy a change. I think I'll have a nice Bloody Mary, if you don't….."

"Keith!" interrupted Vanessa. "Bloody hell! I hardly recognised you. Amazing! You look so smart. Those clothes really suit you!"

Terry's delight at Ian's misfortune was tempered by a burning jealousy for Keith's attention seeking garb. He was quick to inject, "I think we all look quite smart this evening, don't you?"

"For our big night out," said Keith, absolutely elated at his first real compliment in over two years.

"Yeah! I'm ready for a '*gooood*' time," said Vanessa, ignoring Terry's observation, forcing herself to get 'in the swing.' "So that's two pints of Tennant's Extra and one Bloody Mary. Do you want me to make that a double, Dawn?"

"A double Dawn!" laughed Keith. "That's a good one. Hey, I'm not trying to be funny, but as far as I'm concerned Dawn's more like a quadruple if you ask me."

"Watch it!" snarled Terry. "We'll have less of that."

"Leave him alone, you miserable sod! He's only having a bit of fun," said Dawn. She took Keith's remark as a compliment. The word 'quadruple' sounded *dead horny*; like making love afloat a huge wobbly waterbed. She emerged from her aquatic sex fantasy to answer, "Yes please, Vanessa. I will have a double if you don't mind."

Terry noticed, as Vanessa stood at the bar, that she hadn't bothered to dress for the occasion. Nevertheless, she looked positively hypnotic in a loose fitting red check shirt and black pinstriped trousers. Her long dark hair was gathered up in a bob, held captive, save for two lone ringlets like curly sentinels guarding their wispy temple.

103

The Carter's had begun to get busy, and Vanessa exchanged 'hellos' with certain trendy young men, even kissing one on his stubbled cheek. Terry wished he was young, certain and trendy. But he wasn't. Far from it! In the slow motion of her kiss Terry saw her eyes sparkle, and realised his own futile existence meant nothing. A cheap ludicrous joke. He might just as well have lived on the dark side of Pluto for all Vanessa cared. She would never find him attractive. Not in a million years. He was bald, he was painfully thin, he was.... he was repulsive! *Jesus*, he thought, *get a grip on yourself, man.*

"Do you want me to give you a hand, Vanessa, at the bar?" called Terry, above the growing din.

She returned to the table moments later carrying a tray crammed with drinks. "No problem. It's sorted. Now, cheers everyone. Here's to us." They raised their glasses in salutation. "Cheers!"

Gulping down her blood red Bloody Mary, Dawn thought, *Nothing seems to be a problem for you, missy.*

Pointing at Dawns empty glass, Keith asked, "Here's an interesting one. Whose favourite breakfast tipple was that?"

"Easy," answered Terry, quick off the mark. "Elvis Presley's"

Keith struck, sounding like a clock chime. "Wrong!" It was Marilyn Monroe's. Fancy not knowing that!"

"It wasn't!.....It was Presley's! I read it in a book somewhere."

"I think you'll find Keith's right," said Vanessa.

Terry, humiliated, had to concede, "Oh, is he? Well it just goes to show. Anyway, good riddance to the pair of them. Drug addicts."

Dawn snapped, "Don't say that about the King!"

"Well he was. Pumped full of all sorts. They both were."

Vanessa changed the subject. "Quite a number of my friends have said they agree with the article in the *Comet*. They said Terry and I should be proud of it. That there aren't too many people these days with the guts to stand up for what they believe in."

"Believe in, yeah," droned Keith, not really listening but staring at a group of fabulous teenage girls, trying to figure out which one was the lesbian in waiting.

Dawn lit a cigarette and watched the spiralling blue smoke disappear through the extractor fan. Clearing her catarrh-clacking throat, she said, "I must admit, Terry's article sent shivers down my spine."

Vanessa looked at Terry slightly puzzled. He read her mind and immediately offered concessions. "*Our* article, Dawn. Don't forget it was a *joint* effort. We were *both* involved, remember? The *two* of us." Dawn shifted her weight in the chair, desperate to clarify the situation. Luckily for Terry Keith cut in, "Shouldn't one of us be sorting out a cab? It's five to eight."

"That late already!" said Vanessa. "OK, leave it to me." She stood up and walked towards the bar. "I'll ring Wilmslow Taxis. They're usually quick. I use them all the time."

Dawn kicked Terry's ankle and whispered, "I thought you said *you* wrote the thing, on your own. What's all this *we* business?"

"Don't start, lady! The girl's lost her fuckin job over this. The least I can do is let her share in the credit."

Keith didn't like the way this conversation was going. "Come on, you two. We're supposed to be out enjoying ourselves. Don't spoil it!"

"We're in luck," shouted Vanessa from the bar. "There's one on the way right now. Drink up, he should be here in two minutes."

As they waited outside the pub, a furious din emanated across Chapel Lane. It was the horrible whine of an electric guitar being put through its paces, and the source was most definitely Railwayman's Cottage. Bastard! Thought Vanessa. *Attention seeking bastard!*

"Ian doesn't sound too healthy," joked Keith. "Dear me, what's he been eating?"

Dawn laughed, "Keith's on form tonight."

The taxi drove up. Dawn piled in the front; Terry, Vanessa and Keith slid in the back.

"Where to?" asked the driver.

"As far away from here as possible," said Vanessa.

"Come again, luv?"

She composed herself. "The address is, Squirrel's Leap, Mill Lane, Ashley."

The driver, a cryptic crossword fanatic, checked his mirrors and said, "*Poplar* destination is Squirrel's Leap – no pun intended."..........silence........."At least four of our cabs have been sent there this evening."

"Squirrel's what?" asked Keith incredibly, as the taxi gained speed along Chapel Lane. "What kind of pretentious shit is that?"

Vanessa explained, "It used to be called Mill Cottage, but Nigel had the name changed when he first bought the place some years back."

Terry dispatched his sarcastic threepenny-worth, "Squirrel's Leap! The man's a complete tosser. He's worse than Steve Barlow with his Curzon fuckin Mews." (Dawn wished she lived in a house grand enough to be called something. So did Terry). "Speaking of Barlow, is he going to grace us with his presence tonight?"

"Yeah," said Vanessa. "I bumped into Natasha yesterday afternoon outside Hooper's, and she told me they were both planning to go."

Keith got all excited. He whispered to Terry, "Just wait until you meet that Natasha. Fuckin gorgeous she is. Absolutely mind blowing!"

Terry couldn't let on that he'd already met her three days ago in Bank Square Café Bar. Instead he gave his friend a lurid 'I can't wait' look.

"Behave yourselves you two," nagged Dawn from the front seat, noticing in the rear view mirror her husband's greedy expression. She then turned to Vanessa, "Do we have to fetch our own booze to this Do? You know, 'bring a bottle' sort of thing. Only we'd better stop at the next off licence."

"There's no need. When I phoned Nigel last night he said he wouldn't hear of it."

"Brilliant! That's what I call a Do."

"Sounds the business to me. Mind if I come along?" asked the cabby, hoping his bouncy chit-chat might magic a tip.

"Just keep your eyes on the road," said Dawn.

'Squirrel's Leap.' Now there's a name to conjure. A detached gentleman's residence situated along a quiet country lane on the outskirts of Ashley village. In reality it was two stone cottages knocked into one, but with imaginative horticulture – wide box-hedges, hanging baskets, creeping vines and well hoed flowering boarders – over the years Nigel had turned his blessed half acre into a proper little Arcadia. The inside was just as twee; a four bedroomed two bathroomed shrine to Laura Ashley.

Throughout most of Saturday afternoon Nigel had been running round like I don't know what. There was simply *heaps* to do; the caterers were contacted with last minute instructions, the booking of a local jazz band confirmed, and a special delivery by Victoria Wine transit van craved his attention. This was to be no ordinary barbecue! With Roger's help he'd transformed the back garden into something out of the *Mikado*; Chinese lanterns hung from the apple tree and a pagoda-type pavilion had been created by draping silk curtains over the patio trellis. Here the jazz band would perform. Nigel was determined his party would be the social event of the year. He'd invited the entire Prestbury Local Opera Group – from the lowliest dresser to the company's president; his Honour, Judge Saul Greenberg (Nigel would have to steer *him* well away from the holocaust of pork pies and sausage rolls). In addition to the staff from the Comet, there were other members of his various interest groups including the Ashley Village Wine Appreciation Society, Wilmslow Bridge Club, and from his local church choir several young choristers upon whom Nigel was a great influence. In total over eighty people would be coming. He was particularly looking forward to the spleens certain members of the cast would vent when they found out he'd conquered the heterosexual Everest that was Roger Harvey – all 29,160ft of him.

Dawn cooed with excitement as the taxi squeaked to halt outside Nigel's house. Normally a quiet rustic backwater, Mill Lane had about a dozen cars parked higgledy-piggledy along its poppy-strewn grass verge. Vanessa paid the driver and they all got out. Tip secured, he called out a merry, "Have one for me," then sped off back to Wilmslow. The country air felt humid and still, still as abandoned swings in a playground. Invisible birds chirped in the hedgerows. Terry looked towards the horizon and noticed the pink sky's faint edge had begun to bleed dark tints of cloud, like ink seeping through blotting paper.

"Hurry up!" said Dawn. "Don't stand there gawping into thin air."
They crossed the lane, pushed open a picket fence type gate and crunched down the gravel path. Keith knocked at the front door -- a gnarled oak slab studded with capped nails.

"Hello everyone," said Nigel, beckoning them inside his panelled hallway. A grandfather clock stood guard at the foot of the stairs clunking out slow lazy seconds, and there hung in the air a distinct aroma – furniture polish and fresh flowers. It reminded Terry of when he was a boy, waiting patiently in Mrs. Jones' guest house in Colwyn Bay, standing in just such a hallway desperate for his parents to finish their breakfast so he could gather up his bucket and spade and run down to the beach. Nigel kissed Vanessa and Dawn on both cheeks, "I'm so glad you could come." He then discovered Keith.

"My word, what a *transformation!* And all for my little party! Fabulous!!"

Keith blushed and grinned, enjoying his second compliment in less than two hours, "I decided to splash out." He could get used to this.

Their host wore beige trousers, a lilac shirt and a sandy coloured cravat. His mousy hair had been oiled and slicked back. Terry thought he was wearing red lipstick until he realised it was the echo of Dawn's rouged cheeks.

"Listen," began Nigel, staring intensely at Terry and Vanessa. "Before we go in I want to say a few words about what's been happening at the *Comet*. From a personal standpoint I think both of you have behaved with the utmost irresponsibility. You've obviously got your reasons – God knows what they are. Suffice to say, I just want you to promise me that there won't be any unpleasant scenes. I don't want any of this to spoil the atmosphere and get in the way of everyone having a good time. Frank and Jean are here, and I've told them the same thing. So let's forget it. I promise I won't mention it again. As far as I'm concerned the matter's closed. *Fini, kaput*, done and dusted. Agreed?"

"Fine by me," said Terry.

"No problem," said Vanessa.

"Good, that's settled then. Let's go through to the garden and I'll show you where to get a nice *drinky*."

Speech over, they all trooped off behind him. Walking through the house Dawn was struck by how tidy everything was; a tranquil oasis of designer country living. 'Squirrel's Leap' had little use for unruly kids rushing around to upset the neat rows of up-market magazines, such as *Tattler* and *Cheshire Life*, stacked upon the coffee table alongside weighty tomes on opera, renaissance art, gothic cathedrals and Richard Maplethorpe. To her disbelief even the television was switched off!

Shock replaced surprise when she walked out onto the patio. Forty or more people mingled in various cliques while a bow-tied jazz band played smoochy tunes – their temporary silk pavilion flanked on either side by several tables packed with goodies. Dawn froze, gripped her husband's arm and whispered, "Bleedin hell! I thought you said this was going to be a *barbecue!*"

Terry was livid. He returned a savage whisper, "Use your imagination, lady! This is Nigel Harrison we're talking about! He's hardly likely to throw a few sausages on a poxy charcoal grill, now is he? I *told* you not to expect a run of the mill affair. Why do you think we were asked to dress smart? Honestly, you really are a thick cow sometimes."

They followed Nigel across the patio to a makeshift bar set up on the lawn beside a weeping willow. The barmen for the evening were Chris and Tony, two exquisite choristers. Each nudged the other at Dawn's approach.

"Right," said Nigel. "My two young friends here will sort you out. Don't forget to help yourselves to the food, you know where it is. And *don't* stand on ceremony."

Keith stared open mouthed at the many cases of wine, beer, spirits and champagne piled in boxy legions behind the bar. He couldn't take it all in – but he was going to have a damn good try. Finally he said, "You know what? I've misjudged Nigel. He really is a nice guy."

Dawn, though, had other things on her mind. Namely the grub. She hadn't starved herself all day for nothing.

Watching Terry, Dawn, Vanessa and Keith was a disgruntled Frank. He and Jean were standing unnoticed beneath the apple tree twenty metres further down the garden, munching canapés and sipping chilled champagne. It riled him to see that lot enjoying themselves, especially Terry. *The brazen bastard*, thought Frank. *Who the hell does he think he is, swanning in here with his obese wife as if nothing has happened*. He noticed Vanessa, looking so sexy, and wondered why she had allied herself with the bald imbecile. *What a crying shame. We could have been so good for each other.*

"Don't look now," said Keith, after sinking a triple scotch, much to the choristers delight, "but Frank's got his beady eye on us." He then joked, "I'm not sure if I should be seen with you two. It might be more than my job's worth."

"Let him look if he wants. I couldn't give a flying fuck," said Terry.

Vanessa turned and peered through a jumble of guests to see Frank and Jean turn away at that precise moment. Her mind went back to last year's Christmas party. She remembered Frank worse the wear for drink, telling her in hushed tones that his wife didn't understand him. Then, after being lured into Keith's darkroom, his seduction routine peppered with veiled flattery and the promise of promotion. *To think I nearly fell for that*, she thought.

"Never mind about him," interrupted Dawn. "Who's for some grub?"

All three declined, preferring instead to remain at the bar. Dawn made her solitary way back up the garden like a voracious rhino heading for its munching ground. She charged across the patio, elbowed her way to the front of the queue and began filling her plate. The jazz band's drummer – a cool sixty two year old whose 'bag' was female Russian shot-putters – gave her a mischievous grin. Dawn blushed and stuffed a chicken drumstick in her mouth – she'd always fancied musicians. His were not the only eyes to settle on her. Quite a few guests who were milling in and around the house began to notice this outsized ladybird hovering over the food, and their stares became all too apparent. Normally a 'couldn't-care-less' type, Dawn began to feel insecure as she pick-and-mixed her way from table to table.

Suddenly everyone's attention switched from greedy behemoth to glamorous supermodel; Natasha had arrived. She walked hand in hand down the garden with Steve Barlow like some coquette from the Cannes Film Festival attending her first première. Just as Moses parted the Red Sea, so Natasha divided the guests. Envy. Desire. Rapture. Fury. Lust. Jealousy. A tight fitting, ankle length metallic silver dress hanging by the faintest of straps fell straight as armour from the tips of her breasts. The dress slashed dramatic V's into cleavage, thigh and back – her auburn hair tumbling in an avalanche of ringlets. Splendiferous! Steve wore a black Armani suit. Nigel pointed them towards the bar.

"Here comes Mr. and Mrs. Perfect," said Keith.

Steve walked over with a childish grin on his face, ordered champagne and asked, "How's the Wilmslow equivalent of Woodward and Bernstein?"

"Who?" quizzed Terry.

"Unemployed!" said Vanessa. "And if that's supposed to be funny, Steve, let me assure you it's in very bad taste."

He noticed her totally-out-of-place grunge look, and went in for sarcastic seconds, "I didn't realise Nigel was having a barn dance."

"Take no notice of him," said Natasha, sensing the ugly mood.

Keith stood in silence expecting compliment number three, but all he got from Steve was, "Who's this, David Bellamy?"

Terry snapped, "Listen, Barlow. If you haven't got anything sensible to say, why don't you just *fuck off!*"

Steve spotted Frank and Jean beneath the apple tree. He grabbed the champagne bottle off the bar, put his arm around Natasha's silky aluminium waist and said, "Come on, *Tash*, let's mingle. Some people can't take a joke."

The battle lines were drawn.

Meanwhile the late evening sun had begun to fade, inviting the Chinese lanterns suspended from the apple tree to glow reddy-orange in the crepuscular light. The patio had been cleared of tables and chairs and was now a dance floor where elegant couples cheek-to-cheek'ed to the night-time rhythms of Joe Tek's Jazz Band. Nigel was having a rare old time flitting from group to group – a word with his Honour Judge Saul Greenberg here, a joke with the president of Wilmslow Bridge Club there, and everywhere with Roger Harvey.

Dawn inquired about the loo and was directed upstairs – she needed to make room for seconds. After discharging her bowels, she peered inside the toilet rim and noticed a brown stain the shape of India dribbling down the side of the pan; she had failed to assess the correct angle. Never mind, a quick clean with the loo brush would do the trick. *I better open the window and let some fresh air in*, she thought. She opened the frosted pane hoping to disperse the lingerings of her subcontinent splatter. A shadowy Mill Lane came into view, and against the darkening sky the village church seemed etched charcoal black. While alone upstairs, she decided to explore. Desperate for her first ever peek into a homosexual's bedroom, she wondered what Nigel's slaughterhouse might look like. Would it contain whips and chains, or small fluffy toys? Would there be naked men on posters, or picturesque scenes from rural Tuscany? She didn't get the chance to find out! The creaking stairs told her a stranger approached. Dawn nipped back inside the bathroom, counted to ten then opened the door. Standing before her was Frank's wife.

"Oh, hello," said Dawn. "It's Jean isn't it?"

Jean brushed passed without a word and closed the door. *Ignorant bitch*, thought Dawn. But Jean had other ways to communicate – three disgusting tuts and a loud blast from a perfumed toilet spray. Dawn bolted down the stairs thinking, *Oh Christ!*

Outside, the party was sailing full steam ahead. An ocean of booze flowed in such quantities as to suggest the final few hours

111

before prohibition. Keith, like the famous iceberg, sank titanic amounts, while Vanessa and Terry were trying their best not to miss the boat. It was all hands on deck in a glorious mutiny of eating, drinking and dancing. Even the jazz band played on, with a variety of up-tempo favourites. Vanessa, on hearing 'Baby Face,' invited Terry and Keith to join her for a quick Charleston. Keith stood fast. Terry, after scanning the horizon for Dawn, volunteered and followed her onto the dance floor. The leader of the band sang scratchily through a cardboard megaphone, "*You've got the cutest little Baby Face*", as Vanessa showed Terry the ropes. She put her left arm across her midriff, and with her right index finger pointing skyward she pretended to spin an invisible plate while at the same time jigging her head from side to side, taking one step forward then one step back. After a few bars the routine was reversed, so that the right hand went across the midriff and the left hand took over the plate spinning duties. Terry watched for a good ten seconds then joined in. What a lark! Those mobsters certainly knew how to enjoy themselves, "*I'm up in heaven when I feel your warm embrace.*"

Frank and Steve had left Natasha and Jean to their own devices under the apple tree. Together they stood close to the patio, whiskeys in hand, watching Terry cavort like an idiot with their beloved Vanessa. How they hated him, the hairless wonder. They hated everything about him, from the way he gyrated about the dance floor – hips swivelling, eyes closed as if in a deep zombie trance – to the way he'd even managed to get Judge Saul Greenberg involved. In fact most of the guests were now copying Vanessa and Terry's on-floor syncopations, including Nigel. What grated most of all, though, was that *this* man, a man who had done his utmost to sabotage the *Comet*, now seemed to be rubbing their noses in it. Something had to be done in recompense. Steve came up with a plan.

"A fashion photographer! That's very interesting. You must travel a great deal."

"Yeah," said Keith. "I go all over the world. India, South America, New York. You name it, I've been there. Err, you don't know Nigel, do you?"

"Who?"

"Nigel. Nigel Harrison. This is his party."

"Afraid not. I got my invitation through a friend who plays bridge at Wilmslow Bridge Club. Haven't seen her all evening. She's around somewhere."

"Oh, right….. I run my own studio in Paris as well, by the way"

"Fascinating."

Keith had struck up conversation with a lady called Rose, a fifty three year old divorcee from Knutsford who was looking for excitement. Abandoned by her friend, she had spotted Keith leaning against the bar and was enthralled by his Hemingway-esque antics. She was small, blonde, with a trim figure and plumy accent. Her face, though heavily lined due to sun bed fatigue, appeared youthful in the twinkling candlelight. She wore a low cut peach coloured dress a little too short around the thigh, revealing the curse of the creeping cellulite. From Keith's vantage point this volcanic feature eluded him, gazing as he was at her pert cleavage and floating nipples. It wouldn't have mattered if she'd been covered from head to foot in the stuff, it was that long since he'd had his hands on anything other than his own fleshy joy stick. Having read certain tips in *Cosmopolitan* about how to chat up women, Keith slurred, "Tell me a bit about yourself, Rose." He was determined to become a nineties man.

"Oh, gosh! Me? Uhh, my life's nowhere *near* as interesting as yours," she admitted, holding a dry Martini to her bosom while fixing him with a 'take-me-away-from-all-this' blue-eyed stare.

"Go on, give it a go. I'm sure it's not *that* boring."

Rose thought, *Umm, give it a go. I bet you say that to all the young models.* Out came her sad CV. "Well, if you must know, I'm forty five. Divorced, thank God, and live by myself with two dogs in a little house near Knutsford. My ex-husband was a barrister, very dull, and I do voluntary work two days a week helping the blind. So you see, hardly what you'd call stimulating."

"Sound's alright."

"You're only saying that to be nice." She gave his arm a gentle squeeze. "Anyway, I want to hear more about you."

Keith could barely contain himself. All those endless months alone in that hideous flat starved of female company had fired his imagination. "Well, Rose, as you know I'm a fashion photographer. I work for the likes of *Vogue* – and similar mags – and I spend most of the year in America, Europe and Rio."

"Rio! Rio de Janeiro?"

"There's only one Rio in Brazil, luv."

"No there aren't! There are several. Rio Grande do Sul for one."

Cracks had to be papered over, and fast. "I know all about that. But as far as I'm concerned, speaking as *a fashion photographer*, there *is* only *one* Rio."

"Of course, how silly of me," said Rose, desperate not to frighten off her clicking Casanova. "I imagine you're much too busy working to be bothered with such geographical trivia. It's just that I went on holiday to Brazil some years ago, and before I left, typically boring Rose, I read up on anything about the country I could get my hands on."

"I'm not into all that. I like to go where the action is."

"Yes, I can imagine. Tell me, Keith," she cocked her head sideways like a Toucan, "this may sound stupid, I know, but which suburb do you prefer, Copacabana or Ipanema?"

His luck was in. Only last month he'd stayed up late to watch a program on the Open University entitled 'Brazil's Shame.' Presuming it was about the sex industry, he expected to see tits and arses displayed. All he saw, though, was a bunch of scruffy kids being chased by police through the rat infested shanty towns of Copacabana. Keith thought his answer would sound better spiced with a joke.

"Apart from them both being God-awful songs, that's easy," he laughed. "Ipanema. The other place is a right shit hole."

"I agree. But what about…..."

"Do you mind if we change the subject? I'm getting a bit bored talking about work. Would you like another drink?"

Rose found him ever so exciting, and said, "Yes, please! I feel like getting drunk myself."

Dawn had managed to avoid Jean by taking refuge in the kitchen. As with most parties it was full of would-be intellectuals – pretentious jerks lacking in both the looks and self-confidence department. I mean, how many attractive people do *you* know that actually use the public library? She was parked next to the fridge demolishing a chocolate éclair. Glasses chinked and bottles glugged above the muffled *alfresco jazz* band. Surrounding her on all sides were fragmented conversations, -- "Of course Salman Rushdie's a genius. I've never doubted it for one minute. I just wish he'd write the occasional book that made sense, that's all." And, "The whole idea behind Damien Hirst's work, his prognosis for the twenty-first century, is that flesh and time are but one of the same. He's trying to stay, if you'll just hear me out – please, I listened to you. He's trying to say that mankind itself is floating in an existential universe of formaldehyde." And, "Heard about Jim Butterworth? Terrible. Aids. Full-blown!"

It was the sudden increase in whooping and cheering that made Dawn vacate the kitchen. When she stepped outside and discovered the cause – Terry and Vanessa's patio high-jinx – she boiled over. *You! You!*........she thought, unable to think, her piggy features a shifting, buckling landscape of jealousy. Steve noticed she didn't look too pleased. His plan fell immediately into place. He sidled over to the kitchen door and found her rooted to the spot. She was unable to take her eyes off the Charlestoning duo. By this time the dance had progressed to the holding hands and leaning back stage. Steve, an expert in the black art of espionage, (ask Natasha) said, "Hi, Dawn. Enjoying yourself? Great party, eh?"

"So, so."

"They move well together, Vanessa and Terry."

It took a moment for the information to be correlated. Words; so innocent, and yet so deadly. *"Meanin?"* asked Dawn, the night's alcohol spawning demons.

"Nothing. Just making an observation."

"You're very good at that, you reporters."

" I suppose we are."

Dawn still had her gaze fixed to the jiving duo. "You're very good at that as well, aren't you? Supposing."

A more subtle approach was called for to bring down the beast. "It's a shame about what happened at the *Comet*. I'll miss them."

"Will you?"

"Yeah, they were good mates. Listen, if there's anything I can do to help Terry find another job – I know quite a few people – just let me know."

"Thanks, but we'll manage."

Ungrateful cow, thought Steve, even though he hadn't the slightest intention of lifting a finger. His syrupy, "Fancy a drink?" produced an acidic, "No, *ta*." Steve dispensed with the niceties. He went straight for the jugular. "Talking about drinks, I was surprised you weren't in Bank Square Café Bar the other night."

"Come again?"

"Bank Square Café Bar."

"Why should I go to a stuck-up place like that. Have you seen the prices they charge."

"Only, Terry was in there with Vanessa. I thought you might have joined him, you know."

A trickle of hair dye slithered down one side of her rouged cheek like a black viper crossing a sand dune. "Are you sure?"

"Positive! Me and Natasha had a drink with them. I think they must have been celebrating that ridiculous stunt they pulled, because we had a bottle of champagne. "

CHAMPAGNE!!!!!!! "What night was this?"

"Last Wednesday! The Wednesday just gone! We had a great time. Having said that, they didn't stay long. They went off together somewhere. Just before seven I think it was."

Dawn scrambled her brain, *Last Wednesday? Last Wednesday?* It was hard to think, what with the jazz band playing at full throttle and tipsy couples bumping in and out of the kitchen. Eventually the blurred image of Terry stumbling in at two o'clock in the morning materialised. *LASTBLEEDIN WEDNESDAY!* She tried to remain calm, but her vast bulk began to shake within the tented polkadot. Steve's butchery was complete. Natasha appeared from nowhere, grabbed his arm and whimpered, "Stevey, can we go now? I'm really, really, bored."

"In a minute, *Tash*."

"But Steve......."

"I said in a minute." He was desperate to see the effects of his handy work.

Dawn realised that if she stayed any longer a murder might be committed. She asked, "Would you mind giving me a lift home? I've just about had it up to here with this fuckin Do."

"Sure, no problem. What about Terry? Do you want me to tell him you're coming with us?" asked Steve.

"No, better not. I'll see to *him* later."

Roger Harvey looked in the bathroom mirror and examined his handsome face. The last hour had taken it out of him. His hair stood up in strands like demented cockatoo, and his forehead beaded sweat. He dabbed his face with a towel then took out his comb and smoothed the unruly strands into place. Satisfied with the result, he began checking his teeth for stowaways – spinach, watercress, olive shards. An impatient rat-tat-tat sounded on the door.

"Hurry up, I'm bursting," said a voice.

"Just a moment."

After what seemed an eternity, he finally slipped the latch. Terry stood on the threshold holding his crotch like an injured wicket keeper. "You took your time. I nearly had to piss in that plant pot."

He apologised, "Sorry about the wait," and trundled downstairs. Passing the grandfather clock, the hallway sentinel chimed midnight. Roger was surprised to hear, as a riposte, the doorbell ring. *Who the hell's this?* Terry unzipped his fly and joyfully foamed the blue lagoon. Because the bathroom window was ajar he could make out the shadow of someone stretching down the path. Roger opened the front door to be confronted by an enormous shaven headed man wearing a dark suit. Thinking he was a taxi driver, he asked, "What name is it?"

"Arthur Whitman."

Terry saturated the floor.

"Please wait there."

Out on the patio only the closest of couples danced now that the jazz band played soft romantic melodies. Vanessa and Nigel were taking a breather while Keith and Rose snogged beneath the many orange suns drooping from the apple tree. Frank and Jean? They'd left half an hour ago. Roger announced, "Arthur Whitman! Taxi for Arthur Whitman!"

Nigel rushed across the patio, "What's going on?"

Roger explained. When he described the driver in greater detail, Nigel barked, "Please don't tell me you've left him standing at the door?"

"Yes, why?"

Nigel set off through the kitchen with Roger in tow. "Oh for God's sake, man! He owns the bloody *Comet*."

"How was I to know? He doesn't look much like a newspaper proprietor to me."

"Oh shut up, Roger."

Terry finished mopping up the pool of urine with a wad of toilet paper then creaked open the bathroom window a couple more notches. He overheard Nigel grovel, "Mr. Whitman. Words fail me. I'm so sorry to have kept you waiting."

"That's all right. It's me who should apologise. I tried telephoning earlier this evening, to let you know I wouldn't be able to make it, but there was no reply. I had to attend an important business meeting in Manchester. Couldn't get out of it. Been there since eight o'clock. Eight a *soddin clock!* Anyway, to cut a long story short I was on my way home so I thought I'd pop in for five minutes."

"Very kind of you."

"It's the least I can do. After what's happened over the past few days, the last thing I want is another member of my staff holding a grudge against me."

"Nonsense. Please, do come in," said Nigel. "I'll fix you up with a nice glass of champagne."

"Only one, mind. I'm driving."

Good, thought Terry. *I'll stay here until the twat leaves.*

Rose pushed her gin-soaked tongue in Keith's ear and whispered, "You can sleep at my house tonight if you like. No use going back to a half decorated apartment."

"Cheers. You're a life saver."

"How long have you been living at Curzon Mews?"

Keith stroked the back of her dainty neck, thinking how easy it would be to break and put a stop to all these endless questions. "Not long. I only bought the place two weeks ago, so I'm not actually living there at present. If the speed of the decorators is anything to go by, it'll be Christmas before I'm able to move in."

Rose switched her attention to his other ear, "Well at least tonight has worked out. Shall we go?"

"Whenever you're ready, darlin."

His trousered erection pointed the way. But there was one small problem. Making it from the apple tree to Rose's car was extremely dangerous; he would have to negotiate a minefield of home truths just waiting to explode. One mention of 'flat' or 'Handforth' by either Terry or Vanessa would almost certainly blow his cover, and the chance of a precious shag. Keith had an idea. He said to Rose, "Why don't you go and warm the engine up while I nip to the loo."

She started walking towards the house, "Aren't you coming?"

"Let me finish my drink first."

Rose understood; the international fashion photographer wouldn't be seen dead leaving the party with a middle-aged divorcee. *Bad for his image, I suppose*, she thought. "OK, see you in my car in five min-

utes. It's the blue Range Rover Vogue parked halfway along the lane."
Rose disappeared into the house. He waited for a moment, threw back
the clinking remnants of his double vodka, then marched after her. In
the kitchen he came upon Nigel, Roger and Arthur Whitman. He
edged passed nervously, saying, "I'm off, Nigel. Thanks for a great
party. See you on Monday."

Nigel was far too engrossed in his important guest to say anything
other than, "Night." Keith ran upstairs and tried the bathroom door,
desperate to check himself for anything nasty before his sexual
encounter. "Can you hurry up please."

Terry recognised the voice. He unlocked the door. "Come in quick.
Whitman's here!"

"I know," said Keith. "I've just seen the bastard. Is that why
you're hiding?"

" Yeah. I'm staying here until he's gone. Take a seat." He
offered the toilet lid.

"I can't, mate. I'm in a hurry. You'll never guess what's happened. I've met this rich woman called Rose. She lives on her own in
Knutsford. Mad over me she is. I'm quids in. She wants me to stay
the night. Have I spun *her* a fairy tale."

"*You've* got off with a *woman?*"

"Don't sound so surprised, Terry."

"So that's why I've not seen you all night. Listen, talking
about the disappearing act, you don't know what's happened to
Dawn, do you? I've not seen *her* all night either."

"Yeah. I saw her leave with Steve and Natasha about an hour
ago."

"You're joking? She went off with…........?"

"Terry, if you hadn't spent the entire evening fawning over
Vanessa, you might have noticed."

"I've not been fawning over her! I've just been having a
good time, that's all. Surely you don't blame me? Christ, you know
as well as I do Dawn only came for the food. Did you see her earlier
on? Did you see how much she shovelled away. The woman's a
bleedin eating machine!"

"Sorry, Terry. No time for anymore questions. I've got to go.
A certain lady's waiting." Keith noticed Terry's worried expression
and sensed marital discord. He fished in the top pocket of his brand
new corduroy jacket, took out a bunch of keys and prised one off the

ring. "Look, here's the backdoor key to my flat. If you use it, try not to make a mess. See you tomorrow. "

Arthur Whitman strolled with a gorilla-like gait across the patio. Vanessa took one look at him and thought, *You Fascist creep. Come to gloat have we?* She was standing at the bar being chatted up by one of the choristers. Nigel noticed her aggressive body language, so he said to Whitman, "Take a seat by the jazz band, I'll go and fetch you a drink." He walked over to her, "Look, Vanessa, I know you think you've been badly treated, but I'd appreciate it if you'd stay out of Mr. Whitman's way. He's only staying for one drink. So please, as a favour to me, behave yourself."

"No problem, Nigel. Anything you say."

Keith found the correct Range Rover and got in. Rose seemed even smaller at the wheel, like she was driving a combined harvester. She said, "One thing I must ask you before we go. It's very important because you'll be meeting them shortly. Do you like dogs?"

True to his word, Arthur Whitman had one drink then got up to leave. "I must be off. The wife'll be expecting me. Don't want her to think I'm out seeing some floozy. Ha, ha. Shame I couldn't make it earlier. Looks as though I've missed a good party. Still, there's always a next time." He thanked his host, "Nice glass of champagne was that."

Nigel escorted him to the front door, said good night and watched him walk down the path. From the bathroom window Terry saw him open the gate and stroll to his car. Typical Whitman, he'd parked the thing right outside the house, under a street lamp. Terry thought, *Lazy idle swine. Go on, piss off home in your posh car. Yes you, you fat piece of.........*In an instant he sobered up. The magnificent auto was a Seychelles Blue Rolls Royce – and the number plate screamed **AW 2**. *Jesus Christ!* Terry flew downstairs, ran into the garden and grabbed Vanessa by the arm. "We've got to talk," he gibbered. They found a quiet spot. "It was him! It was him. Him!"

"Who was him? What are you talking about?"

"Whitman! That day, at the back of Macclesfield Town Hall, talking to the pro-shopping lobby."

"For God's sake get a grip of yourself and tell me what the hell's going on."

Terry's mouth gnashed like a threshing machine. "They were stand-ing next to his *Roller* in the car park having some kind of private

120

meeting – only I didn't know it was his car until now. I saw it all through the pub window. You've got to be believe me, it was him. Him."

An hour later Terry and Vanessa were sitting round the pine kitchen table in Railwayman's Cottage drinking black coffee. The digital clock shone 1.30am. Their minds raced.

"I knew it," said Vanessa. "I just knew there was something fishy going on. Do you remember what he said when he sacked us – "You're damaging the *Comet's* interests? 'Interests!' Then he changed it to 'principles' – talk about a Freudian slip. I thought it was funny at the time."

"I know. And another thing, Keith told me that Whitman ordered Frank to re-write the article in *favour* of the developers."

"He's probably taking kick-backs, and God knows what else."

"But that's fraud."

"Spot on. And we're going to prove it."

"How?"

Vanessa was taken aback. She stared across the pine table and said, cuttingly, "By undercover investigation, Terry. After all, we are *supposed* to be journalists."

"Point taken. Any suggestions as to where we start?"

"When's the next meeting scheduled at Macclesfield Town Hall?"

"This Monday."

"Right. We'll both go along and see what we can dig up."

The kitchen door swung open to reveal Ian wrapped in his claret coloured dressing gown looking more than annoyed. " Hey, have you seen the fucking time. I can't sleep with you two jerks making all that racket. Give me a break and shut the fuck up." (He'd spent far too many evenings at Salford Quays watching Hollywood movies.) He slammed the door and returned to bed.

"Oops," said Vanessa. "I think we'd better call it a night."

Chapter Ten

Sunday. 11.30am.

The glorious June weather had erupted into a bucketuss downpour, quenching the parched-brown lawns of North East Cheshire. Keith paid the taxi driver and ran up the path towards his flat, dodging the puddles; at least the rain had washed the dog shit away. What a night! Sexual excitement (he gave himself 8 /10) and the drug-like high of living life in the fast lane, albeit incognito. Lying – the Devil's elixir – you can say or do anything you want and blame it all on Mr. Hyde. But it was a double-edged sword this falsifying of the truth, this building castles-in-the-air, because there was no such studio in Paris, and no such half decorated apartment at Curzon Mews. There never would be. Not ever. *Ad infinitum*. Still, lying naked in bed next to Rose beneath a freshly laundered sheet anything seemed possible, and he'd given full vent to his imagination. *If only it was true*, thought Keith, *instead of having to live in this shit-*

tip. He pulled the key from the lock and closed the front door behind him. In the hallway two large suitcases met his eye, and in the background his ears detected a raucous children's cartoon. He opened the lounge door. There sat Terry, feet on the coffee table, sipping tea. "Dawn's kicked me out," he said.

He went on to describe the nasty domestic bust-up that took place in the wee small hours at No.13 Windermere Drive. He'd left Vanessa's by taxi and arrived home just after 3.30am. The lights were ablaze downstairs. Dawn was sitting in the lounge, fag-in-hand, wearing her dressing gown. The television was switched off – a sure sign of trouble. She accused him of having an affair with Vanessa. Terry laughed. Dawn threw a glass at him. It missed and smashed against the wall. She then grilled him about the previous Wednesday. Unfortunately he stuck to his boozy night out with Keith story. Dawn introduced Steve's testimony concerning Bank Square Café Bar. Terry's alibi crumbled. When he tried to explain that it was actually Fat Charlie Peters he'd gone out with, she calmly walked into the kitchen and produced two suitcases. Terry begged her not to leave. He had tragically misjudged the situation. "I'm not going anywhere," said Dawn. "You're the one that's leaving." She hurled both suitcases into the front garden, followed moments later by Terry. "Now piss off back to your champagne bitch," was her final statement before slamming the door in his face. Because he was too drunk to drive he had to leave his car where it was and struggle up to the nearest phone box to order another taxi. More humiliation; it was the same driver that had dropped him off only ten minutes before, and the look on his face as he clocked the suitcases said it all.

"I can't believe she thinks you're having a fling with Vanessa," said Keith, delighted at his friend's misfortune. At last Terry would finally understand the pain and suffering he'd gone through because of Rita. Life was a funny old game. No sooner was Keith on the up and up with Rose, than Terry was on the slippery slope with Dawn.

"I wouldn't mind if I was," said Terry. "All this shit."

Keith glanced at the pathetic suitcases cluttering up the hallway. "I suppose you'll want to crash here for a bit?"

Terry was touched. "If you don't mind. It would really help me out."

"No problem. Stay as long as you want. But let this be a lesson to you. Lying doesn't get you anywhere."

123

"You're right. I've lost my job and now my wife." He slumped forward, cradling his bald head in his hands. "What am I going to do? I can't believe this has happened to *me*!"

Keith was all too familiar with the scenario. "Leave your stuff where it is and let's go for a drink. Come on, there's plenty of time to unpack later. And don't worry about Dawn, she'll calm down sooner than you think."

To celebrate Terry's freedom, as Keith bravely put it, they ordered a cab and drove out to the Bird in Hand pub in delightful, threatened Mobberley – threatened by the second runway, that is. In a tiny oak panelled room opposite the main bar, with its Victorian fireplace, highly polished mahogany tables and quaint sashed window, Keith tried to amuse his dejected friend with last night's adventures. On leaving the party, Rose had driven him at great speed back to her detached house on the outskirts of Knutsford. The journey was memorable for two reasons. Firstly she was drunk, and her Range Rover Vogue kept veering this way and that down the silhouette of country lanes, and secondly she couldn't keep her hands away from his crotch. Arriving at the house, one of her dogs answering to the name of Sam – a golden retriever the colour of cheese & onion crisps – bit him on the ankle and had to be locked away in the kitchen. Rose apologised and they tumbled upstairs with two large brandies, where drunken bouts of frantic sex took place and mammoth lies were told. In the morning she treated him to breakfast in bed – tea and toast and the *Sunday Times* neatly folded on a tray accompanied by a single yellow rose. Rose was mad about him, he confessed, and he was going to take full advantage of her financial situation. Terry eventually cheered up and told Keith all about the Arthur Whitman incident; how he and Vanessa planned to go undercover to expose the corrupt gangster. Keith was delighted, and said he could detect the strange hand of fate behind Nigel's party. Perhaps this moment was a watershed in both their lives. "Perhaps," said Keith, "in six months time when I'm living in Knutsford with Rose and you're journalist of the year, we'll look back and say, 'Yes, this was meant to be.' "

They boozed the entire afternoon and evening, plundering the pub's stock of Ingerbrau extra-strong draft pils and sailing away on a pair of **Giant Yorkshire Dinghies stuffed with spicy sausage. £5.50**.

And so Terry had become a piece of flotsam washed up on Keith's polluted shore. The domestic arrangements were simple. Terry would sleep on a camp bed in the front room, and they'd share the bills. Any port in a storm, he told himself.

Early the next morning, Keith was in the kitchen eating toast when the phone rang. He shook Terry awake – wrapped in a red sleeping bag he looked like a giant chrysalis about to pupate.

"It's for you."

"Dawn?"

Keith shook his head. "Vanessa."

Terry unzipped himself. "What time is it?"

"Half eight. I've got to go." He handed Terry the receiver. "See you tonight."

"Hi, Vanessa. How did you know I was here?"

Her voice crackled down the phone line in staccato shock. "I've just had the most amazing conversation with Dawn. I asked to speak to you, right, and she went completely off her head and called me a whore, then accused me of having an affair with you. Where she got that from, God only knows. I told her it was nonsense but she wouldn't have it. She carried on swearing and calling me a husband stealer. I tried to calm her down but she got more and more upset. She said she'd kicked you out and she never wants to see you again, then she slammed the phone down on me. It didn't take Einstein to guess you'd be staying at Keith's flat."

Terry felt as though a cosmic plug had been pulled and the universe was slowly being sucked down the drain, relatively speaking…...... "Did she," was all he could manage.

"You've not had a very good week, have you?" said Vanessa.

"Not really."

"What can I say? Sound's to me like one hell of a misunderstanding."

"Yeah."

She came to the point, "Listen, if you don't want to go to the public enquiry this morning, I fully understand." The world just keeps on turning, leaving us stranded in its wake.

"I think I better had. It'll do me good to take my mind off things."

"I was hoping you'd say that. I'll pick you up in fifteen minutes." Terry gave her the address and she rang off.

When they arrived at Macclesfield Town Hall a nasty shock awaited. The council official at reception – the old man who Terry threatened to report to his superiors the previous Monday – took great delight in saying, "I'm afraid you're going to have to queue up like everyone else. Your press passes have been revoked. They're not worth the plastic they're printed on."

He slid them back under a gap in the glass-fronted cubicle as though they were radioactive. "Don't look at me like that," he said, all too aware of Terry's vicious temper. "I'm only following orders."

Walking up the stone staircase towards committee room three, Terry said, "And I bet I know whose orders he's following. Whitman's."

Vanessa agreed. "You're right. But Whitman's gone and made his first mistake. Just because we don't work for the *Comet* anymore, doesn't give him the right to ban us from the press box. Those passes were issued by our union, not Whitman, so it's against the law what he's trying to pull. Unemployed or not, we're still journalists."

She stopped outside the committee room door and grabbed Terry's arm, her lovely brown eyes widening with excitement. "You know what this means? He's worried. We've got the gangster worried."

Inside the packed council chamber they sat as close as they could to the press contingent, most of whom gave a sympathetic wave. News of their heroic deeds had elevated them to cult status. Just as the public inquiry was about to start, Fat Charlie Peters came across to offer his support. "Speaking on behalf of all my colleagues, I think you've both been very brave in standing up for what you believe. To be perfectly honest, most of us here aren't bothered either way about the shopping complex. But we realise it must have taken a hell of a lot of guts to go against Frank like that."

Terry said, "Thanks, Charlie. But it wasn't Frank who sacked us, it was Arthur Whitman." He was about to add 'The fat Yorkshire bastard', but thought better of it. Instead he waited for Charlie to return to his seat, then pointed to the table holding the pro-shopping delegation. He whispered to Vanessa, "They're the ones I told you about who had a secret meeting with Whitman at the back of the Town Hall."

Three loud *Rap-Rap-Raps* sounded from the distinguished looking chairman. "Order. Order."

A hush fell over the council chamber, punctuated by the odd cough and scraped chair.   "Ladies and gentlemen, this is the second in a series of three public meetings to decide the fate of the proposed Mottram Hill Shopping Complex. As you may or may not know, the first dealt with legal technicalities. Today, the Anti-Shopping Development Lobby will put forward their case, followed next Monday by the Pro-Shopping Development Lobby. By the power invested in me by Macclesfield Borough Council, I call upon Joanne Alloway to begin her opening speech. A slender young woman in her late twenties rose to her feet. *Wow*, thought Terry, *the environmentalists always have the best lookers*. She wore a pair of tight blue jeans and a striped Breton T-shirt. As she began to speak, her curly dark hair and soft doe-eyed features appeared all the more innocent by the shy girlish tilt of her head.

"Jo's a friend of mine," whispered Vanessa. "I've arranged to meet her for lunch."

Terry's thoughts dipped below the whys-and-wherefores of shopping malls and came to rest on the stormy outcrop that was Dawn. As far as he could see there was only one person to blame for putting such adulterous notions into her head – and that was Steve Barlow. It was obvious; he hadn't given her a lift home out of the goodness of his heart. Terry wondered what kind of malicious fabrications would have caused her to explode in the way she did. Steve was well known in the office for his vivid imagination; he could make a boring nil-nil draw between Altrincham and Northwich Victoria sound like a classic European Cup final – **desperate defending, scintillating free kicks, wave after wave of attack and counter attack. A veritable smorgasbord of unbelievable skills to nourish the Saturday afternoon punter.** In other words he was a pathological liar.

Three hours later, following lengthy statements, heartfelt pleas, a variety of expert witnesses, graphs illustrating the area's declining wildlife, and a video showing the disastrous effects suffered by local shopkeepers after a similar shopping mall was built outside Newcastle-upon-Tyne, they adjourned for lunch.

"Is that it?" asked Terry, bored ridged.

"No," said Vanessa. "There's a lot more discussion this afternoon." She stood up. "Come on, let's go over and see Jo. She's dying to meet you."

They pushed their way through the outgoing crowd towards the front of the council chamber. Joanne was deep in conversation with the rest of the anti-shopping lobby until she noticed her friend.

"Hi, Vanessa. Glad you could come." They exchanged continental-type kisses. "Let's go for a bite to eat. I know a nice little

Italian restaurant round the corner that does an *amazing* lasagne." She looked at Terry. "You must be Terry Howarth. I've heard a lot about you. I can't thank you enough for what you and Vanessa have done to help the cause. I'd be interested to hear your opinion on our presentation." To her colleagues around the table she said, "I'll see you later." This minx had more energy than the sun.

Inside Bachi's restaurant on Canal Street, with its terracotta-tiled bar, red checked table clothes, and token Chianti bottles whose slender necks were strangled by a frozen avalanche of candle wax, Joanne ordered the food. "*Tre lasagne verdi e un litro di vino rosso della casa. Grazie.*"

"*Prego,*" said the waiter, from Buxton.

Terry gave a nervous snotty-sniff, thinking that whatever it was sounded very expensive. Joanne thought his mannerism rather uncouth, not at all a social nicety. When the wine arrived Vanessa poured out three glasses and made a toast, "Here's to the cause." Chink, chink.....chink. She then described to Joanne Terry's revelation about Arthur Whitman. Joanne could barely contain herself. She put down her glass and said, "Please tell me you're not winding me up. Oh my God, wow, this is fantastic! We've got them by the balls. If these allegations are true, that he's using the *Comet* as a vehicle to promote his business interests, then we can stop the shopping development dead in its tracks. What Whitman's doing is fraud. He can be sent to prison for it, along with the whole damn pro-shopping lobby."

"Hold on a minute, Jo," said Vanessa. "Let's not get carried away. We need proof before we can go any further. I mean, all we've got at the moment is Terry's eyewitness account of Whitman having a shady conversation at the back of the Town Hall. That won't stand up in court."

Terry didn't half fancy this Joanne, this firebrand, and it irked him to see her enthusiasm dampened by Vanessa's pessimistic comments. He took on the guise of Mel Gibson in *Lethal Weapon*. "We're gonna have to prove it then, aren't we. Even if it means breaking in to Whitman's house. There's no way I'm letting that gangster get away with it, scott free."

"I'm impressed," said Joanne. "That's just the attitude we need in a situation like this. For the good of the environment we've all got to stand up and be counted."

Vanessa's Eco-worrier instincts rose up to drown her reservations.

128

"Right! The gloves are off. Terry, if you're serious about wanting to bring Whitman down by whatever it takes, then I'm with you all the way. But first we'll have to work out a plan."

Joanne offered, "If there's anything I or my colleagues can do to help, don't be shy in asking."

Three piping hot lasagnes arrived at the table, bubbling lava-like in their cast iron tureens. During the meal an ingenious strategy was formulated. Joanne would plough through the mountainous paperwork dealing with the shopping complex, to see if Whitman's name came up, while Terry and Vanessa gathered hard evidence such as photographs of any clandestine meetings he might have with the developers. This would entail staking out his house in Prestbury, and following him to and from his office. Also the *Comet* was to be studied for editorial bias. In short, an undercover operation of such covert complexity it would equal Watergate but for the tall white buildings and important personalities.

"We're going to have to work fast," said Joanne, pouring out more wine. "Two weeks from today the council will make their decision, and if we haven't got anything concrete to put before them, then I'm afraid we're sunk."

Terry slurped back the vinegary vino and thought, *Why am I getting myself involved?*

Ineluctable anarchy.

Chapter Eleven

"New balls please," ordered the posh voice emanating from Keith's television set. "Miss Arancha Sanchez Vicario leads by five games to love, and by one set to love."

It was Thursday, the fourth day of Wimbledon, and the dumpy Spaniard was cruising towards another effortless victory. *It's a pity Steffi's not in it this year*, thought Terry, *My golden legs would pulverise that ugly bitch.* If there was one person he hated more than Sanchez Vicario, it was Monica Selles. Terry couldn't stand her grunts and groans, her hideous toad-like face-pulling, as she went on to thrash say a dainty Swede or lithe Lithuanian. What chance did these feminine sweethearts have against an Eastern European gargoyle whose powerful back muscles thwarted an assassin's blade? And Tim Henman, the great British hope – with his craggy-featured father perched eagle-like in the player's box – deary me, when will he get it into his thick Android bonce that he simply can't play the game; that the only thing he's fit for is advertising cardboard tasting *Bran Flakes* nobody ever eats. Terry thought he was an overrated schoolboy, and reckoned Professor Stephen Hawking had more chance of winning the title. Another thing that got on his nerves was the BBC commentary team. Proper men didn't gush – "*Ooh I say*," or "*That was simply breathtaking*" or "*He really is a lovely man*" – like those effeminates.

Terry was waiting for Vanessa to come and pick him up. Due to his cowardice, he still hadn't ventured home to pick up his rusty Uno. She had promised to be at the flat by twelve o'clock sharp. It was now 12.30. They were about to start another day's stakeout of the Whitman offices in Altrincham, followed by a late evening shift outside his Prestbury mansion. Three days had gone by, producing a big fat zero. Terry had armed himself with one of Keith's spare cameras, but so far the only thing he'd shot was Arthur Whitman sitting alone in his Rolls Royce and a couple of him out walking the dog. There was no sign of any developers hiding behind trees, and definitely no secret rendezvous in multi-storey car parks.

"Game, set and match to Miss Arancha Sanchez Vicario. Six love, Six love." The crafty piglet had triumphed yet again. The BBC commentary team oozed, "*Wonderful*," "*Marvellous*," "*How charming*," as Terry got an eyeful of curtseyed knicker.

Finally Vanessa arrived. She wore black denim jeans and a grey sweatshirt proclaiming 'Save the Whale'.

"Sorry I'm late," she apologised, hiding her disgust at the flat's unwashed fatty smell – Keith's dirty laundry combined with Terry's cooked breakfast. "I've been speaking to Jo on the phone for the past half hour. Major developments."

"Yeah. Like what?"

"Do you mean to say you've not seen the *Comet?*"

"No. Keith told me that the little swines paid to deliver it round here sometimes chuck bag loads of them into the nearest skip." Vanessa produced her own copy, handed it to Terry and said, "Read this."

He scanned the front-page editorial. Frank's name headed an article so biased towards the shopping complex, so virulent in its condemnation of Terry and Vanessa – who it described as **rogue reporters bent on some kind of anarchic crusade** – it was obvious Whitman must have been behind it.

"The man's breaking every ethical law in the book," said Vanessa. "I mean, look at this." She had also brought along a copy of the *Comet's* rival paper, the *Wilmslow Gazette*. Its editorial trod a careful path between the developers and the environmentalists, ending in banal statement: **justice and common sense would no doubt prevail**.

Terry read both articles and said, "Whitman's way out of line. He's worse than Goebbels with his propaganda."

"You're right. But to nail the bastard, to show the public inquiry that he's in cahoots with the pro-shopping lobby, we still need hard evidence."

"Where that's going to come from, God knows."

"Let's not get too down hearted," said Vanessa. "You never know, today might produce something. Well, shall we go?"

He grabbed his jacket and a plum coloured bag containing sandwiches, a thermos flask, and Keith's spare camera loaded with film. They set off in Vanessa's Honda Accord to begin another stakeout.

The head office of Allied Northern Newspapers, the name of Whitman's publishing empire, was located behind the Metro station in Altrincham. A three-storey chrome and glass fortress, its entrance could easily be observed from the station's car park. This meant shelling out for an all-day permit, which annoyed Terry, but the vast number of cars provided valuable camouflage. Vanessa parked her Honda close to the building's perimeter fence, offering an excellent view of any suspicious comings-and-goings. Two drizzly hours later though, boredom had set in.

"Typical Manchester weather," said Terry, pouring from his thermos two steaming coffees. "It's hard to believe the sun's beating down at Wimbledon."

Vanessa hated small talk, so she asked, "How are you getting on at Keith's?"

Terry thought for a moment. "So far we've done nothing but get drunk every night."

She laughed, "I noticed the Hawaiian drinks bar."

"I know. Hideous isn't it? The man's got no taste. Still, it's good of him to put me up for the time being."

"What about Dawn? Have you been in touch with her yet?"

"No.... Actually, yes. I tried telephoning the other night but Kath answered. She's the Mother-in-law by the way. I asked to speak to Dawn but the old cow shouted down the phone that I had a 'bleedin cheek' and hung up."

"Do you miss her?"

"Who, Kath?"

"Of course not Kath! Your wife. Do you miss her?"

This personal question embarrassed him. He wasn't used to sharing his inner most feelings, especially with a woman. He took a paper tissue from his trouser pocket and wiped away a misty blanket of condensation formed on the windscreen. "There," he said, "we can see better now."

She squeezed his arm. "Come on Terry, don't avoid the question. You can tell me."

In the three years he'd known Vanessa, this was the first time she'd ever touched him in a genuinely affectionate way. Alright, she'd pushed passed him at the coffee machine, but this was different, more profound. It had the effect of releasing an emotional tidal wave built up over the past few days. "I do miss her, if the truth be told. I didn't think I would, but….. Funny isn't it, the words of that song are so true, 'You don't know what you've got till it's gone.' I never thought I'd say this, and I never in a million years thought I'd be sat here right now saying it to you, but although she's a lazy fat lump, and that's not really her fault you know, it's her glands, I still, I still love…......"

"Look! Over there!" shouted Vanessa, putting an end to Terry's pathetic drivel. "It's Whitman! And he's carrying a load of files."

They watched as the terrifying ogre walked towards his blue Rolls Royce cradling a bundle of heavy files under his left arm. He opened the passenger door, placed them on the front seat, then got in the other side and drove away. Vanessa was quick to start her car. "Let's go!"

Pissed off that his love ramble had been cruelly hijacked, Terry asked, "What are you getting so excited about, those files could contain anything?"

"We'll never know sat here, will we!" she barked.

Whitman turned left on to Stamford New Road and headed through the centre of Altrincham towards The Downs. The traffic as usual was moving at a snail's pace, so Vanessa found it easy to keep up. Eventually they picked up speed, following him along Hale Road to the roundabout at the Four Seasons Hotel where he carried straight on and cruised through the airport tunnel towards Wilmslow. From there he drove directly to his home in Prestbury.

The Whitman residence was a detached Georgian mansion nestling in four undulating acres on the outskirts of the village; the type of place Terry would consider buying if his lottery numbers ever came up. Surrounded by a high wall, the house was invisible from the road, so Terry and Vanessa had to make do with parking in a lay-by opposite the entrance gate.

"I reckon he's going to have a meeting with the developers tonight," said Vanessa, switching off the engine but giving the windscreen wipers autonomy to deal with the constant drizzle.

Terry was flabbergasted at her vivid imaginings. "How have you worked that one out?"

"I haven't, exactly. It's just a sort of feeling I've got. A kind of serendipity."

"Who do you think you are, Mystic Meg?"

Within the Accord, tempers were beginning to fray.

"Serendipity means stumbling on something by good fortune. It has nothing to do with psychic powers. If you must know, the phrase was first coined by Horace Walpole in the eighteenth century – long before the National Lottery was ever thought of."

"How interesting. I'm really glad you've told me that. I might have had trouble sleeping otherwise."

Vanessa snapped. "Listen, Terry, if you don't want to be here just say so, and I'll drive you back to Keith's flat right now. You're getting on my nerves! All you've done all day is moan, moan, moan. You're worse than an old woman! At least *I'm* trying to be optimistic about the situation."

He realised he'd gone too far, and that any more insensitive comments would jeopardise the only thing in his life keeping him sane. So he pulled back from the brink. "I'm sorry, Vanessa. I can't apologise enough. I know this business with Whitman's important to you. It is for me as well, by the way. But it's not been easy this past week. My whole world's suddenly turned upside down; starting with Nigel's barbecue and ending in that fuckin camp bed. I'm trying my best to cope, I really am." He laughed. "If you think I'm being miserable with you, spare a thought for Keith; my mood swings must be driving him up the wall. I've even been shouting at the television set, that's how frustrated I am. I mean, what harm have any of those tennis players ever done to me?"

Vanessa didn't understand the question, but his sentiments struck a chord. Her thoughts returned to Railwayman's Cottage. She peered through the car windscreen across the rain-swept country lane and said, her voice tinged with emotion, "You're not the only one having domestic troubles. Losing my job has put a real strain on my relationship with Ian. He keeps going on about how stupid I was writing that article, and how futile all this is. He said we'll never expose Whitman, that people like him are too powerful, and we're just wasting our time. That's why I'm clutching at straws."

Terry felt the urge to put his arm around her shoulder and tell her everything was alright. Instead he asked, "You don't really believe that, do you?…….That we're wasting our time?"

She wanted to say yes, but her natural fighting instincts told her otherwise. "No. I think if we keep at it something's bound to turn up."

134

"You're right," said Terry, trying to appear uplifted. "Tell you what, I'll pour us two more coffees should I?" He rummaged in his bag. "We'll give it until nine o'clock, if no-one shows up by then we might as well call it a night. Agreed?"

"OK." She glanced inside the plum coloured holdall. "Have you got anymore of those chocolate biscuits left?"

Dejected after another fruitless evening, Vanessa dropped Terry off at Keith's flat. It was 9.30pm. The angry wind whipped low black clouds across the sky while the rain continued to hammer down, splashing the pavement with a million full stops, drumming on the car roof like galloping hooves.

"See you tomorrow, around twelve'*ish*," she said, then disappeared up the street in an accelerating spray of tumbling mist. He wanted to shout back, *Why, what's the point?* but thought better of it. He hurried inside and found a mechanical Keith standing behind the Hawaiian drinks bar pouring himself another massive scotch.

"*Aloha*," said Terry. "I'll have one of those if you don't mind. I've had a shite day."

Keith did as he was asked and a second tumbler got the glugging treatment. He set the drinks down on the coffee table, sat opposite his boozy buddy and announced, "You'll never guess who I saw today." Terry raised his glass to sip the petroly scotch, "Cheers. Who?" Keith looked horrified. He stood up and clasped both hands together like a demented evangelist, his eyes full of madness. "Rita! I saw my Rita! After almost two years there she was, plain as day." He fell back into the armchair spent, his bread cast upon the water.

"Bloody hell. How did that come about?"

Outside, above the meat packing factory, a slash of lightning tore open the sky, followed moments later by a deafening, window-pane-shaking clap of thunder. For a stroboscopic second Terry saw the words – Everett Wholesale Meats – flash in the gathering darkness. Slowly, feverishly, Keith developed his amazing revelation.

"Me and Steve had to go into Altrincham to…........."

"That's a coincidence, I was there today. Where about's…......?"

"*Terry*, for *fuck's* sake will you not interrupt when I'm talking. You're always doing it, and it gets right on my tits. Just let me finish for once, will you. Christ!"

"Sorry, mate. Please, carry on. I won't say another word.

135

Promise."

A further rumble of thunder preceded, "Like I was saying, me and Steve went into Altrincham to interview the new captain of Wilmslow Cricket Club. Seeing as he's a barrister, Frank thought it would be a good idea to do a profile on him – you know the sort of thing, pictures of him dressed in his wig and gown, all that shit." (Terry instantly saw the headline – **Battling Barrister Gets Wilmslow Out Of Jail**.) "Anyway, the stuck up bastard, after the interview me and Steve decided to go for a pint in the Orange Tree. Just as we were about to walk in I happened to look through the window," – it was at this point Terry noticed his friend begin to disintegrate – "Well…..there she…was….working behind the…. bar."

"What did you do? Did you go in?"

"No…I just froze. I grabbed Steve by the arm and pretended there was someone in there I owed money to. He believed me, so we went next door to the Hog's Head."

"You should have gone in and had a friendly word with her. A quick hello, to show you're not bothered."

"But I am bothered!"

Keith sat down and drained the tumbler of scotch. "Seeing her again, Terry, it's brought it all back. She looked fantastic. She's lost loads of weight, and her hair's different – shorter, you know, more 'with it'."

"Are you sure it was Rita?"

"Don't take the piss! I'm fuckin devastated here."

"You sound it."

Keith returned to the Hawaiian drinks bar for another liquid truncheon. He looked, standing behind the fake grass awning, like some latter day Robinson Crusoe desperate to leave his isolated beach hell. Outside, the storm cracked and reverberated.

"Listen to that," said Terry. "I bet it'll be nice in the morning."

"Tomorrow's weather is the last thing on my mind…..I want Rita back. I still love the woman."

Terry was startled. "But what about Rose? I thought you were really into her. I thought you had plans."

"I did, until I saw Rita again. Anyway, Rose found me out."

"How do you mean?"

Keith began pacing the room. "That I'm a liar! That everything I said was a load of bullshit."

"Calm down. When did this happen?"

"Tuesday afternoon."

" You never let on."

"I was too embarrassed. Thinking about it now makes me want to throw a rope over the nearest tree."

He sat down again and began his tragic litany. "I bumped into her at the Shell garage on Hawthorn Street. She was at the next pump. I didn't notice her at first. Talk about humiliation."

"What's wrong with her seeing you at the garage? It's a free country. "

"Terry, I'm suppose to be a freelance fashion photographer."

"Yeah, well?"

"Well international fashion photographers with studios in Paris don't go around sloshing half a gallon of petrol into a fuckin moped!"

"Point taken. You should have said you were incognito. It's always best to lie in a foreign language."

"It was too late for anymore lies. She walked over and gave me a vicious look, then she said, all cocky, "A little bird told me you work on that shabby *Wilmslow Comet* as a mere staff photographer. I must say I didn't believe a word of it at first – stupid, trusting old Rose – until I checked through the newspaper and saw your name printed beneath a picture of an hysterical old woman."

Terry couldn't help himself. "Sounds to me like Joey's been telling tales."

Keith ignored the budgie-gag and said, "I don't want to go into anymore detail, but she carried on hassling me right there on the forecourt, accusing me of living in a horrible little council flat in Handforth." He paused for a second as if to digest the truth. "Then she said something along the lines of men being absolutely pathetic, called me a lying insensitive creep, and drove off."

"I bet that hurt, her calling you insensitive."

"Don't remind me, I'm just getting over it."

"I wonder who told her?"

"She must have found out from her friend who plays bridge with Nigel. He was making funny remarks in the office all yesterday, asking me when I was going to Milan to do the next photo shoot for *Vogue*."

"Nigel's a right stirrer."

137

"Never mind about that faggot. Terry, I want to ask you a favour?"

"Shoot."

"Will you come out with me tomorrow night?"

"Let me guess. The Orange Tree. Correct?"

Keith offered a false laugh to drown his embarrassment, his see-throughness. "You can read me like a book."

"Listen, I don't want to be a killjoy, but in my opinion I think you're wasting your time."

Keith raised his voice, "Why?"

"Because Rita's living with a woman for God's sake, and by all accounts she's shaved her head."

"I didn't say she's *shaved her head*!' What I said was, she'd had her hair cut short, that's all. Stop putting words into my mouth." In his mind's eye Terry imagined this 'new Rita' to be a cropped-haired, ear- studded, combat-gear wearing sapphic. This barbarous image forced him on the defensive. "I'm only trying to make you see sense. No use getting hurt twice."

"You *say* she lives with a woman. How do you know for sure?"

"It's common knowledge!"

Keith felt an invisible blow to his self-esteem. His eyes darted about the room as if searching for this 'common knowledge.' "Even if she is, it might just be a sort of phase she's going through. I read some-where that women are more likely to experiment with each other than men. The dirty bitches. Anyway, she's hopefully realised her mistake by now, and when she sees me again I'm sure she'll want me back."

"After living as a lesbian for over a year? Do me a favour. You've seen the kind of tricks they get up to in those porn films. What possible interest do you think she'll have in you after experiencing all that? This gay business, you know, it's not like suddenly changing your regular brand of toilet paper. People don't just swap horses in mid-stream for the sake of it."

Keith felt his path to happiness was being unfairly blocked. He leant forward, put his head in his hands, and said wearily, "All I want to do is walk in the Orange Tree tomorrow night wearing my new gear and show her that I've *changed*. Surely that's not too much to ask? I promise that if she doesn't want me I'll call it quits and never mention her name again."

138

Terry thought, *Some hope*.

Chapter Twelve

The next morning Frank Piper was sitting at his desk wrestling with a serious problem. Arthur Whitman had sent him a fax inviting everyone at the *Comet* to attend a special night out. The fax read, 'Due to the disgraceful incident concerning Terry Howarth and Vanessa Garland, which in my opinion has badly affected morale, my wife and I have decided that all members of staff from the Wilmslow office might benefit from an evening's relaxation at a French restaurant of your choice. This Monday would be preferable. Sadly partners are not invited. Please report back A.S.A.P. with time and venue. A. Whitman.'

Frank's problem was simple. He'd recently accepted the honour to captain Wilmslow Tennis Club's men's fourth team, and, as fate would have it, an important fixture had been arranged on the very evening of the dinner. The opponents were Lymm Tennis Club, and the match was to inaugurate their new clubhouse. What was he to do? He didn't want to let anyone down, least of all Whitman. He studied the fax a second time, then did a quick cross reference with his diary. An ingenious solution presented itself. The match was scheduled to start at 7pm and finish around nine, so Frank reckoned that if he booked a local restaurant in Lymm village, say for 9.30pm, he could play the fixture and attend the dinner without too much hassle. Game set and match! Later that afternoon, after making sure Nigel, Steve and Keith were free to attend (Keith in particular complained that 9.30pm was far too late to eat, before Nigel tut-tutted and said that not everyone had to have their tea on the dot of six o'clock) he faxed Arthur Whitman back with the details, plus, 'Thanks again for the invitation, we are all looking forward to taking up your most generous offer,' as a grovelling postscript.

Throughout the afternoon Keith was ensconced in his dark-room, developing several rolls of film he'd taken the previous day.

Frank had sent him to a nearby farm in Mobberley to photograph the pathetic inmates of 'Caroline Bowker's Donkey Sanctuary'. Skin and bone mooching round a shit-splattered yard, the animals were also in a bad way. Keith wondered why this emaciated lady – wearing thick brown corduroy trousers and a green polo-neck woolly jumper – bothered to look after these biblical creatures with their designer crucifixes and doll-like eyelashes. What kind of heavenly force drove such people to perform acts of wanton kindness was a complete mystery to him. Nevertheless, he chose to use a rather touching image of six scrawny donkeys being fed by their anorexic saviour. Whilst enlarging the photograph, his mind percolated with excitement at tonight's encounter with Rita. How would she react seeing him again? Would his smart clothes and alcohol-free manner do the trick? If they did get back together would their sex life be extra kinky? Thoughts, like rats, just keep on multiplying.

Keith arrived home at 5.30pm to find Vanessa's car parked outside his flat. He imagined her lying naked in bed waiting for him to return, waiting for the sound of his key to scrape the lock before shouting, "I'm in here, baby. Come and get it." Instead he found her fully clothed chatting to Terry in the front room. He'd seen far too many porn films. The unemployed pair looked serious, as if they'd been caught discussing a secret missile instillation. Keith asked, "How did it go today?"

"Terrible," answered Terry. He saw Vanessa's reaction to his negative comment and quickly made a joke. "This undercover lark's not as glamorous as they make out in the films."

"Talking about glamorous," said Keith, bragging. "Arthur Whitman and his wife are taking me, Frank, Nigel and Steve out to a posh French restaurant in Lymm on Monday night. Frank called it a 'bonding exercise.' Should be interesting, I've never met his wife before."

Vanessa looked as though the winning lottery ticket had dropped into her lap. She gave Terry a wide-eyed stare, then confirmed with Keith, "This Monday night? You're all going out for a meal this Monday night?"

"Yeah, that's what I said."

"Which restaurant?"

"Er.. Frank did say…. I remember now, it's a place called Lymm Bistro. Sounds dead expensive doesn't it. *Bistro*." He repeated the word, luxuriating in its promise of free French cuisine. It seemed an age since he'd last perused a decent menu without the prices almost giving him a heart attack. And all that wine. Gratis!

"What time?"

"Just a minute," said Keith, concerned his free night out might be spoilt. "You're not planning on turning up are you? Well I wouldn't if I were you."

"No way!" said Vanessa. "We wouldn't be seen dead out with you lot. I'm just being nosy, that's all." She got up from the chair, smartish. "I must be off. Terry, will you walk me to my car, I want to discuss something with you."

He followed her outside like a lap dog. Keith watched from the kitchen window as they both stood on the kerb, deep in conversation. Terry felt as though ice water was being poured down his spine. Vanessa said, "Well, that settles it. Monday night's the night. Funny how fate intervenes. Just when it seems you're beaten, something always turns up." She noticed Terry's frightened expression. "I hope you're not thinking of backing out? After all, it was your idea in the first place."

"Me? No." His bowels slackened. "Once I say I'll do something, I'm always true to my word."

"Good. I'll be in touch over the weekend. Bye." The clunk of car door was followed by a hastily revved engine then a scattering of loose chippings.

He stood on the pavement, flummoxed. That just about put the top hat on it, crowning a miserable day. It had begun amusingly enough. They were sitting in Vanessa's Honda Accord overlooking the entrance to Allied Northern Newspapers when she told him about her massive row with Ian. Terry loved every second of, "I couldn't stand his childish behaviour any longer, his mood swings, so I threatened to kick him out." It was at this point that things started to go wrong. "Well, Terry, it certainly had the desired effect. We sat down, and for the first time in ages we actually communicated like adult human beings. We had a long talk covering a whole host of subjects. Ian was marvellous. He set the record straight. He said he'd been miserable because of me. He said that because I'd lost my job, he felt helpless and blamed himself for not trying more."

Terry thought, *Bullshittt!*

"Anyway, to cut a long story short, Ian's decided to help the cause."

This idea incensed him. "How? What can *he* do?"

The bombshell descended, whistling through the air with callous ease. "What can *he* do? Terry, I've not told you this before, and it mustn't go any further, but Ian's spent some time in prison – for burglary. Evidently he has a talent for getting in and out of other people's houses."

"Do you mean to say you're living with a jail bird?"

This stung Vanessa. "It all happened a long time ago. He's a reformed character now."

"So what are you suggesting?"

"As I say, for the good of the cause Ian's decided to come out of retirement and do one last job."

"And?"

"He said he'd be more than happy to lead the raid on the Whitman mansion."

Terry imploded, "That's a bit drastic. I mean, I know the Whitman's live on their own, but you know as well as I do from all the hours we've spent outside their house, they hardly ever go out. At least his wife doesn't. When would we get the opportunity?"

"We'll just have to make one. All this hanging around staring out of the car window, it's getting us nowhere. Don't forget, we've only got a little over a week. If we haven't managed to find anything concrete to put before the public inquiry, we're sunk."

"But the house is bound to be alarmed like a soddin fortress! Places like that always are! And you've seen that pack of Dobermans he's got running loose in the grounds!" Terry instantly saw the headline – **THREE UNIDENTIFIED BODIES TORN TO PIECES BY GUARD DOGS.**

"That's why Ian's coming along. Like I said, he's an expert."

"Sounds like one hell of an expert to me, spending time behind bars."

"He wasn't caught on the job. Someone grassed him up."

Terry knew it was useless to argue. He also knew, sitting there in the car, about to delve into a pale Tupperware box for yet another cheese sandwich, that with God's grace an opportunity to embark on such a lunatic escapade would never present itself. The Lord, however, moves in mysterious ways.

He walked back inside the flat feeling utterly dejected, and not a little scared. Fate makes criminals of us all whether we like it or not. Keith appeared half naked wrapped in a towel. "What was that all about?" he asked, drying his hair.

"Oh, nothing. Just going over the itinerary for next week."

"Anything interesting?"

"Nope."

"Right then, fancy a drink? Might as well start the evening off with a bang."

Keith was a nervous wreck, shuffling about the front room in time-lapse fashion like a robber caught on a security video. In between lethal amounts of scotch poured from the Hawaiian drinks bar, he kept shouting at Terry to hurry up and get ready. His friend obliged, eventually, wearing black denim jeans and a mauve coloured sweat-shirt. Finally at 7.15pm the taxi arrived and they were on their way. Terry had to admit, his friend did look smart, even though he'd over done it with the aftershave. Rita wouldn't stand a chance.

The plan was to have a few scoops in Wilmslow, then catch the 288 bus into Altrincham. The Swan being their first port of call, double vodkas were thought necessary. They next tried the newly opened Blue Lamp, on Green Lane, an ex-Police station transformed into a public house. Keith recalled how he was arrested years ago by two burly officers and brought to this place on a trumped-up drunk and disorderly charge, being dragged through the same double doors that now introduced a welcoming bar instead of a gruff sergeant's desk. He remembered passing out on the station floor, then coming-to surrounded by several policemen bending over him, their black uniforms and silvery buttons a mini universe above his spinning head. Forced to spend the night in the cells, he took revenge by joyfully pissing up the wall.

Directly outside the pub they clambered aboard the Star Line bus to Altrincham. The evening sun shone buttery-yellow, slow-ly baking cherry Ferraris and nut-brown Porsches locked inside Stratton's crystal matrix. Terry and Keith loved passing this ultra-building, a glass temple to speed, and like two schoolboys they craned their necks and peered through the shifting bus window at the latest dream machines. Morley Green, Hale Barns, Hale, then the long sweep down Stamford New Road to be deposited alongside the terminus clock tower. 9.10pm. Just enough time for a quick few in the Bricklayer's Arms before tackling the Orange Tree. Inside the set-back-pub on George Street, Keith looked a worried man. Pensive, nervy, dry-mouthed, he attacked the fresh pint of Guinness put in front of him.

"*Whoa*, steady on," offered Terry. "You don't want to be slurring your words. I thought the whole point of this mission was to show Rita you're a changed man."

"I won't," he burped. "And I am."

Glass-eyed Keith. Funny how one's clothes tend to droop and crumple the more alcohol one tends to pour down one's neck. Stagger was probably an exaggeration. They tottered out of the *Brickies* and turned left along George Street's pedestrianised causeway, deserted save for the odd gangly youth haunting the precinct. At W.H. Smith they took a short cut through a narrow passageway. Here Keith put both hands against the wall as if trying to prevent it from toppling over, then spewed up, a steamy cascade splattering against the brickwork, running down the pointing in chunky rivulets.

"Fuckin hell!" growled Terry. "I *told* you not to drink too much. You've had double what I've had."

"It's not the booze, it's the nerves."

Passing under a streetlight, Terry noticed bits of vomit clinging to the lapel of his friend's jacket. "You can't face Rita looking like that," he said. "We'll have to go to the Malt Shovel and get you cleaned up."

"Cheers, mate."

The Malt Shovel was crowded; heads, shoulders and elbows surrounding the smoke filled bar. An ageing jazz band miraculously containing a blind piano player played 'When The Saints Go Marching In'. After visiting the gents to remove shards of tomato skins from Keith's jacket, they re-emerged smiling into the foggy bar parlour.

"Let's have one more round before we go to the Orange Tree," shouted Keith, above the jazzy hullabaloo. "Otherwise I don't think I'll be able to go through with it."

Terry shook his head and ordered two Carlsberg Specials, threatening, "You better had, making me come all this way."

"What's wrong! We're having a good time aren't we?"

This question led them to finish their drinks in speedy silence and begin the two hundred metres or so walk up towards the Old Market Place high on Dunham Road. It was now 10.05pm. Dusk had given the streetlights halos, and the moon shone an Islamic crescent. A crowd meandered in the square before the Orange Tree, their laughter and tinkling glasses percolating the warm summer air. Hanging

baskets dripped from the pub's creamy façade while a yellowish light blazed from within. Keith bore witness to this pleasant scene and felt his stomach give instant birth to a billion wriggling maggots, each one burrowing, Rita, Rita was inside. They crossed the busy A56. Terry saw his friend's petrified face and asked, "Do you think you can handle it?"

Keith slumped down on a wooden bench outside the pub. "No, I don't think I can. Not at the moment, anyway. Why don't you go inside and get the drinks, then report back. I just need a few minutes to compose myself."

Terry walked in and joined the scrum at the bar – it seemed half the population of Altrincham needed a drink. He looked around and noticed Pete the landlord, an amiable chap in his late forties, chatting to Denis Irwin of Manchester United. *Fifteen grand a week for kicking a ball about*, thought Terry. A woman in her late forties next caught his eye, pushing through the crowd collecting glasses. It took a few seconds and a couple more furtive glances before he realised it was Rita. My God, she'd changed alright, changed for the better. His expectation of her having turned into a Bull Dyke was totally unfounded. She wore a pretty white blouse and a lime green skirt, her brassy hair cut short over her ears in a cute demi-wave. She'd also lost weight, at least two stone, and she moved through the crowded pub with the confidence of someone at ease with life, laughing and joking with the drunken punters.

"What can I get you?" whined the South African barman. Terry ordered the drinks and suddenly felt his sixth sense being invaded. He glanced sideways to catch Keith's face peering at him through the leaded window. He was gesticulating wildly, pointing towards Rita who was now washing glasses at the other end of the bar. Terry gave him an annoying look that said, 'I know, I can see her, you stupid bastard'. He took the drinks outside.

"Did you speak to her?" asked Keith frantically, his watery eyes bulging like a frog about to croak. "Did you tell her I was here?"

"Give me a chance. I can't just walk up to her and say, 'By the way your ex-husband's outside, you've not seen him for two years but I was wondering if you could possibly take him back,' now can I?"

"I didn't ask you to say that. You sarcastic twat!"

"Look, if you're not satisfied, if you won't let me go about it in my own way, you're perfectly welcome to go in there and do the job yourself. Don't start giving me grief."

"I'm sorry. I'm all on edge. You see, I've been looking forward to this moment for over a year. I guess I'm a bit impatient for the right result." He took a long swig from his pint, licked his lips and said, "But *was* I right or *was* I wrong? Doesn't she look *fantastic*?"

"Alright, alright," said Terry, getting more uptight by the minute. "I'll go and have a word with her. Christ! Oh, and by the way, don't be spying on me. If Rita catches sight of your hideous visage, you'll ruin it for yourself. Your best bet is to go to the Hog's Head right now and I'll meet you in there when I've finished."

"Sound tactics those."

Before walking the short distance to the Orange Tree's competitor, Keith took one last peek through the window to see his cohort push his way to the corner of the bar where Rita stood busily washing glasses. She looked up, recognised Terry with a friendly smile, and they began talking in earnest. Keith felt his bowels give way. He quickly downed his *alfresco* pint and hurried over the cobbled road into the Hog's Head. The place was full of kids, no wonder they need-

147

ed security staff on the door. One of the bouncers in particular – wearing a black nylon jacket, combat trousers and Doc Martens – was a vicious looking skinhead; the type capable of gleefully throwing his own crippled mother head first down a lift shaft, followed by her guide-dog, on Christmas Morning. Keith ordered half a pint, thinking a clear head might come in handy later. Only when he tried to focus on a beer mat did he realise how intoxicated he'd become.

"He'll be absolutely devastated when I tell him," said Terry. "But if that's your final word."

Rita plunged another pint glass into the swirling soap-suds. "It's his own fault. All those years he took me for granted." Her voice was calm and measured, baring no hint of malice. "The funny thing is, and you can tell him this if you like," – here Rita's oval face lit up, her bright green eyes with their flecks of gold alive, vibrant – "If it wasn't for him being such a terrible husband, I never would have met Sam."

Sam, she uttered the name with real devotion. This confused him.

"Sam? I thought you'd shacked up with a woman?"

Rita laughed. "I have, her name's Samantha."

He felt ridiculous, like a hungry child biting into a plastic banana. "Oh, I see," was all he could muster.

"I want you to understand, Terry, that for the first time in my life I've found out what true love really means," – the word love always made him blush – "It's not just sex," Rita explained, noticing his crimson tint, "I know that's what most men think when they imagine two gay women living together. It's tenderness and understanding. Basically what I'm trying to say is, I've found my true soul mate and she just happens to be a woman. Someone kind, gentle and sincere. Three things Keith knew very little about. Or ever will, come to that."

"So you don't want him back, then?"

Rita shook her head and gave a terse, "No, not really."

"I better go and put him out of his misery. He's waiting for me in the Hog's Head right now. As I said, he'll be devastated."

"I'm sorry I can't talk for longer, but as you see we're mad busy."

"That's alright, don't worry about it. Anyway, it's been nice talking to you. I think I understand what you've been trying to say."

As he turned to go Rita said, "Oh, Terry, I forgot to ask, how's Dawn keeping?"

He blushed a deeper, claret red. "We've spilt up," was his epilogue.

Keith had parked himself at a table near the window. He kept scanning the doorway of the Orange Tree for signs of Terry's emaciated figure, willing it to appear. His drunken state had induced a fit of extreme melancholy. Trying to recall at least one happy event from his ten year marriage proved useless. Instead, a kaleidoscope of arguments, broken promises, abusive language, back-handers, thrown-up meals, obscene sexual demands and coarse insults flitted through his memory banks like an MTV video. And that was just his wedding night! Where were all the good times? He simply couldn't remember. At last Terry reappeared, walking towards the Hog's Head with grim determination. Keith's head swayed puppet-like. "Well, how'd'it go?"

Terry grabbed a chair and straight away realised his friend was in a bad way, a human dam filled with alcohol ready to burst it's emotional banks. Sensitive diplomatic phrases were needed in order to avoid a catastrophe, but he ended up sounding like a police spokesman on *Crimewatch*. "Not good. Rita said she was extremely grateful to you for asking, but at the present time she's quite happy with her lot. She did add, though, that if in the near future she did become unhappy, with her lot, you'd be the first person she'd contact in order to rectify the situation."

Keith felt a whirlpool dragging him down. " Is it true she's living, living with a woman?"

Terry nodded.

"That's it then. Finished." Tears began to seep through his crinkley lids. "I might as well kill myself."

"Don't talk rubbish. Look, last orders have just gone, let me get you a nice double malt."

They stayed for another twenty minutes before the terrifying skinhead turfed them out. Terry had to prop Keith up against the side of the pub, hoping the fresh air might bring him round. It wasn't the fresh air that put the life back into him, though, it was the sight of Rita strolling nonchalantly out of the Orange Tree towards a waiting taxi. Keith wanted to run after her, throw himself onto the ground and beg her forgiveness. Even in *his* drunken state he knew this action would be useless, knew she would only end up hating him even more. Instead he watched her approach the taxi and open the passenger door….. Something was wrong, she didn't get in. She just stood there on the kerb calm as you like. Who was she waiting for? A madcap idea splashed through Keith's brain. She was waiting for *him*! The door was being held open so that *he* might run across the square and dive in! Terry was a fucking liar! She *did* want him back after all! No sooner had he decided to make a move than a rather tall female hurried from the Orange Tree and caught Rita up. Keith froze Medusa style as both women embraced and shared a long lingering kiss full on the mouth. The taxi drove away moments later with its love cargo snuggled in the back. Terry acted swiftly to prevent his friend achieving melt-down right there on the pavement. "Let's jump in that other cab and get back to the flat. I don't know about you but I've seen enough to last me a lifetime."

"You're not wrong," slurred Keith, hanging on to Terry's shoulder while he dragged him across the square and shoved him into the second taxi.

"Where to?" asked the driver.

"Handforth."

"Your mate looks in a bad way." (He was one of those chatty types).

"Yeah."

Heading out of Altrincham, the cab driver, a hunched-up sixty year old with a bulbous nose and splintered teeth, kept glancing in his rear view mirror at the miserable pair sat in the back. They'd definitely had a bad night, he could tell. He hadn't spent half his life ferrying people around without learning a thing or two about body language. A regular Freud on wheels, he prided himself on being able to suss out his punters problems in an instant, then, once sussed, to dispense some philosophical witticism that would immediately cheer them up. Yep, no doubt about it, by the look on their faces they were suffering from women trouble alright. Probably blown out by a couple of tarts on the trawl for rich businessmen from Hale. Well, Handforth, you've got no chance have you? Should have lied and said Wilmslow. He gave them a cheeky grin via the mirror, coughed and said breezily, "Hey, did you see those two dykes kissing? Absolutely disgusting. And they weren't bothered were they? Flaunt it in front of you they do nowadays. I honestly don't know what the world's coming to, do you? Gay rights! I'd give them gay rights. I tell you what, Hitler had the right idea if you ask me."

Chapter Thirteen

The Break-in

Monday. 6.20pm.

The twelve seater minibus hired by Wilmslow Tennis Club left the M56 motorway at junction seven, negotiated the massive roundabout and headed towards Lymm along the A56. It contained the men's fourth team; an assorted bunch of middle-aged, middle-class professionals keen to leave their wives at home on this glorious summer evening and do battle with their opposite numbers at Lymm Tennis Club. Also in the minibus, sitting along the back seat next to Frank, were the reluctant threesome Keith, Nigel and Steve. Frank had enticed them along with the kind offer of a lift. "No use driving or getting a taxi," he'd said to them that morning in his office. "If Arthur Whitman's treating us we might as well all go together and have a good drink, seeing as it's free."

Frank's real objective behind this generous act was this; as newly appointed captain he was keen to impress some of the wealthier members of the team – so what better way than to publish an article in the *Comet*, accompanied by classy photos, of the team's fabulous exploits. People just love seeing themselves featured in the newspaper.

Tucked away in the inside pocket of Keith's corduroy jacket was Vanessa's mobile phone. This was to be used as a direct line of communication throughout the evening to inform the burgling trio of Whitman's whereabouts. When Terry mentioned the plan to him over the weekend Keith was flabbergasted, saying they could all end up inside if it went wrong. Terry finally convinced him to become a fifth-columnist by playing the loyalty card – hadn't he done his level best to help with the Rita situation, and wasn't he the one who punched the obnoxious taxi driver in the face after the fascist bastard dropped them off.

The minibus swept passed Lymm Dam – its dark waters entertaining a host of fishermen whose concentration was peppered by the quarterly chimes of church bells -- then turned right along Brookfield Road and arrived at the tennis club spot on 6.30pm. From the back seat Frank rallied the troops. "OK everyone, let's get one thing straight. Although this is a friendly to inaugurate their new clubhouse, I want total commitment. Focus on the job in hand, try not to hit the ball too hard, none of us are Boris Becker, and remember one thing, all fifty-fifty line calls are to be argued over; don't let the home team bully you into giving up a single point. Is that clear? Good. Now, I want you changed and out on court in fifteen minutes. Best of luck everyone."

As they clambered from the minibus Frank was met by the club's president, Alan Ranscome. He was a portly chap in his late fifties with thinning grey hair and clipped moustache. Keith thought he resembled Eric Pollard from *Emmerdale*. He bounded forward, hand outstretched, and spoke with the hint of a scouse accent. "Hello, Frank. Nice to see you again. We'll, what do you think of our new clubhouse? Not bad, eh? Isn't it about time Wilmslow invested in one? Ha, ha."

"Hi, Alan. Yes, I'll have to mention it to our committee. Still, call me old-fashioned, but I was a big fan of the old wooden place. Dilapidated it may have been, at least it had charm. If you don't mind me saying so, these new brick buildings, and I see you've modelled it on Bowdon's, to me they lack a certain amount of character."

The president thought, *Typical snobby Wilmslow. The bastards are only jealous*, but managed a smile and said, "We'll make it a quick two setter, then afterwards I'll given you the grand tour and we can have a few drinks."

"Afraid I won't have time to look round the place. Thanks for the offer, but I've got a dinner engagement at nine thirty."

"Nine thirty!" spluttered the president, "It won't take us *that* long to beat you."

Keith detected a touch of needle creeping in. He checked his camera and said to Steve, who was eyeing up one of the female members sitting out on the veranda, "This might not be that bad after all."

"Humm, you're right," answered Steve, noticing the faint smile of a 'come on' pass across the lips of the short skirted young lady.

152

Nigel said, "I'm just popping into the men's changing rooms to see if any of them require a drink before the start of play. Won't be long. *Traa.*"

7.05pm.
Ian began grinding up the sleeping tablets with a pestle and mortar while Vanessa rolled chunks of mincemeat into tight little globes the size of golf balls. Terry watched as Ian impregnated all twenty with the powdered pacifier.

"These little beauties would knock a fuckin elephant out," said Ian proudly, standing back from the kitchen table inside Railwayman's Cottage to admire his handy work. "Those guard dogs you were telling me about won't stand a chance. They'll be fast asleep in ten minutes. Guaranteed!"

Vanessa, concerned for the animals welfare, said tentatively, "Ian, you're sure no harm will come to the dogs? They'll just fall asleep and wake up in a couple of hours feeling a little groggy, right? Is that right?"

"Yeah, they'll be fine."

Terry, nervous as hell about the night's venture, pronounced, "I don't know why you're so bothered about the bleedin dogs. I can assure you that if any one of those vicious swines wakes up and gets hold of us, we'll be feeling more than a little groggy."

"Animals have rights too you know!"

"Well I tell you what, why don't you climb over the wall on your own and try giving them a dog biscuit? Let's see how far you get doing that!"

Ian intervened. "Come on you two, this is supposed to be a precise operation. No use losing your cool. We've got to rely on one-another, remember."

"It's alright for her, she'll be sat in a lay-by outside the house. We're the one's risking our necks."

"Hang about, Terry. This *was* your idea in the first place," shouted Ian. "Don't think you can change your mind and back out now! Anyway, we need Vanessa to keep watch."

"I'm not thinking of backing out. I wouldn't dream of it," said Terry, dreaming of it.

"I hope not. I've gone to a lot of trouble over this. A lot of trouble. Now, let's go over it one more time."

153

"Coffee anyone?" asked Vanessa.

It was a simple enough plan – drive over to Prestbury, wait for Keith to call on the mobile phone to say the Whitmans had arrived in Lymm, then, under the cover of darkness, drug the guard dogs, climb over the wall, break in and begin the search for any incriminating documents. What could be simpler? The layout of the house was provided by Terry. Eight years ago, well before Vanessa's time, he and the rest of the *Comet's* staff had been invited to attend the Whitman's silver wedding anniversary. The bash was held in a huge brightly coloured marquee close to the house. He remembered slipping away while the tented knees-up was in full swing, and wandering around the empty mansion on the pretext of looking for the loo. He certainly got a privileged glimpse into this mini Murdoch's kingdom. It was like strolling through a glossy edition of *Cheshire Life*! Talk about plush! He entered the house via the conservatory – not really a conservatory in the true sense of the word like you see advertised in the newspapers; a poxy-Perspex lean-to they charge the earth for, this was more like an aristocrat's Hot House, with giant palms and a bubbling fountain – from there he took a nosy down a long corridor, carpeted in the finest shag-pile, passing room after room filled with expensive antique furniture. (You had to hand it to Whitman, he may have been a vicious gangster but the man certainly had taste). About to enter – I've-just-got-to-see-what's-on-the-other-side-of-these-two-big-bastard-doors – Terry was discovered by Mrs. Whitman who asked him what on earth he was doing. When he replied innocently that he was looking for the little boy's room, she replied, all sarcastic, "You certainly won't find it in there, that's my husband's private study. Now I must insist you leave the house immediately and use one of the outside lavatories provided for your convenience."

So the upshot was, with the knowledge gained from Terry's drunken escapade, at least when they broke into the place they wouldn't be running round like morons ransacking every drawer in every room.

"Yes please, Vanessa," said Terry. "I will have a coffee if you don't mind."

8.11pm.

Frank was getting absolutely slaughtered at tennis. His entire team were. It was nothing short of an embarrassing fiasco. Everything seemed to be going wrong. Their serving was appalling; they were either hitting the ball too hard so it flew miles out or dropping it pansy-style over the net making for easy, killer returns. It was sod's law, once one player gets the jitters it affects everyone else. Out of the eight singles matches played thus far, Lymm were ahead in all eight. After a short break the doubles were to be played. A humiliation was on the cards, one that would go down in gold-leafed history as, **Lymm Tennis Club** (inaugural match to celebrate opening of new clubhouse) **12, Wilmslow Tennis Club 0.** It looked as if Frank might be the first ever captain to preside over a whitewash. Not only that, but the whole thing was being captured for posterity by a smirking Keith, his camera snapping every duff shot and contorted expression, and boy was he enjoying it. At one point, after a particularly gruelling rally where Frank had been given the run-around, Keith took a photo of him prostrate on the ground. Even Nigel had to laugh, though he kept his amusement well hidden, as Frank yelled, "You're putting me off, for Christ's sake! Point that thing elsewhere!" But it just made matters worse, because the very members of the team Frank was trying to impress, the ones he'd promised instant fame, "I think I can safely say we'll all look good in the sports pages. Something to show the grandchildren, eh boys?" were so busy looking at the camera their incessant posing put them off their game. At the break, a red faced Frank gathered together his beleaguered troops who all agreed that Keith should be banned from the courtside. When he was informed of their decision he wasn't the least bit bothered. He'd managed to collect more than enough hilarious shots to last him a lifetime thank you very much, and it meant that for the second half of the match he had the freedom to give the bar a good seeing-to. Steve's job was the hardest, though, having the unenviable task of writing a laudatory article excusing the pantomime-like performance that would meet with Frank and his wealthy cohort's approval. It was nigh impossible! My God, how could anyone! It would be like saying Belsen was a complete misunderstanding.

9.02pm.

Vanessa walked into the living room carrying two black jogging suits and two pairs of black leather gloves. Ian and Terry were glued to the TV watching an episode of The X Files.

"Here," she said, holding the night fashions out in front of her. "You'd better get changed into these."

Ian grabbed his and went upstairs saying, " Move over Scully and Mulder."

"How can your boyfriend make jokes at a time like this?" asked Terry, his inner gut tightening in spasmodic waves.

Vanessa laughed, "That's what I love about him, he just doesn't give a shit. Anyway, talking about the time, you'd better get changed. We'll have to go in ten minutes."

Go? He didn't want to hear the word Go, he wanted to here the word Stay. Stay, and forget the whole thing. Silence. Not silence, Scully was talking in that monotone way she has without moving her lips. He couldn't put it off any longer. He walked into the kitchen with his black bundle. It smelt musty……...as if the cat had been sleeping on it. How he wished he was that cat; running around outside chasing mice without a care in the world. He noticed the cat-flap and wanted to dive through it. That's the thing about animals; when you're having a good time there's no way you'd even consider change places with them, but put something distasteful on the horizon like a terrifying visit to the dentist or a gut wrenching job interview and the idea of turning into a mangy crow suddenly becomes attractive.

Terry re-appeared in the living room resembling a spindly extra from a James Bond epic, the faceless type that always gets killed even before the opening titles have been shown. Ian was next, a suave member of S.P.E.C.T.E.R. He threw Terry a tin of black shoe polish and said, "Put this in your pocket, for later."

Terry thought this crude camouflage idea not only over the top but down-right dangerous. He wasn't stupid, he knew that guard dogs are trained to attack black people. On sight. He remembered seeing a documentary on TV about South Africa during apartheid. Those savage police dogs couldn't wait to slip the leash and attack the stomping Townshippers. He did as he was told, and without a word put the shoe polish in his pocket.

"Let's go," said Vanessa.

9.15pm.

Frank and his defeated colleagues showered and changed in silence. They'd just about managed to avoid the dreaded whitewash but still the score was a humiliation. **Lymm Tennis Club 10. Wilmslow Tennis Club 2**. Keith reckoned he heard the president of Lymm order his two final doubles partners to throw their matches so as not to cause bad blood between the two clubs. After all it is only a game. Frank left the changing rooms and joined Steve, Nigel and Keith in the bar. He said to them, "Hurry up and finish your drinks, we're meeting Mr. and Mrs. Whitman in fifteen minutes and I don't want us to be late."

"What about the rest of your team mates?" asked Keith. "I thought you said they were going to give us a lift to the restaurant in the minibus."

Frank was loathed to explain, he wanted to leave the club as quickly as possible. "Don't be so bloody lazy, man. It's only a ten minute stroll into the village. Now come on." "Yeah," said Steve, swallowing the dregs of his half pint. "The walk'll do us good."

Keith had never been to Lymm village before and he didn't half think it was posh, with its quaint Victorian sandstone monument, its silvery weir enclosed on one side by a row of whitewashed cottages, its jumble of shops and pubs climbing steadily towards a narrow canal bridge. Nigel adored the place, often coming for long dreamy walks on crisp autumnal afternoons. On more than one occasion he'd been sorely tempted to buy a property, but the larger louts hanging round the cross swigging Tennants Extra put him off. His part of Ashley, thank God, was a thug-free zone.

Lymm Bistro was tucked away down a side street opposite the Spread Eagle public house. Much to Frank's consternation, Arthur Whitman and his wife were already seated at the bar perusing the menu when they walked in.

"Terribly sorry we're late," grovelled Frank. "The er…....."

"Nonsense. You're not late at all," said Whitman, full of himself. "In fact you're five minutes early. Anyway, sod the time, we're here to enjoy ourselves. Now, what's the drinks order?"

Keith asked for a double scotch, then went off to use the toilet. He made sure the place was empty before pulling out Vanessa's mobile phone. He dialled the number and pressed 'enter'. Within a few seconds the other phone rang (it was Ian's – when Vanessa bought her's Ian was so upset she had to buy him one just to stop the moaning).

"Hello," answered Vanessa.

Keith closed the cubicle door and sat on the loo. "It's me, Keith. Arthur Whitman and his wife are in the restaurant right now."

"Good, that's good. Try to make sure they stay as long as

possible. And don't forget, ring me the moment they're about to leave. Thanks Keith."

"I will. Good luck. Over and out."

He slipped the phone back into his inside jacket pocket, flushed the toilet for effect, then pretended to wash his hands before rejoining the others in the bar. *This espionage lark really whets the appetite!* Thought Keith. He picked up his double scotch and all five were shown to their table by a rather pretty waitress Steve couldn't keep his eyes off.

9.50pm.

Food was the last thing on Terry's mind as he sat in the back of Vanessa's Honda Accord blacking up his face. Due to the late evening cloud cover, the break-in had been brought forward by half an hour. The car stood in a deserted lay-by opposite the house, its perimeter wall seemingly as tall as a castle's. And getting taller by the minute. One of the unseen guard dogs suddenly let out a God Almighty howl, icing the blood in Terry's veins.

"I'll soon put a stop to that," laughed Ian.

"The smell of polish always reminds me of school," said Vanessa, turning round to inspect her brave back-seat burglars. "You two look really funny," she went on. "Like a pair of chimney sweeps from Mary Poppins."

Jesus Christ! Thought Terry, the whites of his eyes enlarging, *The woman's on another planet.*

Ian inspected his brother-in-arms and noticed a glaring mistake. "I hope you don't mind me saying this, man. It's just that, your bald head, I really think you need to, sort of, you know, cover *all* of it, in polish, otherwise….........."

Terry felt himself blush beneath his ebony outer coating. He realised what he must have looked like and grabbed the tin. He took off his gloves and reluctantly finished the job, even going so far as smearing the stuff in his ears.

"OK," said Ian, picking up the Tupperware box containing the knockout meat balls. "It's feeding time." A gleaming grin appeared across his camouflaged-face. "You two stay put while I administer the sedatives." He got out of the car, crossed the lane and clambered atop the perimeter wall. Terry and Vanessa watched him carefully shimmy up an overhanging tree branch, then vanish into the thick foliage. He began shaking one of the branches wildly.

"What's he *doing*?" asked Terry.

Ian's plan took immediate effect. The rustling branch was answered by several distant barks that soon became a single cluster of growls beneath the tree. One by one, over a ten minute period, the growls subsided as each dog gobbled up three or four paralysing pellets. Ian's figure could be seen moments later perched on an outside branch of the tree, beckoning.

"Right," said Terry, petrified. "I'm going in."

"Don't forget the tool bag," said Vanessa, handing him a black holdall. "Oh, and remember, three blasts on the horn means Whitman's on his way back. So get the hell out of there as fast as you can. Good luck to both of you."

"Cheers. I'll need it."

He hurried across the lane, his legs whirling spindles, flung the holdall grenade-like over the wall and climbed over. He hit the dewy ground with a thud. Getting to his feet, he noticed Ian stood at the base of a tree surrounded by five sleeping Dobermanns – a dark star of snoring snouts.

"They're out cold," he said. "Let's get on with it."

They ran toward the Wh.itman mansion, which could be seen huge through slices of trees. It would be nice at this particular moment to say an owl hooted, but it didn't. Just the rustling of summer leaves and the occasional sound of a car swishing by the perimeter wall. They reached the back of the house, both men crouching down out of breath beside a rhododendron bush, its perfume glorious at this late hour.

Terry gasped, "As….far….as…I…can….remember, the conservatory's over there." He pointed to a shadowy crystal mass reflecting the moon. "And the entrance is behind that pillar."

Ian delved into the holdall and produced two black Balaclavas. He handed one to Terry and said, "Here, you better put this on."

"I don't believe it!" whispered Terry, fuming. "I just don't fuckin believe it! You let me spread all that shite over my head when all along you had these tucked away in your bag. You stupid twat!"

"Hey, calm down. I didn't know they were there until now. Blame Vanessa. She must have packed them, cause I certainly didn't." Terry wanted to get this thing over and done with, the prospect of those Dobermanns sleep walking twanged at his already elasticised bowels. "I'm not arguing with you," he said. "Let's go."

Both men stood up and ran towards the house, their hurrying feet a snap, crackle and pop across the gravel drive. Reaching the entrance doors to the conservatory, Terry said, "This is it. This is the place where I got in last time."

Ian peered through the glass, but all he could make out was mini jungle of palms, dangling vines and the silvery spray of an indoor fountain. He asked, "Where's the door into the house?"

"Over there."

"Where? I can't see anything."

"Just get me inside and I'll show you. It'll come back to me, I'm positive."

"You better had be."

Ian took out a pencil torch from his back pocket, unzipped the holdall and shone in its baby beam. Terry expected to see an array of sophisticated electronic equipment necessary to thwart a country house, such as jammers and by-passers, like those fancy gadgets used in *Mission Impossible*. He was shocked instead to find illuminated nothing more than a lump hammer, chisel and crowbar. He studied the contents of the bag for a good thirty seconds, then asked, tentatively, hoping above all hope there might be a secret compartment, "Ian, what's this lot?"

"It's the gear."

"To be used for what, exactly?"

Ian scoffed, "To be used for what. To be used for breaking in."

"But I thought you were going to disable the alarm first."

"Disable the alarm! Who do you think I am, The Saint? You've seen too many fuckin films, man."

"But…......."

"Listen, there's no way I can even attempt to mess about with this alarm system. I wouldn't know where to start. It's too complicated."

"But Vanessa told me you were an expert at breaking into houses."

"I am. Terraced houses. Nothing along these lines!"

"But you said…......"

"I said I'd get you in the house, right. Well that's just what I intend to do."

"How?"

160

"Like this."

Ian picked up the lump hammer and smashed a large pane of glass, sending triangular shards crashing onto the conservatory's stone floor. He pushed his way through the broken window. "Come on, we've got half an hour."

Terry froze. "You fuckin nut case!"

"*Come on*, that's how long it takes before the security firm gets here. Hurry up, I'm not standing here all night. Do you want to call it off or what?"

Terry's heart was pumping like a sprinter's. He didn't know whether to run back to the car or follow Ian into the house. Lord knows why, he chose the latter. They ran past the trickling fountain towards a door that Terry remembered led into the main house. Ian began forcing the lock with the crow bar.

"How do you know we've got half an hour?" asked Terry, hyperventilating.

"Give me some credit. I have done a *little* research. Two nights ago, from the lay-by, I phoned the security company on my mobile and said I thought I saw someone breaking in. I timed how long it took before one of their cars got here. It was exactly thirty four minutes. Rich bastards like Whitman don't bother using the police for protection anymore, private security's all the rage these days."

"They must be a bunch of cowboys."

"Why?"

"The alarm's not gone off."

Ian laughed. "It has, I can assure you."

The door popped open and they were inside. They followed the torch beam and ran down the corridor towards Whitman's study. Terry got handed the crowbar, it was his turn to jemmy the door. "Ughhhh. Come on, budge you bastard."

The lock broke and he crashed through the door. "I'm in. Ian, where are you? I need the torch."

His partner had disappeared. Terry heard a noise in the next room; it was the unmistakable sound of looting.

"What are you doing, for Christ's sake? You're wasting time! We're not here to rob the place!"

Ian was busy choosing porcelain figurines from the mantelpiece. "I'm coming. I just thought if we robbed a few things it might put the police off our scent. Make it look as if common burglars had broken in. I'd help yourself if I were you. There's loads of decent gear. It's an Aladdin's Cave."

"I'm not interested! Hurry up will you! We've only got twenty five minutes!"

Ian hid a few choice pieces in his bag then joined Terry in the study. The room smelt of cigar smoke and was full of bumpy shadows; two curved Chesterfields, an oval drinks table and a Louis XIV desk hazed into view as their eyes got used to the dark. Suddenly, a shaft of moonlight lit up a colossal oil painting of Arthur Whitman. He was pictured wearing trunks, standing arms aloft in the centre of a wrestling ring – the glorious slayer – while his unfortunate opponent lay prostrate on the canvas. Ian and Terry were transfixed. They both stood rooted to the spot as Wildman Whitman stared down at them menacingly from his vantage point above the fireplace.

"I presume that's the main man," said Ian, awe-struck. "Spoo—ky. I wouldn't like to bump into him on a dark night. He looks a mean bastard."

"You might be doing just that if you don't stop pissin about. Now cut out the thieving and start looking for evidence will you."

While Terry took the crowbar to Whitman's desk, forcing open each ornate drawer, Ian had a go at the filing cabinet. After a ten minute search they both drew a blank; nothing but bills, ancient invoices, pornographic magazines and several half eaten chocolate digestives. Nothing that would tie him in with the shopping development.

"This is useless," said Ian. "I told Vanessa we'd never find anything. He's probably got all his important stuff locked up in the safe. And don't ask me where that is."

Terry glanced at the oil painting and thought, *No, it can't be. Only in the films.*

By this time Ian had had enough. He began stalking the room like a caged leopard, searching for anything of value, anything that might make this futile evening worthwhile. He spotted a small gold statue of a wrestler perched on Whitman's desk. A lap-top computer also caught his eye. Terry saw him craftily tuck both objects in the holdall. He was about to tell him to put them back when he felt something hard against his foot. On the floor, under the desk, was a black attaché case. He bent down and picked it up.

"Right, this the best I can do. Let's get out of here."

"Hang about," said Ian. He dragged a chair over to the fireplace, stood on its red velvet seat then produced a penknife from his back pocket. There followed a glorious ripping sound. To Terry's amazement, in less than ten seconds he'd managed to peel away from the inner frame the terrifying portrait of Arthur Whitman.

"What…...What do you think you're doing?"

Ian jumped to the floor, rolled up the canvas and said, "Spoils of war, man. I'm kidnapping the fucker."

"You're insane, do you know that?"

"No time to argue, Terry. We've got five minutes to get out."

They ran down the corridor, through the conservatory and out into the night. The air tasted cool and fresh as they hurried towards the copse of trees where the dogs…........... The dogs! *The dogs!* thought Terry.

"The dogs!" said Terry.

"Well, what about them?"

"Won't they *be* waking up?"

Ian stopped and leant against the perimeter wall, desperate to catch his breath. He started sniggering. "Terry, they won't be waking up."

Before he could explain, in the distance a rapidly approaching siren could be heard. Ian looked at his watch. "Two minutes early, I'm impressed."

Terry scrambled up the wall but was instantly pulled back. Ian grabbed his collar. "Do you want us to get caught? Do you? *Do you?* Well you're going the right way about it."

"I'm trying to get away. What's your problem?"

The security car, sirens ablaze, whizzed passed and screeched to a halt outside the main gate. Ian whispered aggressively, "That's my fuckin problem. You'd have been half way across the road by now, wouldn't you? A sitting duck in their headlights."

"You're right," admitted Terry. "I'm sorry. I panicked. I'm not thinking straight. What do you suggest?"

"Stay put until the car's half way down the drive. *Then* climb over."

The plan worked a treat. As the security car roared towards the house, Ian scaled the wall, booty strapped to his back, closely followed by Terry. On seeing her two desperados, Vanessa fired up the engine and they were soon heading back to Wilmslow along the back lanes.

"Watch your speed," said Ian. "We don't want the police stopping us looking like this." He rubbed his face with a towel.

163

"Jesus!" said Vanessa, driving with one hand while pushing the hair off her face with the other. "When I heard the siren I nearly shit myself. Talk about a close call."

Ian, his body surging adrenalin, let rip, "Wow! That high beats drugs any day!"

Ensconced in the back seat with the black attaché case on his knee, Terry remained silent.

10.45pm.

Arthur Whitman rose from the table and raised his glass in salute. He was more than a little drunk. "Cheers everyone. Here's to the future of the *Comet*. God bless her and all who sail in her, etc."

"Cheers."

"And another thing," he slurred. "I don't want what's happened in the past few weeks to spoil the good relationships I have with you people. You're a fine bunch, and well worth putting up with."

Applause from around the table induced Whitman to order another two bottles of vintage claret. Keith was really enjoying himself. They all were. From the very first double scotch he hadn't given a moment's thought to Terry's burgling escapade. Why should he? Why ruin a five star gourmet meal thinking about that idiot. And what a meal! Lymm Bistro had done them proud. Frog's legs for starters, and for main course, roast duckling in orange sauce with all the trimmings followed by raspberry pavlova; the whole shooting match washed down by never ending amounts of wine. *And* it was still flowing. *And* they still had brandy coffees and after dinner mints to look forward to. People could say what they like about Whitman, he was a generous sod when the mood took him.

Frank puffed on a Havana cigar and said, "On behalf of myself and my colleagues sat around the table. Mr Whitman.......`"

"Nay lad, Arthur, Arthur. Please, we're not in the office now."

"......... Arthur, then. On behalf of myself and my colleagues, I'd just like to thank you and Mrs. Whitman for a most splendid and generous meal. To the Whitmans!"

Keith, Nigel and Steve stood in unison with Frank. "To the Whitmans!"

"Very nice," said Mrs. Whitman. It was the first thing she'd uttered all evening.

Twenty minutes later the bill was mysteriously paid and another pretty young waitress brought to the table a bundle of jackets. Keith suddenly remembered his promise. He slipped off again to the toilet and made the call.

11.15pm.

"Thanks, Keith," said Vanessa. "Yeah, the whole thing went smoothly. No, none of us got caught. Yes, that's right, including Terry. We're all back at Railwayman's Cottage as I speak. You've had a good time, then? That's good. Thank's again for calling. Night." She put the phone down on the kitchen table. "Jesus, he sounds pissed. Let's hope he spews his guts up in the back of Whitman's Roller!"

Her vain attempt at humour failed to lift Terry's spirits. He just sat there staring into space; a frozen vegetable. The night and its bag of tricks had been a complete screw-up. Oh yes, they got away undetected alright, but the whole point of the break-in – gathering incriminating evidence powerful enough to stop the shopping development – was a dismal failure. Terry's stolen attaché case, prised open with a screwdriver, contained nothing more than several old golfing magazines and a crinkly copy of the *Financial Times*. Even Vanessa had to concede defeat. With less than a week to go before the final public inquiry, she knew the last roll of the dice had been thrown. Ian, though, was delighted with the night's outcome. The kitchen table quickly became a show ground for his booty – four Meissen figurines, one gold statue, one lap-top computer, and the ultimate in trophies, Arthur Whitman's gigantic portrait.

"Let's take a look at the evil fucker, shall we?" joked Ian, unfurling the canvas. "Clock that expression! Pure monster. What I wouldn't give to see the look on his face when he gets home and finds…..."

Terry exploded, "It's all been one big fuckin joke to you this, hasn't it! You fuckin bandit. I can see now why you volunteered. You just wanted to plant your sticky fingers on anything moveable, and balls to anyone else."

"I think you're over reacting," said Vanessa. "Ian *did* say he was going to take a few things so the police…......"

"Bollocks! And you believe him? You're even more naïve

165

than I thought. Can't you see, he's used the situation to his own ends. You should have seen what he was like, he couldn't wait to start thieving. We were only in the house five minutes and he was at it."

Ian found Terry's outburst extremely comical. The mere fact he hadn't bothered to get changed, or wipe the polish off his face gave the scene a surreal edge. He had to admit, Terry did bare an uncanny resemblance to a boisterous Malcolm X.

"Calm down, man," said Ian. "You'll give yourself a heart attack."

"He's right," added Vanessa. "You shouldn't let things get on top of you."

"Shouldn't let things get on top of me!" screamed Terry. "That's it, I've just about had it up to here with you people. Phone me a taxi, now!" He started pacing the floor. "On second thoughts I'll phone one myself."

"For God's sake calm down," said Vanessa.

"Stop telling me to calm down will you!"

Terry stormed out into the hall. Before slamming the front door, he shouted, "I never want to see either of you again."

An eerie silence descended, then, "I don't rate his chances of getting a taxi very high looking like that, do you?" laughed Ian.

Chapter Fourteen

The first Terry knew about it was when Dawn phoned Keith's flat the next day. Keith had gone to work, and he was fast asleep on the camp bed. He was shocked to hear his wife's voice. Within her harsh tones there was a hint of friendliness that puzzled him. She said that Robert Acott, the owner of the *Wilmslow Gazette*, the *Comet's* rival, had telephoned the house to offer him a job as senior reporter. The reason being, Fat Charlie Peters had collapsed and died of a heart attack while leaving the Swan on Monday evening. Terry was flabbergasted. Poor old Charlie, one packet of Pork Scratchings too many. Always happens to the decent types. Dawn went on to say that Mr. Acott needed a replacement as soon as possible, on a higher salary, and he was giving Terry first refusal. If he was interested, he should go to the *Gazette's* office in Wilmslow this afternoon and discuss terms. There was more good news; Dawn said she thought this "living apart business" had "gone on too long" and that he should "come back home" and "try to work things out". "If only for the kids sakes," she added. Terry got down on his bended knees to thank God for taking Fat Charlie. He also thanked God for making Dawn see sense, finally.

He took a shower, frenziedly scrubbing away the remnants of shoe polish from his head, hands and face. (He'd managed to remove most of it last night with the help of a large fluffy bath towel stolen from a washing line. Even so, the taxi driver thought he'd been shifting coal). He stood close to the pondering shower head, allowing needles of water to sparkle across his bleach-white nakedness. If all went well this afternoon, and why shouldn't it, he could sign off the dole and leave this rat-hole of a flat for good. What would he tell Keith? He didn't have a chance to tell him about last night's break-in, he was so pissed. The break-in! My God, with all the excitement he'd completely forgotten about it. Who knows, the police might be on their way round right now! No, calm down, if there was any hint of him being under suspicion Keith would have phoned. *Must think positive*, he thought.

Terry had a spot of lunch, tidied the flat, wrote Keith a short note then pressed his best suit into action, ironing wise. He left the flat at one thirty and caught the bus. The *Gazette's* office stood opposite Hoopers department store, sandwiched between an estate agents and a solicitors. Not wanting to appear too eager, he purposely dawdled up Alderley Road, stopping for a second outside a newsagents. It was there he saw the stomach-churning headline plastered across a *Manchester Evening News* billboard: **LOCAL TYCOON'S HOUSE ROBBED**. Terry rushed into the shop and bought a copy. He feverishly read the article, looking for any clues as to who the police might suspect. To his relief, a short paragraph halfway down the front page supplied the answer. He didn't know whether to laugh or cry. It read: **The police officer leading the investigation, Inspector Alan Monroe, admitted to being completely baffled by the crime. He said that on the one hand, because of what was stolen, it appeared to be the work of an obsessed wrestling fanatic; a twisted individual or individuals with a passion for wrestling memorabilia. Yet on the other hand, Inspector Monroe went on to say, the police also suspected a barbaric gang of mindless thugs. When pressed to explain this, the Inspector revealed that an autopsy carried out this morning by a local vet proved a large quantity of rat poison had killed the guard dogs.** He walked in to the *Wilmslow Gazette's* office thinking, *So that's what Ian meant when he said, "They won't 'be' waking up". The cruel swine!*

An hour later the plumb job of senior reporter had landed in Terry's lap, with a salary increase of two thousand a year. He was due to start work the next day. Robert Acott said he was "delighted" Terry had agreed to join the *Gazette*, explaining in flowery terms that he wanted someone with "a superior knowledge of the locale and all its nuances," someone who could "fill the enormous gap left by Fat Charlie Peters." Mr. Acott made it plain he had "admired" Terry's work for years, saying his "talent as a journalist was wasted at the *Comet*." While he "entirely understood" the personal reasons behind the inflammatory article condemning the Mottram Hill Shopping Development, he cautioned he "could never allow such cavalier behaviour to take place at the *Gazette*." Terry assured him it would "never happen again." It was, he admitted "a regrettable episode" brought about by "outside forces" beyond his control. He was "looking forward to rejoining the local news network" and Mr. Acott wouldn't regret putting his faith in him.

Deep down Terry knew why he'd been offered the job; it was partly to spite Whitman, and partly for his insider knowledge of how the *Comet* operated. Still, he wouldn't tell Dawn that. He'd tell her that at long last someone had recognised him for what he was – a talented journalist. To celebrate, he popped across the road to Sainsbury's and bought a bottle of French champagne. During his triumphant return to Windermere Drive, the taxi was ordered to stop outside a florists while he jinked in and purchased a dozen red roses. They hadn't gone more than three hundred yards when to the driver's irritation he was asked to stop again, this time outside a chemist, where cash was converted into candy flavoured condoms (ribbed). He arrived home around 4pm. Much to Terry's surprise he noticed the privet hedge had been cut! *And* the front lawn looked as if the mower had rattled its way across once or twice! He checked to see if he was standing outside the right house. Yes, number 13. What could possibly happen next – his wife appearing semi naked in the doorway having lost a staggering five stone, about to inform him that his mother-in-law Kath had died from a brain tumour the size of a grapefruit? No such luck. Still, it was nice to see Dawn waving at him from the front window. The surprises continued. She grabbed hold of him bear-like inside the hallway, smothering his face in kisses, then pulled him into the lounge.

"Mind the flowers," said Terry. "Here, they're for you. I hope you like them. I've got some good news…........."

"Oh Terry, luv. I'm so glad to have you back. You don't know what I've been going through. I've been racked with guilt for kicking you out. I really have. I'm so sorry. I'm so, so sorry for even thinking you were having an affair with that Vanessa. The whole idea was bloody ridiculous, I realise that now."

Terry wanted to ask her why it was so bloody ridiculous. Instead he remained silent, hugging her enormous back while she continued to blub in his ear, "The kids have missed you. I've missed you. We've all missed you. Please say you'll forgive me. Please. I know I don't deserve it."

"Course I forgive you. By the way, where *are* the kids?"

"I've packed them off to mum's. I thought we could have a quiet evening in all by ourselves. You don't mind, do you? I mean, if you really want to see them I can always ring her up and tell her to bring them back round."

"No!" said Terry. "You've done the right thing. It'll give us time to talk. Now sit down while I tell you the good news."

"Hang on. Before you start, I'll get us both a nice glass of white wine."

White wine! Thought Terry. *Bleedin hell.* He took out the bottle of champagne from the Sainsbury's carrier bag and said, "Here, put this in the fridge to chill."

You should have seen Dawn's face. *Champagne! Bleedin hell.* While she was in the kitchen, attending to his every whim, Terry noticed the lounge had been given the Mother of all spring-cleans. Everything shone like a new pin. It was as if he'd wandered into a show house by mistake. But he realised this was no mistake. This was love.

If food be the music of love, eat on. Dawn certainly did. The meal she prepared that evening was stupendous – prawn cocktail to start, followed by rabbit stew and dumplings, followed by mint chocolate gateaux. It was a candlelight job. Alright she had to close the curtains to get the effect, but so what, it's the thought that counts. 'The best part of breakin up,' as the old song goes. Over a mound of steadily drying rabbit bones sucked and discarded in the centre of the table, they gazed dreamily into each other's eyes and laughed at their silly pasts. While Terry imparted his vision of the future, a future that included a terraced house in Wilmslow, Dawn poured out the champagne. She didn't half look cute in her tight black leggings and low cut blouse. A knock at the front door ushered in reality.

"I'll get it," said Dawn.

She got up from the table. Three murmuring voices were a prelude to, "Terry, it's the police!"

The rabbit certainly tried its best to burrow out of Terry's arse, closely followed by the dumplings. He sat there ashen faced as two Darth Vader-like police officers walked through into the lounge.

"Mr. Howarth?" asked the sergeant.

"Ye…Yes."

"Mr. Terrance Howarth?"

"Yes, that's me."

"Are you the owner of the silver Fiat Uno, registration BYC

354 K, parked out front?"

"Yes, that's me."

"Well, my colleague and I happened to be passing when we noticed your tax disk is one month out of date. Are you aware of this, sir?"

"Yes, that's me."

Dawn came to the rescue. "Sorry for butting in, sergeant. Perhaps I can explain. You see, my husband's been away for a couple of weeks, haven't you, luv? He's had a lot on his plate. It's probably just slipped his mind. The car's not moved, honestly, I can vouch for that. Ask next door if you don't believe me."

The younger PC was having none of it. "That's as maybe, it's still a criminal offence."

The old sergeant, who'd witnessed his fair share of council house strife, took one look at the candlelit scene and guessed that either a joyous home-coming or a domestic reconciliation was in progress – why else would a couple from Handforth be drinking expensive champagne, with the curtains closed. The wisdom of Solomon was called upon for backup.

"Now, now," he said to his eager young colleague. "Let's not get too carried away. Mr. Howarth, I'm giving you until tomorrow to sort out a new tax disk. If you haven't done it by then, I'll be forced to book you. Do I make myself clear?"

In a millisecond Terry was transposed from nodding mannequin to exuberant host. "Crystal clear, sergeant. That's very understanding of you. I'll do it first thing in the morning. Promise." He picked up the champagne bottle. "Would you care for a glass?"

"Trying to bribe a police officer?" laughed the young PC, already learning a thing or two about public relations from the old man. Well, perhaps a little compassion did beat rattling someone's head with the nightstick.

"Thanks for the offer," said the sergeant, "but we'll have to be going. Good night. And don't forget to renew your tax disk."

"I won't," said Terry, showing them out.

Chapter Fifteen

After a terrible night's sleep, punctuated by sex and nightmares – sea shanties and jail chains – Terry woke up early. His first day at the *Wilmslow Gazette*! A new job! A new beginning! A new Dawn? No, she lay sprawled beneath the duvet as usual, snoring her head off. Gently out of bed for a quiet breakfast, then try to start that awkward swine of a car. He needed to see Keith, urgently.

He left the house a little after seven, arriving outside his flat as the dustmen were making their rounds. Terry saw the dog shit was back with an avengeful splatter – a crude concrete canvas in the style of Jackson Pollock. The door swung open to reveal a sun-fazed, pyjama wearing Keith.

"Jesus, you're early. You'd better come in."
Walking through the darkened hall Terry could hardly contain himself. "Well?"

"Well what?"

"What do you mean, 'well what'. I'm asking you what happened at the *Comet* yesterday. You know, the fallout from the break-in."
Keith strolled into the kitchen and began filling the kettle. "Yesterday? That'd be Monday, wouldn't it? Let me see now. Oh yes, I remember. Would that be the day you happened to get a new job, and happened to go back to your wife, and happened to leave me a poxy note saying 'Gone out. Phone you later.' After all I've fuckin done for you!"

"How….........?"

"Don't look so surprised. News travels fast. If you must know, we had a whip-round in the office yesterday afternoon for Fat Charlie. Me and Steve took the money over to the *Gazette* and that smarmy bastard Acott couldn't wait to tell us all about his new recruit. And get this, he said, 'Terry's gone back to his wife.

Apparently, due to some domestic problems, he's been staying with an acquaintance. In a real slum by the sound of it.' A real slum? You cheeky bastard!"

"I never said that. Honest."

Keith's voice blasted from the kitchen, "Well how does he know I live in a fuckin slum then if you didn't say it?"

"You don't live in a slum."

"I fuckin do!"

Terry had to negotiate a sticky minefield. "Listen, mate, I'm *really* grateful to you for putting me up. I can't thank you enough. And I'm really sorry for not being here yesterday to tell you about Dawn and the job at the *Gazette*."

Keith wandered into the lounge with two brews. He handed one to Terry and said indignantly, "You didn't even bother telling me about the break-in."

"I did! Monday night! But you were that pissed when you came back from Lymm you just went straight to bed."

Keith off-the-cuffed, "I know all about it, anyway. Vanessa told me. A right shambles by all accounts."

"Did she. When?"

"Last night. I went round to her house to return her mobile phone. I found the poor girl in tears. Terry, you should have seen the state of her. She was heartbroken about those dogs."

"I hope she didn't think I had anything to do with it."

"No. She knows Ian's to blame."

"Was he there?"

"Was he balls. According to Vanessa, as soon as the *Evening News* got delivered he scarpered."

At last Terry saw an opportunity to ask the question, "What's been the reaction at the *Comet*, concerning the er....?"

Keith saw right through him. "Don't worry, you're the last person in the world they suspect. Frank's theory is, a load of yobs from Wythenshawe high on drugs carried out the raid. So you can rest easy in your bed."

"What about Whitman?"

"Funny you should ask that. No-one's seen him."

Terry's first morning at the *Wilmslow Gazette* was spent familiarising himself with his new surroundings – computer system, coffee machine, toilets. He knew most of the staff by name, and within minutes everyone was cracking jokes about Fat Charlie: "Gone to the great boozer in the sky," "The shares in Pork Scratchings will plummet," etc. It wasn't long before Robert Acott issued Terry with his first assignment – a local cemetery had been vandalised. "I want you to go over to St. Wilfreds this afternoon and see what you can dig up." He was going to enjoy working for the *Gazette.*.

Around lunchtime a phone call was put through to Terry's desk. It was Vanessa, and she sounded agitated. Her voice machine-gunned, "I've got to see you. It's really important. Please, can we meet."

The hairs on the back of his neck rose icicle-like. Had the police been round to Railwayman's Cottage asking awkward questions? For that matter, had she been arrested? And if she had been arrested, had she cut a deal with the police? And if she had cut a deal with the police, would she be wearing a wire at their lunchtime meeting in order to save her own skin and entrap him?

"Christ, what's wrong? Is it the police?"

"Of course it's not the police. It's something that'll blow your mind. Terry, you won't believe what's happened."

"Go on."

"I've found evidence. A shit-load of evidence that's gonna put Whitman behind bars and stop the shopping development dead in its tracks."

Terry thought, *Oh, no. Not this again.* Relieved to hear the authorities weren't closing in, he asked, "What evidence?"

"I don't want to discuss it over the phone. Look, can we meet for lunch? I'll explain everything when I see you."

Terry had heard it all before – finding the missing piece to the jigsaw, uncovering the last bit of crucial evidence. Why didn't the woman just give up? She was obsessed! He started to get annoyed. "Listen, Vanessa, I don't think having lunch with you's a good idea. To tell you the truth, I'm not interested in what you've found."

"But Terry…….!"

"For God's sake when are you going to admit defeat? You can't beat people like Whitman. The man's too powerful. We tried our best, but it wasn't good enough. Let's just leave it at that shall we. The other thing is, my life seems to be heading back to normal. I've got a new job, I've got my wife back, and I certainly don't want to jeopardise the situation by going on another wild goose chase."

174

Vanessa wanted to assure him it wasn't a wild goose chase, but realised by the sound of his voice he meant business. She calmed down and said, "If that's your final word."

"It is, Vanessa. I'm sorry."

"Well can I ask you something, Terry?"

"Sure."

"You don't mind if I go ahead on my own. You know, and use the evidence."

"No problem. I wish you all the luck in the world."

"Thanks, Terry. Goodbye."

Chapter Sixteen

Three days later Terry was driving to work when a special report on the early morning news almost caused him to crash his car. The radio announcement said, "At midnight last night, police arrested eight high ranking council officials and four prominent local businessmen in what is believed to be a major corruption scandal concerning the proposed Mottram Hill Shopping Development. A warrant has also been issued for the arrest of Arthur Whitman, who, according to a report in today's *Daily Telegraph*, is the alleged ring leader behind what is now being dubbed *Wilmslow-Gate*. A police spokesman said that Mr. Whitman disappeared the day after his Prestbury mansion was burgled, and hasn't been seen since. Other news: Manchester United have signed..........."

Terry swung his *Uno* into Wilmslow station's car park and bought a copy of the Telegraph from the kiosk. Halfway down the second page was the dramatic headline **CHESHIRE BUSINESS-MAN IN HUGE FINANCIAL SCANDAL, by Vanessa Garland**. Terry felt dizzy. He had to lean against the wall in order to read on. The article was a *tour de force*. It alleged that not only was Whitman a major shareholder in the shopping complex, he'd also used his own newspaper as a vehicle to sway public opinion. It went on to report – **crucial evidence has come into my possession proving that over the past year vast sums of money have been transferred from the Whitman account into the accounts of several local councillors. These councillors, pictured below, are the very people whose job it was to ensure a fair and honest public inquiry. This evidence has now been passed on to the DPP**.

The Mottram Hill Shopping Complex was dead. On the following Monday, eight newly appointed members of the public inquiry voted 8-0 against the proposal. Vanessa was hailed a local hero – Woodward and Bernstein rolled into one. That evening, the

Manchester Evening News editorial column described her as – **a brave and passionate journalist whose tireless efforts to protect the environment should be a lesson to us all. Finally, we would like to congratulate Miss Vanessa Garland and wish her all the best in her new appointment as investigative reporter for the Daily Telegraph**.

Terry was sick.

****

Two weeks later he was sitting at his desk putting the finishing touches to an article out-lining the dangers of weed killer in the home, when the phone rang. It was Vanessa. She was in Wilmslow for the day and wanted to meet him for lunch. This time he decided to accept. They met in the Nose café bar on the corner of Water Lane and Hawthorn Street. Vanessa wasn't hard to spot, sitting out on the veranda wearing blue jeans and a baggy white shirt.

"You're looking good," said Terry, pulling up a chair. "Living in London seems to agree with you. What's brought you back so soon?"

Vanessa ordered two espressos and said, "I needed to sort a few things out. I've put my house on the market and stuff." She leant forward and touched his arm. "Anyway, never mind about that. We did it, Terry."

"Did what?"

"Did what? Stopped that shopping development from going through."

Terry laughed. "You did it, you mean."

"No. We both did."

He took off his jacket and sat down. "Can I ask you something that's been puzzling me? Where did you get hold of all the evidence about Whitman's dodgy bank accounts?"

Vanessa smiled. "You know that lap-top computer Ian stole from the house? It was all in there -- names, dates, the lot. I gave the police a floppy disk and told them it was sent to me by persons unknown. You know, someone with a grudge against Whitman. Apparently, he didn't even report the computer as being stolen. As soon as he found out it was, he did the disappearing act."

"Fancy leaving something like that lying about."

177

"Well, Terry, that's the arrogance of the rich for you. They never think they're going to get caught. I suppose I have to thank Ian for nicking it in the first place."

"Is he living in London with you?"

"No. After what he did to those dogs, I decided it was time we split up." Her eyes fell to the floor and she sighed, "Honestly, you think you know someone."

"What's it like working for the *Telegraph*?"

"Really exciting. I'm still finding my feet. What's it like working for the *Gazette*?"

"Shite."

"Any news about Whitman?"

"That crooked bastard! The police think he's in South America. A regular Ronnie Biggs."

"Best place for him."

Vanessa ordered lunch – two ham baguettes and half a carafe of chilled white wine – then asked, "So tell me, what's the latest gossip from the *Comet*?"

Terry sank into his chair and smiled, "Humm, where to begin. Well, for a start they all thought they were going to lose their jobs after Whitman disappeared. Keith said Whitman's wife came into the office a few days after the shit hit the fan and told everyone she was taking over the running of Allied Northern Newspapers. She laid the law down good and proper and said she intended to run a tight ship. According to Keith, Frank didn't know whether to laugh or cry. You know how much he hates taking orders from women. Anyway, after what's happened, I just think he's grateful he's managed to hold on to the editor's job. You can bet your life there'll be no more skiving off to the golf course during the day."

Vanessa laughed, "Yeah, nice one. And another thing, I'd love to see Frank's face if Mrs. Whitman ever tries it on with *him* at the Christmas party!"

"Can you imagine it!"

She refilled both glasses with chilled wine and asked, "How are Nigel, Steve and Keith doing?"

"Cheers. Oh, Keith's still the same. Still obsessed with getting his wife back. That's another story, by the way. I'll tell you about it one day. I'm seeing him after work for a drink, actually. I'll let him know you were asking after him."

"That'll be nice."

With a hint of triumph, Terry went on, "Steve and Natasha have split up. *He* said he finished with her. He's a lying bastard. No man with any sense would do that."

"You're right. Barlow's such a plonker. Natasha was far too good for him. What about Nigel?"

Terry grinned, delight spreading across his ravaged face. "Now you're talking gossip!" He leant forward and put both his elbows on the table as if holding a winning poker hand. "You know Nigel was in charge of that Pirates of Penzance thing his opera company were putting on? Yeah, well, one of our reporters from the *Gazette* went along to cover the first night. Fuckin disaster! Get this. Roger Harvey, Nigel's bum-chum from the barbecue, who was playing the lead, talk about favouritism, was so nervous he forgot most of his lines and could hardly sing. Not only that, but because the character he was playing was supposed to be eighteen, Roger had that much make-up on he resembled a soddin drag queen. The bloke from the *Gazette* said he ponced about the stage looking like a cross between Peter Pan and Widow Twanky. They had to replace him with the stand-in after the first act. Anyway, to cut a long story short, Nigel resigned and they've both shacked up together at Squirrel's Leap. Very cosy."

Vanessa laughed, and realised she just might miss parochial Wilmslow.

After lunch Terry walked Vanessa to the station. Before getting on the train she gave him an envelope. They said their goodbyes and he stood for a while on the platform watching the London bound express slowly pull away from the station. It could have been him on that train. He opened the envelope. It contained four hundred pounds and a note that read -- Dear Terry, here is exactly half the money I got from writing the article exposing Whitman. Please accept it. Without your help it could never have been written. If you and Dawn ever fancy a weekend in London, please don't hesitate to contact me. My address is on the back. Good luck for the future. Lots of love Vanessa. xxx

Throwing caution to the wind he went straight to the travel agents and booked a weekend for two in Paris. In bed later that night an excited Dawn nudged Terry with her elbow and rasped, "Are you asleep?"

"Yes."

She whispered in his ear, "Don't be daft. Listen, luv, can I ask you a favour?"

"Go on."

"You know when we're in Paris?"

"Mmmm."

"Well, do you think we can hire a car and drive through that tunnel where Princess Di got killed?"

"I don't see why not."

"Brilliant. I can't wait to tell all the girls down at Bingo."

"You do that, luv. You do that."